JACK: GRIME AND PUNISHMENT

THE BROTHERS GRIME, BOOK 1

Z.A. MAXFIELD

For everyone who was there for me after my house burned:
I want to tell a story about loss and new beginnings.
Let's punch a hole in the empty shell of our old dreams and blow
in new life, shall we?
You come too.

I'm going out to clean the pasture spring;
I'll only stop to rake the leaves away
(And wait to watch the water clear, I may):
I sha'n't be gone long. –You come too.

I'm going out to fetch the little calf
That's standing by the mother. It's so young
It totters when she licks it with her tongue.
I sha'n't be gone long. –You come too.

The Pasture, Robert Frost

CHAPTER 1

THE CAT WAS NEW.

Jack was pretty sure when he'd gone to sleep there hadn't been a cat in his house, much less a bowl of water or a dish of food. He stood still while it made its way sinuously between his legs, over his shoes, sniffing him and getting friendly with the rubber tip of his cane.

To be fair, it seemed like a nice cat. It was an attractive shade of gray that appeared almost blue, and it blinked up at him with green eyes. Its pupils seemed vertical, though, and vaguely reptilian. Jack couldn't help worrying what a cat like that could get up to.

He lived alone, and he was sure the cat was new.

Jack heard a footstep behind him and jumped out of his skin.

"Sorry, boss." Skippy, a ham-fisted, olive-skinned mountain of a man froze and looked him over from behind a thick, black five o'clock shadow. "Didn't mean to scare you."

"How'd you get in here?"

"Uh..." Skippy flushed and glanced at the back door. "I think you need better locks."

"I think I need employees with fewer dubious skills." Jack put the filter and grounds in the basket of his coffeemaker and turned it on. His kitchen was neat; he kept everything in reach. The fewer steps he needed to take, the better, even before he had a cat slithering between his feet. Skippy reached his colorfully tattooed arm down and picked the cat up.

"Can you cat-sit?"

"I have no clue." Jack glanced at the cat again. "What does cat-sitting involve?"

"Okay, well. This is *Tasha*." Skippy shot Jack a wry sideways glance. He must have thought Jack was kidding. "Even though it's called cat-sitting, you don't actually *sit* on the *cat*. That's not what you do."

Jack rolled his eyes. "What does the cat need?"

"I put her food in the cupboard where you keep crackers, and the litter box is in the bathroom. It's the clumping kind, so you just scoop it and throw it in the trash or—"

"Don't cats shred shit and run away and bring in dead bats and rabies and—"

"Tasha's fine." Skippy pulled her closer to his chest. "She's a good cat."

"Is she likely to run away if I were to leave the door open?"

"You probably shouldn't do that."

Jack eyed them both. He could *maybe* handle a cat. "For how long?"

"Four days?"

Jack thought about that. "I'm not responsible if anything goes wrong."

"Okay." Skippy tried to hand the cat over, but Jack stepped back.

"Scooping I can do. Bonding is out."

"She's a good cat," Skippy repeated as he let her fall to the floor. "She's smart."

"Right. If she wins the Nobel Prize, I'll help her endorse the check."

Jack made his way to the office and turned his master switch to the On position.

All around them, electronics whirred to life. A printer, a fax machine, several computers and fans.

His cousin Gabe teased him about turning the power off every night, assuring him that all his stuff could stay plugged in but powered down, but if eight years in Orange County Fire taught Jack anything, it was that his decrepit wooden house with its mostly century-old wiring didn't need any help burning down.

"I'll get the coffee. You want yours black?" Skippy asked.

"Like my sin-riddled soul," Jack answered automatically. He sat in his rolling chair and put his cane aside. "Unless you've got whiskey."

"Fresh out. So you'll watch the cat for us?"

"Yeah." Jack figured Skippy earned what he wanted. He was a damn good employee, even if he came on a little strong. Even if his gang tats and hard good looks sometimes terrified the clients.

"And I can take today and tomorrow off, huh? On account of that last job went so late? Me and Kelly Ann want to get out of town for a few days. Her mom's got the baby."

"I guess I should thank God I didn't wake up and find him crawling around in my kitchen."

"So it's okay? About the days off?"

"Yeah, fine."

Jack marveled at Skippy's energy when he returned with two steaming mugs. The man had worked all day the day before and well into the night, but here he was, cheerful as fuck at oh-dark-thirty, wearing khakis and a clean red uniform polo, even though he'd planned to take the day off.

"You're all right, Skippy. Yesterday go okay?"

"That was the best fucking job yet." Skippy's enthusiasm

took Jack by surprise. Muscles bulged on his furry forearm as he held Jack's coffee out for him. Eyes the color of pine tree bark radiated giddy happiness. "Yesterday was *gorgeous*."

Jack gave Skippy the once-over. He didn't think an employee had ever said a job was gorgeous before. Particularly not after a long day at one of the worst fresh crime scenes they'd ever taken on. "Are you kidding?"

"Yesterday we did twelve hours, start to finish." Skippy sighed, lifting a hand in that finger-rubbing motion that universally indicated money. "Cha-ching! Bunch of punks, living in a rental in Brea. Guess someone musta come in and blam-blam-blam. Blood spatter everywhere. I never seen nothing like it. I'm like...*dude*. This is some sick shit."

"Twelve *hours*?"

"God, yeah. It was fucking grim. I guess the fun started in the upstairs bedroom. We had blood and tissue everywhere, and then there's more in the hall, down the stairs, family room, living room, kitchen. It's like they was finger-painting with their bodily fluids. Then I go outside, and what do I see?"

Jack leaned back in his chair. "I cannot imagine."

"There's bloody footprints out the back door. Someone hadda be hauling ass. There's blood all over the patio. So I look, and god*damn* if there's not still a little bit of our guy's head in the strainer of the pool filter. There's stuff the cops *missed*. I swear to God, I could die a happy man today. That was the worst scene I ever been at."

"I'm glad you're so delighted by all this."

"Would you feel better if I said they had naked pictures of underage kids all over the walls?"

"Did they?"

"Nope." Skippy cackled. "What do you care? It's money. Sloppy work, though."

"How do you mean?"

"I mean, what kind of asshole killer keeps getting off near-miss shots over and over, chasing after his deadees for, like, miles before he can kill them? There was blood all over the walls, man. Zombie-apocalypse shit. Nom, nom. Fucking amateurs."

"The killers were amateurs?" Jack worried whenever he caught a glimpse inside Skippy's head. He really did. Things looked pretty scary in there.

"Twelve hours! That's my longest job yet, and you know I don't waste a minute. Me and Vasquez don't screw you over like some of these punks."

"I know." Jack unlocked his strongbox and counted out two thousand, four hundred dollars in cash. "Here you go. When Vasquez gets in, I'll give him his cut."

Skippy picked up the stack of hundreds and kissed it. "Come to daddy, *benjamenz.*"

"We've still got to talk about whether you want to go with a PPO plan for dental or an HMO."

Skippy's happy smile collapsed. "Oh, now. Why you gotta go and spoil it? When I get a big cash bump like this, I can pretend I'm still in the enforcer business and not the damn cleaning-up-shit business. Why you gotta go talking about dental plans?"

"Sorry, but you know I do things legit, even if you want to get paid in cash." Jack shot Skippy a warm smile. "You're still all thug to me, baby."

"Damn right, I'm all thug. But I gotta eat. And no one better judge me for how I bring home my bacon. Once Kelly Ann and me had the baby, I got all shiny."

"You earn it, Skippy. Every last dime."

"Hell yeah, I earn it. I hadda open the fucking pool filter to replace the diatomaceous earth. You know what? That shit gets everywhere. Hadda call the Five-O and tell them they missed something. *Hilarious!*" he sang. "Your detective kept trying to wipe that fine-caked mud off his little Italian shoes."

"My detective?"

"Your boyfriend, Detective *Hung*ley."

"He's not my boyfriend," Jack said too quickly.

"Yeah, yeah, he's just your friend, *except* when you're both ass-plowing drunk, and I ain't supposed to know about that. Whatever. I've gotta tell Kelly Ann we're going to Vegas. Don't call me until Monday."

"Have fun." The office phone rang, and they both saw it was Detective Huntley calling. Jack felt his cheeks heat. "All right, get out. That's Dave on the phone now."

"I'm supposed to go right now? 'Cause he's not your boyfriend. Nuh-uh. That's some sick shit you homos get up to. Calling each other on the phone, going out for drinks and what-not. Ending up blind drunk and fucking." Skippy shook his head and backed out, making rude hand gestures. "Where I come from, that's called *dating*."

"*Out*." Jack answered the phone. "Dave?"

"You working already?"

Three words in Dave's perfect whiskey voice had Jack shifting in his chair. "Mm-hmm."

"One of these days I'm going to plant something on your boy Skippy, and he's going to jail, which he richly deserves."

"You don't like him finding shit your crime scene guys missed?"

"I don't like how happy it makes him."

"He's thorough, is all."

"That's not the point, is it? He used to break people's kneecaps for a living."

Jack's artificial knee wanted to crawl up his ass at that. Even if he couldn't exactly remember his body shattering, the thought made him sick. "You got proof of that?"

"Would he be walking around free if I did?"

"Quit bitching me out for something I didn't do. Why'd you call?"

"I got something, but I didn't know if I should call your outfit."

"What are you doing there if—"

"It's my mom's neighbor's place. I was having breakfast with her, and"—Dave covered the phone somehow, but Jack could still hear him telling someone in the background he'd be right there —"her neighbor started ringing the bell. He got home from his night shift at St. Jude and found his cousin, who lives with him, dead. Ate his gun. I guess the neighbor couldn't face talking about it right then, so he came here to ask my mom to call the cops."

"Are the cops there yet?"

"Not yet. Any minute, I expect."

"You're not supposed to throw me business, are you? You'll get in trouble if—"

"It's Nick Foasberg. That's why I'm calling you. I wanted you to hear it from me."

Jack froze. "My Nick Foasberg?"

Dave replied, but Jack couldn't process what he was saying. The unnatural hammering of his heartbeat drowned out the annoying squeak of his oscillating fan. He turned the damn thing off, because suddenly the room felt cold.

"*My* Nick is your mother's neighbor?"

"Ah, God, Jackie. No." Dave had a perfect voice, all right. Perfect for phone sex. Perfect for shouting at perps. Perfect for making a death-notification call. "I'm so sorry to have to be the one to tell you this. Nick Foasberg is dead."

CHAPTER 2

JACK GOT in his truck and programmed the Sunny Hills address Dave had given him into his navigation system. The drive over was fairly quick considering morning rush-hour traffic.

It was going to be weird between him and Dave, now that he knew where Dave's mom lived. He and Dave had been acquaintances as far back as high school, but even then Dave didn't seem to have a mom. As far as Jack was concerned, Dave shouldn't have a mom, 'cause he didn't do guys with moms.

Jack didn't do much more than collide with guys in the blank oblivion of alcohol-fueled sexual encounters anyway, but guys with *mothers*? No.

Hit-and-run fucking was his thing. That was the only way to learn a guy's most intimate secrets and still be able to walk past him the next day without recognizing his face.

He and Dave, they had that, but with the added bonus that they could get together most Friday nights and bitch about work. What they did wasn't complicated.

And that was just how Jack liked it.

"You *asshole*," Jack muttered as he made his way past rows of

older Spanish colonial houses in the hilly upscale neighborhood.
They were glamorous two-story places, most on oversize lots with
wide green lawns. Here and there he got a glimpse of dazzling
gardens.

With every square inch of Orange County real estate highly
prized even in this shitty economy, big yards were as scarce as
faithful husbands.

You never said your mom lives in East Upper Crustia.

Jack rounded a corner and found the place he was looking
for. Two police cruisers and the coroner's van were parked out
front. A small crowd of curious neighbors clumped on manicured
lawns—gawkers held back by a thin thread of decency and the
suspicious glares from a handful of uniformed police officers.

He spotted a couple of guys he knew—his competition—and
was pulling to the curb across the street just as someone wheeled
Nick's body out the side gate.

Jack gripped the wheel and simply sat there, stuck in his
truck, unable to move through the gut-twisting pain of seeing
Nick Foasberg in a body bag.

Jack's phone rang, and he adjusted his Bluetooth out of habit
more than need. When he answered, he kept his voice profes-
sional. "Masterson."

"Are you okay?" A new voice from Dave. *Tender.*

"Nick Foasberg can't be dead."

"Take a deep breath for me."

Jack pulled air into his lungs, then blew it out again, but his
heart hammered on unhappily. "How do you know it's my Nick?
There could be more than one Nick Foasberg. It's not an
uncommon name."

"The cousin went to school with us a few years behind."
Dave's voice could hold back oceans. It could order the cosmos. "I
recognized him. You don't think I'd put you through this if I
didn't know for sure."

"I don't know what you'd do."

"Yeah, you do. I know how you feel about Nick Foasberg, even if you never let yourself admit it."

"What do you mean, I never—"

"You *love* him. Even after he—"

"I know." Jack couldn't have this conversation. *Not now.* "I know that."

Dave was silent for so long Jack thought the call had dropped. "Who are you sending over? God, do not send Skippy. The neighborhood watch will burst into flames if you send Skippy."

"No. Not Skippy." Jack managed the latch on the door of his truck. Once it was open, he pulled the strap of his messenger bag over his head so it would stay put while he got his cane on the ground.

"Is Gabe going to bid it or Eddie?"

"No." Jack closed the door of his truck and started across the street. He looked over the houses on either side of Nick's cousin's place. God. Dave's mother had to be doing pretty well to have a place like that. These houses were worth millions. Who had that kind of money?

The cousin's place had typical Spanish colonial features and the look of old Hollywood: thick stucco walls complete with arches, wrought iron over the windows, and a red tile roof. Precisely sculpted boxwood flanked a cement-and-brick pathway that seemed to flow in tiers like pools of lava from a soaring rustic front door. It was pretentious but not unpleasing. "Are you still at your mom's place?"

"Oh, no." Dave swore. "Fuck no. You are *not* going to that scene yourself."

"It's my company."

"Not the point. You get other people to bid this one."

"I'll talk to you later." Jack ended the call while Dave was still trying to talk sense into him, telling him to walk away, or better yet—run.

Maybe Jack *could* have walked away if he hadn't noticed the pale-faced man who stood on the porch talking to one of the uniforms. Jack could have picked Nick's cousin out of a lineup— he would have known him anywhere. Maybe they had gone to school together, but he didn't remember. Now, however, seeing the man's big frame, his pale skin and blond hair—lightly kissed by a tinge of coppery red the Foasberg family had been blessed with for generations—there was little doubt.

Even from across the street, Jack recognized that echo of Nick's Irish bad-boy looks. The way the man held himself was so goddamned *familiar*.

Foasberg's cousin was the final proof Jack needed.

The final nail in Nick's coffin.

It was a damn good thing Jack had his crutch, because halfway up the walk, his knees buckled.

"Masterson?" Ty Chang, an officer he knew fairly well, put an arm around his shoulder to steady him.

Mouth dry, Jack could only nod. He knew most of the uniforms around the Fullerton area from when he worked at Station 2. Some he'd known pretty well, and they had followed up with him in the four years since his injury in the Freeway Complex Fire. He'd worked with Chang in the past, and they'd remained friendly.

Jack had also met a lot of new people in law enforcement since he'd begun the Brothers Grime with his cousin Gabe and their friend, Eddie. Grime's red-shirted employees had to be familiar to the police by now, because *yes*, Jack actively ambulance chased, listening to scanners and sending his people out to bid on local jobs.

Chang stepped forward. "How the hell are you, Masterson? You look a whole lot better than the last time I saw you."

Jack flushed. He'd lost twenty pounds of muscle since the accident. His buzzed-off hair and hollow, nondescript brown eyes gave him the look of someone who'd seen some seriously hard times, and now he walked with a cane. If that was better, he'd been an awful mess.

Somehow Jack found a way to make words. "Look at you. Hitting the gym?"

"Can't say I have." Chang rubbed his flat stomach. "But I'm running my ass off coaching my kid's soccer team."

"You got time for that?"

"I have a great assistant coach."

"Lucky." On the porch, Nick's cousin—*what is his goddamned name?*—seemed numb with shock. He stared blankly beyond them.

"You have to stay back here until we get through."

"I know the routine."

"I thought you had people for the grunt work?"

"Sometimes I do this myself."

Chang nodded and leaned over to speak confidentially. "This one isn't too bad. Contained to the bathroom on the first floor. Guy ate his gun. Small caliber."

"I—"

"It's like he was trying not to make a mess. The tidy ones usually do it in a car. They think they can go somewhere and family won't have to see. This guy was bottomed out. I guess he didn't own a car."

Jack's skin tingled as gooseflesh stippled his arms. "I knew the victim, so—"

"Oh, God. I'm sorry." Chang frowned at him. "Hey, you okay there? Maybe you should call one of your guys?"

"No, I got it. It's hard to do the job when it's someone you know. My guys are all busy with other things," Jack lied. Sweat cooled his clammy skin. "How long, you think?"

"We're just finishing up now." Chang leaned over to whisper. "You've got competition."

Jack nodded. "I'll get the bid, though."

"Used to be there was nobody to do this shit. Now I'm noticing more and more outfits. Violent crime is a growth industry."

Jack shrugged. "It's what pays my bills."

The coroner's van rolled out, and the cousin spent a few more minutes talking with the police on the porch.

Jack felt a light touch on his shoulder. "Are you Jack Masterson?"

He turned to find an older woman, blonde and pretty, peering up at him. She wore slim-fitting trousers and a high-necked blouse under a soft brown cardigan that matched her eyes. He didn't need to be introduced to know this was Dave's mom.

He didn't want to meet her. "Yeah."

"Dave asked me to come over here and talk to you. He said to ask you to come have a cup of coffee with me." Her eyes were just like Dave's. Golden and warm. Kind.

"I don't think—"

"He said I shouldn't take no for an answer because the man who shot himself was a friend of yours." Those eyes still shone with warmth when she got tough. *Interesting.*

"I need to bid this job."

"There are other jobs." She wrapped surprisingly strong fingers around his upper arm and tugged, but he braced his legs and didn't move.

"And I need all the jobs I can get."

"Dave said—"

"Dave is a good cop and a great guy, ma'am, but he can't tell me what jobs I can take." Jack pointed out a guy leaning idly against the door of a white truck with a camper shell on the back.

"See that guy? He's going to bid this job, and so is the guy in the red sedan. They're all waiting to tell your neighbor how they'll do the best job for the lowest price. The guy in the red car is retired LA Sheriff's Department, and I know his company is legit. He's okay. He does good work. I've never seen this other guy before. Seems a little skeevy to me."

She looked the guy over. He was sipping from a cup of doughnut-shop coffee and using his car keys to dig something out of his ear. "Is that normal?"

"I doubt it. They say you shouldn't put anything in your ear smaller than your elbow."

"Pffft. No." Dave's mom gave his arm a happy shake. "I meant people standing around like vultures, waiting to—"

"Maybe you never gave this much thought, but suppose something awful happens in your house. Say someone breaking in gets shot by the police. Afterwards, your place is a crime scene, and the police dust for prints and search through everything you own. When they let you back in, who cleans up the mess? Are you going to be up to that?"

"I guess I never thought about it."

"Say you got a massive sewage backup, and they fix your plumbing, but you're still knee-deep in sh—excrement when the plumbers leave. You're sitting on a major biohazard. Do you want to wade in and get yourself a case of hepatitis C?"

Her eyes widened. "God, I never—"

"Do you want to wipe up fecal matter and blood-borne pathogens with a kitchen sponge?"

"Holy cow." She blanched, and he felt bad he'd started his even-vultures-have-a-purpose speech.

"I'm sorry." He glanced over her head at the cousin, then back.

"I didn't introduce myself. I'm Karen Huntley. My son is

worried about you. He asked me to try to talk you out of taking this job."

"It's fine, ma'am. It's nice to meet you." *Even if it's the last thing I needed today.* "Most people don't think about this until it happens to them, and then believe me, we try to be sensitive and take care of their needs efficiently. This might be the worst moment of your neighbor's life. We understand that. We're here to help."

"I'm sorry. I don't think I realized."

"I don't deny the money is good. But we earn it." Jack held his hand out to shake. She took it and gave it a squeeze. "Dave looks like you."

"Call me Karen," she said gently. "And come for a cup of coffee—at least come over until they finish up here."

"I can't do that. This is my business. If I don't approach as soon as I can, your neighbor could be pressured into signing with the competition. I can't take that chance."

"You want to pressure him into signing with you?"

Jack stiffened. It looked like Dave's mom was determined to be honest. "That's how it's done, ma'am. This is just business."

"Even if the blood and tissue and fecal material belonged to someone you once loved?"

He flinched. "You don't do this job if you get emotional. I am uniquely qualified for it."

She searched his face and appeared to make up her mind about him. "Then let me help you, and we'll get that coffee." She took his hand and walked him to the door, surprising both the police officer and Jack's cousin.

"Ma'am," the uniform addressed her, but she ignored him.

"Excuse me, gentlemen." She kept Jack's hand while she reached out and curled her fingers around her neighbor's wrist. Touchy-feely. Dave was too, come to think of it—when they were alone. "Ryan, this is my son's friend Jack."

Ryan. That was his name. Jack offered his hand. "Have we met?"

"Yeah." Ryan eyed Jack before he took it. "We've met."

"Ryan," Karen said patiently, "I'd like you to come over as soon as you're done here and have a cup of coffee with us."

"Jack and I went to high school together." Ryan continued to stare at Jack.

"If you need anything else, you can call this number." The police officer talking to Ryan gave him a card. Clearly he didn't know what to do since it wasn't considered good form for Jack to interrupt. This was a gray area because Dave's mom was the neighbor, and she'd done just that.

High school. Right. Did I have a class with him? "You were in my—"

"I was a freshman when you were a senior. You were friends with my cousin, Nick." His voice broke, and his expression said, *As if you didn't know.*

"Could I maybe talk to you? You feel up to a cup of coffee with me and Karen?"

Ryan glanced down at himself. He wore green scrubs and a hooded sweatshirt. "This isn't really a good time."

God bless Dave's mom. She ordered Ryan to lock up his house and come along, *right now.* She talked the whole time about nothing, low-voiced and soothing.

Given the situation, Jack had to smile while he watched his competitors try to muscle in. Karen answered for Ryan, taking brochures, saying how he'd look over what they had to offer and give them a call at his earliest convenience.

Bill Engstrom, the retired LEO Jack knew from past scenes, left gracefully, but the new guy was high pressure.

He got Jack's back hair up.

"I'm so sorry for your loss, Mr....?" When Ryan ignored him, the guy stepped in front of them and held out his hand. "My name is Daniel Sanders, and I represent KrimeKleen Services. Losing a loved one is so devastating, especially when the loss is violent. I'm sure you're wondering how you're going to face going back inside your home right now."

"No, I'm not." Ryan tried to move around him.

"Wait." The man held his hand up. "Since you're wearing scrubs, I won't insult your intelligence by telling you how dangerous blood-borne pathogens can be, and how great a growth medium blood is for—"

"You can stop right there," said Jack. Karen maneuvered Ryan around the salesman and herded him toward her house. Surely there was no need to paint a terrifying picture of the consequences of improper disposal of biologically hazardous waste, even if that was *exactly* what Jack had done to Karen only minutes before. "Give me your information, and I'll see that he gets it."

This new guy just irked Jack, who couldn't forget the guy *dug for earwax* with his keys. The man turned and took off after Karen in a display of persistence Jack thought smelled too much like aggression. Did this guy get paid by the word?

"Wait. I'd like you to look this over. It's a brochure explaining why KrimeKleen Services outranks the competition by nearly two-to-one in an independent poll of—"

"Thank you." Karen was clear she wouldn't welcome further conversation. "He'll call if he needs your services."

"But the pathogens are—"

"I know all about biohazardous waste," barked Ryan, who'd apparently had enough. He gave Jack and the salesman the hairy eyeball. "I work at a *hospital*."

Karen, Earwax Guy, and Jack all gaped at him.

"I don't *need* anyone to come clean this shit up for me. I can do it myself."

CHAPTER 3

JACK COULDN'T SAY EXACTLY how he ended up sitting at Dave Huntley's mother's kitchen table, drinking coffee from delicate, gold-embossed teacups. When she brought out a bag of shortbread cookies and turned the whole thing into a teddy bear picnic, he pinched himself discreetly.

Because he didn't want to think about Nick, his thoughts settled on Dave.

This is where Dave comes from.

This explains so much.

Karen's voice interrupted his thoughts. "What Jack is saying, I think, is that while you might be able to clean the room yourself, it might be better—emotionally speaking—to have a third party come in."

Ryan slid a glance Jack's way. "Is that what Jack is saying? That I might be emotionally scarred by cleaning my cousin's blood from the tub, and he won't?"

She bit her full lower lip. "Jack, I believe what Ryan is saying is he's worried—"

"I heard him." Jack sighed. *I'll have to ask Dave if his mom is a marriage counselor.* "We both knew the deceased."

The phone rang, and Karen left them alone while she answered it.

For a couple of minutes, silence consumed them. Jack heard the number on the stove clock flip over from 10:56 to 10:57. Then 10:58.

"Why are you here?" Ryan finally asked.

"To bid the job like everyone else."

"Right." Ryan's tone of voice indicated he didn't buy it. He'd wrapped his arms around himself.

Jack put his cup into the saucer none too gently, then pushed it away. "Christ. I should not be using something as fragile as that."

Ryan's lips curved into a faint smile. "They're pretty, though."

God. Pale skin, pale brows. Freckles dusted the bridge of his nose and were scattered by the thousands over his forearms where he'd pushed up his sleeves.

Eyes the lightest shade of blue, like shadows in the snow.

Ryan was so like Nick. Yet...they were as individual as snowflakes.

Where Nick Foasberg had been built brutal in the way of Irishmen with the blood of Vikings in them, Ryan had softer edges. He was all lean muscle mass and just as tall as Nick, but he wasn't keen like Nick had been. He wasn't sharp or hard.

Ryan's body language said he had nothing to prove.

He was intelligent. That much was clear. Was he a Foasberg? Or a cousin with a different name?

Jack said, "Look, you don't know me, but—"

"I know *of* you." Ryan's gaze locked with his. "I know what Nick did to you. I was there."

Jack's heart dropped like an elevator with a broken cable. "You—"

"I know he humiliated you. How he and his friends beat you." His gaze was searching. "What did you think would happen when you asked him to senior prom publicly, when you made a circus out of it so everyone knew you had a thing for him?"

Jack's heart contracted. "I don't know."

I didn't expect my best friend—who was also my fucking lover, goddamn it—and six other assholes to beat the hell out of me. I didn't expect I'd barely escape being sodomized with a broom handle because someone called the cops.

No, sir. I did not expect that.

Ryan's hostile expression turned to one of pity. "I would *never* condone what he did. Violence is wrong. But you should have gone to him in private. Told him you were gay. Talked to him about it. He was your friend. He would have understood. But he felt cornered when you did your whole rose-between-the-teeth thing. He was desperate."

"You're seriously going with that?" Despite years of practice controlling his reaction to Nick's betrayal, Jack's voice rose. Ryan clearly remembered things differently than he did. "Gay-panic defense?"

"No. Never." Ryan's fists tightened in his lap. "But I'm certain he never meant the situation to get so out of control."

More minutes of silence—measured by the mechanical sound of numbers flipping—ticked by.

Jack felt bone tired already, and it was still early. "What the hell happened to him?"

"He killed himself."

"I know that. I guess I meant...do you know why?"

"Things haven't gone well for him for a while."

Jack sat back. "I didn't know."

"You heard the Foasbergs lost the dealership, right?"

"Yes." Foasberg Chevrolet had been their family business for about eighty years. Jack heard they lost the dealership when GM restructured after the bailout.

Jack took a cookie to give his hands something to do. "That was a nice place."

"He tried to keep the service bays open for a while, after. Tried to get a different franchise. It finally closed, and they sold the land. The market was shit, and they pretty much lost everything."

"I didn't know."

"After that, things just"—Ryan lowered his lashes—"went downhill."

"But—"

"I'm sorry." Karen reentered. The heels of her shoes tapped briskly on the tiled floor. "I have to go pick up a friend whose car quit on her."

Jack rose to leave. Karen picked up her purse from the kitchen counter.

She must have realized leaving meant Ryan would have to face going back to his house alone, because suddenly she turned to him. "Ryan, you could stay here and finish your coffee. I won't be very long. You can make yourself at home until—"

"I couldn't." Ryan stood up. "I've abused your hospitality enough today."

"But you shouldn't have to go back there, not when—"

"It's fine. It's not like I can unsee the scene."

Ryan started toward the door. Jack and Karen followed.

Jack wasn't ready to give up on the job just yet. "Mind if I come with you? I could give you a quote."

"I told you—"

"I understand, Ryan. I really do. If you know how to clean and disinfect and dispose of waste materials, then you'll be able to save money if you do it yourself. But you might find it's more emotional than you imagined and change your mind. Even if you don't use Brothers Grime, my bid will give you a ballpark idea of what any reputable firm would charge you for the job."

Karen smiled. "All right. That sounds reasonable, doesn't it, Ryan?"

"Yes." Ryan didn't look Jack's way.

"Excellent." Karen pulled Jack into a hug before he had a chance to make that impossible. She did the same for Ryan, and he welcomed her. "I'm so sorry I have to leave. Expect me to stop by later with food."

"You don't need to go to any trouble."

"It's no trouble." Karen practically shook him. "I'll worry about you."

"Yes, ma'am." Ryan smiled.

"Jack, it was a pleasure meeting you," she said.

"You too, ma'am."

She closed the door behind them, presumably because she had to go through the house to get to the garage. A minute later, the heavy steel door rolled up, and Karen's import sedan backed down the driveway. Still awkward around Ryan, Jack waved from the porch as she sped away.

Then they headed toward Ryan's place, the final stop on Nick Foasberg's short and troubled journey through life.

CHAPTER 4

"HERE. LET'S GO THIS WAY." Ryan led Jack down the path toward the sidewalk, even though it looked like it would be easy to get from the Huntleys' house to Ryan's place over the grass. "The grass is pretty spongy there, and the ground's uneven. We get gophers. Tough with a cane."

Jack didn't acknowledge the kindness, if that was what it was, but he posted a chalk mark on an imaginary scoreboard. *One point for grace under pressure.* Ryan seemed gracious, even in these awful circumstances. People could take lessons from him and Dave's mother. Maybe that was the kind of thing you could expect from the moneyed class.

That led Jack to wonder how Nick's cousin Ryan had come to be among them.

"This your place?"

"Yeah." Ryan unlocked the door but hesitated before pushing it open. "I—"

"We could talk out here, if you feel more comfortable. It might be good for you to find somewhere else to crash for a while."

Ryan gave the door a hard push. "After you."

Jack crossed the immaculate marble-tiled entry and waited. Ryan followed, locking the door behind them. When he slipped off his shoes, Jack started to toe his shoes off as well. Probably that was how Ryan kept the floors so nice.

"You don't have to take yours off. I do that for comfort more than cleanliness." He raked a hand through his short, wavy hair. "I know it's early, and you're here to see the—" His mouth snapped shut.

"Bathroom," Jack supplied.

"*Bathroom*, yes." Ryan watched him with those pale, cool eyes. "You're here to see where my cousin killed himself, but I need a drink first. Would you like one?"

"No, thank you. I'll be driving."

"Mind if I have one?" Ryan headed toward the back of the house. "I'm pretty sure I don't care what your answer is."

"You go right ahead." Jack followed. "If you like, you can just point me in the right direction, and I'll leave you to it."

"It's this way." Ryan led him into the kitchen and pointed down a narrow hallway. "That used to be the maid's quarters and what my grandmother called the service porch."

Ryan turned his back and began rummaging through the cupboards.

Jack left him. He didn't bother asking why Ryan put his cousin up in the maid's quarters. He was probably going to see Ryan differently now, knowing his house once had a live-in maid.

The wood trim, cabinetry, and crown molding were likely all original, but the floor tiles looked relatively new. On one side of the hallway there was a washer, a dryer, and a deep sink. Farther down, there was a tall, thin cupboard Jack figured contained a built-in ironing board.

Overall, the place seemed torn from a different era entirely, where the maids lived off the service porch and anyone who actually counted lived upstairs.

The last door on the left was ajar. Dirty footprints traced where the coroner had removed the body. The tracks led to the end of the hall and out the back door. Jack took disposable boot covers from his bag and slipped them over his shoes, then pulled on thick latex gloves and a simple mask. He used his cane to push the door the rest of the way open, leaving his bag behind.

Careful where he placed his feet, he walked inside. There wasn't much there. An unmade twin-size bed with a wrought-iron frame. A trunk, open at the foot of the bed, half-full of blankets and bedding. Clothes had been piled on a chair in the corner —mostly jeans and T-shirts. A worn sweatshirt hung from a hook on the door.

Nothing adorned the walls except a simple wooden crucifix. When Jack toggled the light switch, a ceiling fan stirred the air in lazy circles. The only light came from the window, which looked out onto a block wall and some garbage cans.

Flagrant nosiness compelled Jack to open the closet door. Inside there were several suits and long-sleeved tailored shirts, white and French blue, neatly pressed, still wrapped in dry cleaner's plastic. A pair of worn dress shoes lined up with trainers and flip-flops on the floor.

A quick perusal of the bedside table—*Nick's* bedside table, Jack reminded himself—turned up the *Alcoholic's Anonymous Big Book*, a Hazelden series meditation book, and a tattered paperback copy of Tom Clancy's *Ghost Recon*.

Jack turned a full circle where he stood, taking it all in. This was so...desolate. So much worse than he'd expected, and he hadn't even crossed the threshold of the bath yet. He hadn't even seen where Nick had died.

He steeled his heart and stepped to the bathroom door. Remnants of crime scene tape hung limply from the door frame.

A biohazard warning was prominently posted on the door. A peculiar combination of curiosity and dread made Jack's heart race. His eyes burned, and his throat seemed clogged by a thousand things he wished he could say now that it was impossible.

The old-fashioned knob turned easily in Jack's hand, and he stepped into the bathroom and switched on the light.

The room was larger than he'd expected. It contained a pedestal sink, a claw-foot tub with its plastic shower curtain shoved aside, and a brand-new dual-flush toilet. Louvered windows let in daylight and a soft breeze that did nothing to help dissipate the choking smell of death.

A newer, one-piece shower-and-tub enclosure would have contained the mess better. As it was, gore spattered the wall behind the tub. Blood flecked stretches of white plaster. Red lines drawn by gravity ended in dark pools of congealed blood inside the tub and on the black-and-white floor tiles.

If it hadn't been Nick's blood, Jack would have written it off as fairly commonplace stuff. It would take a two-man team half a day, if that.

Jack knew he should turn around and leave. He *should* write a proposal, get into his truck, and go home.

What made him stand there mesmerized by the impersonal aftermath of Nick's gruesome death when he'd seen it so many times before?

What made him ask useless, stupid questions like how had Nick come to this awful end? What could Jack have done differently? How could he have helped?

How did the world keep on spinning without Nick Foasberg in it?

Jack closed his eyes.

Every breath he took stung, chilled to icy finality by the death of his first love. Jack thought he'd come for closure when the reality was he was opening a wound that had never healed and would never close now, ever.

God, Dave was so right to warn me off.

"Seen what you need to see?" Ryan's voice came from directly behind Jack. Warm, whiskey-scented breath puffed over the skin on the back of his neck.

Jack turned. "Yeah."

"'Cause you've been standing here for over an hour."

"I—" *Over an hour? Really?*

"Did you come here so you could get the last laugh?"

"Laugh?" Jack pulled his mask down. "Why would I laugh?"

"I figure you wanted a chance to look down on your child-hood tormentor"—he gestured drunkenly toward the old tub—"or what was left of him to prove you finally won. Right?"

"You think this is about *winning*?"

"What else?" Ryan crossed the room, picking his way with more care than he probably would if he'd been sober.

Jack followed just as carefully, because he was stiff from standing in one place for so long. He tore off his gloves and bootees, leaving them on Nick's bedroom floor. "God, I can't... Slow down. *Ryan!*"

Ryan waited at the end of the hall, his face a mask of pale fury.

Jack asked, "What about you?"

Ryan frowned at that. "What do you mean, what about me?"

"Why was your cousin living in the maid's quarters, in a room no bigger than—"

Ryan's blue eyes turned to ice. "That's none of your goddamn business."

"Did you look down on him?" Jack asked, meaning to chide him gently.

Ryan sucked in a sharp breath. "You bastard."

"I'm sorry." Jack was sorry for everything. *Everything.* God, he was so tired.

Ryan's Adam's apple bobbed in the long column of his pale throat. "I couldn't let him live upstairs anymore. He stole my wallet, my credit cards. Anything he could get his hands on."

"Christ." Jack glanced at the door to Nick's small, tidy room. Had to be drugs. The place didn't have the disorganized-rat's-nest look of a meth user's room. "Prescription drugs? Vicodin, Oxy?"

Ryan bobbed a brief nod.

"Christ."

"He was working on things." Ryan looked back toward the room. "He was going to counseling."

"Let me just..." Jack tried to salvage things by going back to his original purpose for being there. "The average hourly rate for a job like this is four hundred dollars. I send a truck and two men. If you go with another service, you shouldn't be charged for more than four hours. If you're interested in outside help, show me all your bids, and I'll do it for ten percent less than the lowest of them. I'll go even lower if that's what it takes."

"Maybe I don't want you in there with the evidence of Nick's darkest, most hopeless hour." Ryan's eyes narrowed. "Maybe I'm angry because people like you cross the street to get away from someone in Nick's kind of trouble, yet you're happy to take our money to clean up the mess."

"I'm sorry for your loss, Ryan," Jack whispered. Anger was simply one of the stages of grief. He'd bungled this so badly he couldn't think anymore. "I've handled this all wrong. I normally don't spend time out in the field. My cousin Gabe usually talks to survivors. He has a gift for making people feel safe, but I"—he hesitated before telling the awful truth—"I couldn't stay away."

"Where were you when he was losing his business?" Ryan asked. "When his wife divorced him and took the kids. Where were you when he lost his identity and turned to oblivion for comfort?"

"That's not fair. I'm where I *always* was." Jack pounded the rubber tip of his cane on the tile. "In the *same* goddamn house I grew up in. I have the *same* goddamn phone number."

Ryan's energy seemed to evaporate, and he heaved a deep sigh. "Nick wouldn't have called you anyway."

God. "I know that. I don't know what I'd have done if he did."

"So how is cleaning up the mess he left behind going to help you?"

"I have no idea," Jack admitted woodenly. "I only know I need to do it."

Ryan's eyes were suspiciously moist. "Maybe I do too."

"You were here for him until he made it impossible. You have nothing to be ashamed of."

"I did everything I knew to do, and it wasn't enough." Ryan shook his head. "It's never enough. I need you to go."

Ryan walked past Jack, face expressionless. He opened the front door, leaving no room for further discussion.

Jack fished out his wallet. "I've got the number of a local bereavement group, Survivors of Suicide, here. They've all been through trauma like this, and they volunteer to help survivors cope with loss. Please call them. *Please.*"

"I can cope with loss." Ryan took the card from him and glanced at it briefly. "It's failure I despise."

Jack swallowed his pride. "I'm so sorry, Ryan. I've really fucked this all up. This is about *you*, and what you need. Let me help you."

"I'll let you know what I decide." Ryan closed the door between them.

CHAPTER 5

JACK HAD BEEN SITTING in the booth at Steamers for an hour already, listening to live jazz and trying to decompress when Gabe came in and sat down opposite him. Gabe's curly brown hair looked freshly washed, and he'd dressed in his normal off-duty wear: a lightweight Henley and jeans. Jack looked him over. They were first cousins, and they shared hair color, skin tone, height, and build. Except now Gabe looked like the before picture, and Jack felt like...the aftermath. Thin and broken and light-years older.

Their coolly efficient waitress had already supplied Jack with three 151 and Cokes, and she was ready to whisk the last empty drink away and get him another, but Gabe ordered himself a beer and waved her off.

Gabe's expression gave Jack chills.

"I know. I shouldn't have gone." Jack tried a preemptive apology. "I'm sorry."

"Dave's on his way. I told him he should never have called you."

Jack rubbed his face with both hands. "Gabe, I—"

"Do I need to point out that going to see the scene where Nick killed himself was probably a bad idea?"

"Don't start." Aware of Gabe's unspoken objection, Jack nevertheless signaled the waitress for another 151 and Coke when she brought Gabe's beer.

"I wouldn't know where to start." Gabe's softly controlled voice grated on Jack's nerves. "This could break you for good."

In theory, Jack agreed. Control was Gabe's thing. Nothing—neither violence nor gore nor emotions—got the better of Gabe. Sometimes Jack lost his shit. They all knew that.

Gabe probably figured Jack was mostly broken already—that the accident and the loss of his identity as a firefighter had blown him apart, and Nick's death crushed what was left. The truth was far simpler. He had never been whole to begin with.

"It won't. Besides," Jack admitted what was really bothering him, "Nick's asshole cousin thinks he's going to clean it up himself."

Gabe snorted. "No way."

"He's some kind of doctor. Says he knows what he's looking at, and how to disinfect and dispose of the waste materials."

"That shit's going to get personal fast." Gabe looked up and motioned to someone. "That's why you should never have gone over there in the first place, Jack."

Jack followed Gabe's gaze and saw Dave standing by the bar, wearing a charcoal suit that fit his broad-shouldered frame perfectly. White shirt, striped blue tie. Detective Dave must be coming from work; he still had his cop face on. He acknowledged them, his expression none too happy, before ordering a drink from the bartender.

Jack waved. "Why'd you have to invite him?"

"He invited himself. What have you got against Dave all of a sudden?"

"I met his mother this morning. Did you know he comes from

that neighborhood in Sunny Hills with the old glam houses? Why the hell did he go to our high school?"

"He grew up around here. His mom remarried and moved to Sunny Hills later."

"How do you know that?"

Gabe flushed. "I just know."

Together, they watched Dave make his way over, beer in hand. He slid into the booth next to Jack. "And the award for most stubborn motherfucker goes to..."

Gabe drummed on the table with both hands. Jack could barely hear him over the music.

"*Jaaaaaaaaaack* Masterson, for My Dead Lover's Crime Scene, directed by—"

"All right, all right." Jack accepted his rum and Coke from the waitress without interacting.

Dave's brows drew together. "You okay?"

"I am feeling no pain. But I'll need a ride home." Their gazes met, and Dave's lip curved up into a half smile.

"I'll take you," Gabe said, too loud. "I'm going that way anyway."

Jack glanced back at him. "If you're planning on lecturing me some more tonight, I think it only fair to warn you it will fall on deaf, drunk ears."

Dave eyed Jack speculatively. "My mom said you talked to her neighbor, Ryan?"

"Yeah. He seems like a good guy." Jack picked up his drink and took a deep swallow. "Tried to help Nick when he was pissing his life down the toilet. Gave him a roof over his head. Nick stole drug money from him."

"Addicts," Dave muttered cheerfully. "Can't live with them, but on the bright side, eventually they kill themselves."

"Don't' be a douche, Dave." Gabe kicked him under the table.

"Sorry." Dave looked away.

Jack turned his drink like a combination lock. "He's making up his mind if he'll use us. He'll call when he decides what he's going to do."

"He *thinks* he can do it by himself," Gabe informed Dave.

"To be fair," Jack murmured, "he knows what he's up against."

Dave took a sip of his beer. "So why not let him? Why not simply give him the opportunity to lay his dead to rest?"

Because I need that same opportunity. "He's family. He shouldn't be the one to do it."

"Neither should you." Dave looked irritated with him. "You're locked in a death spiral with Nick Foasberg. He was a loser."

"Yeah, yeah."

Dave leaned over, bumping Jack's shoulder. "You're better than that."

"How do you figure?" Jack asked.

"Nick's dead. He didn't give a shit about you, even when he was supposed to be your best friend."

Jack blew out a deep breath.

"Dave's right," Gabe said quietly.

"Do you know his cousin had no clue about us? He told me I should have outed myself to Nick in private, given him time to come to terms with the fact I was gay."

"Did you tell him what really happened?" asked Gabe.

"No."

"Suppose you come clean." Dave smirked. "No pun intended. What's the worst that could happen if you stop keeping Nick Foasberg's secrets?"

"End of the world as we know it." Jack shrugged. "And I'd feel fine."

"I'm serious. Maybe you should set the record straight."

"And how am I supposed to tell a dead man's secrets? Why

would I come clean now except as some sort of sick revenge? I'll look like an asshole."

Gabe rolled his eyes. "Why worry? You look like an asshole anyway."

"Ha-ha." Jack listened as the jazz combo played something he vaguely recognized. Brubeck, maybe. The waitress came by again, but he cashed out. He'd had plenty to drink. Way more than enough. They sat in silence for a while, and it was good.

Dave watched the musicians, and Jack watched Dave.

Being with Dave—drinking, watching a game, or listening to music—was nice. As Dave relaxed, he shifted down so their shoulders pressed together. The heat of Dave's skin warmed Jack's even through the fabric of his suit. It was almost pleasant, sitting there like that.

Almost enough to make him forget he'd had tea with Dave's *mother*. Better not to make any decisions about that on a snootful of alcohol.

"Time for me to go. If I don't, I'll fall asleep right here."

"What's wrong with that?" Dave asked. "We'd wake you before last call."

"I don't want you hauling my ass out of here over your shoulder." Jack motioned for Dave to move so he could get out of the booth. Dave offered to help, but Jack shrugged him off. He managed to rise awkwardly, bracing himself on the booth's edge while he got his cane and gripped the handhold. *People who can't walk right when they're sober have no business drinking.*

Gabe stood to leave. "I've gotta hit the head first."

"I can run Jack home," Dave offered. "It's no trouble."

"I'm beat. I'm heading out anyway."

They both looked at Jack.

"I'm on Gabe's way. He can take me tonight." Jack read the disappointment in Dave's eyes. "Maybe some other time."

Dave gave him a brief nod. "Sure."

Jack let Dave walk away. While he waited for Gabe outside the bathroom, he wondered if he'd done the right thing. Maybe he'd be better off with company than alone.

Jack followed Gabe to his SUV in silence.

When they edged away from the curb, Gabe asked, "Will Skippy bring you to get your car tomorrow?"

"Skippy's in Vegas. But I'll get a ride from someone."

"It's none of my business..." Gabe hesitated like he had something to get off his chest and wasn't sure the best way to go about it. "It seems to me like you've got something going on with Dave."

"You're right. It's none of your business."

"You gotta stop looking for love in the closet, coz." Gabe's voice was even but chiding.

Jack closed his eyes, but he smiled. *As if.*

He could have let Dave take him home, and they'd have probably broken the land speed record up the stairs to bed. But he'd met Dave's *mother.* He'd sipped tea from her little china cups.

Whatever had happened with Dave—sport-fucking or friends with benefits or whatever they called what they'd had with each other—he wasn't sure he could do it after the way Dave's mother patted his hand and said, *"It was a pleasure meeting you."*

Whatever he and Dave were, it wasn't *that.*

After a while, Gabe asked, "If we take Nick's scene, who're you going to send out?"

"I don't know yet. The cousin seemed pretty sure he didn't need us."

"How's he doing?"

"He's processing." Jack knew Gabe expected more than that. Gabe could go on for hours about how people felt about shit. "Angry. I gave him the SOS card."

"This is some fucked-up shit, Jack. I'll be happy if he doesn't call."

"Maybe he'll change his mind."

Gabe turned down the street that led to Jack's neighborhood. It was a study in contrasts: shotgun houses that were either pristinely kept—little smurf cottages—or so run-down they barely looked like they'd last through a strong wind.

A lot of the houses were rentals now, full of teens who didn't want to live on campus at the local university, or—in the worst of cases—squalid flophouses for addicts who lived a hairbreadth from homelessness.

Jack's place was too close to the train tracks. Too far from the brand-name supermarket.

Jack had lived in the house he was raised in ever since his parents had taken off in an RV. He'd purchased the place from them, and his monthly payments along with social security made their golden years possible.

Jack's neighborhood wasn't particularly safe, but Jack had never had trouble there, except in high school when he'd fallen afoul of Nick and his fag-bashing posse.

When Gabe pulled up to the curb, Jack grabbed the latch to get out. Gabe caught his arm. "I have a joke."

"Tell it."

"What do you get when you combine a guy who has no idea how good he is, a guy who has no idea what's good for him, and a blood-soaked crime scene?"

Nothing's as irritating as family. "I don't know. What?"

Gabe slanted a dark look at Jack before he let go. "I guess we're going to find out."

CHAPTER 6

THE PHONE RANG at 3:00 a.m.

Jack fumbled for it, drunkenly knocking everything else on his nightstand to the floor before he finally got hold of it.

"Wait," he ordered, taking the time to right a bottle of water before he sat up and put the phone to his ear. "What?"

"Hello?" A vaguely familiar voice.

Jack had to swallow before he could speak. "Jack Masterson. Who's this?"

"It's Ryan Halloran."

Ryan Halloran... *Not a Foasberg, then. Why the hell are you calling me at 3:00 a.m.?*

"Hello." Jack waited.

"I'm sorry to call so late."

"It's not late," Jack argued. "It's early."

"Right. I couldn't sleep." An audible sigh. "I couldn't even stay drunk. I went through a whole bottle of whiskey, and I can't seem to...let things go."

"I'm sorry." Jack's tongue was shaggier than his bathroom rug.

He took a few swallows of water before speaking again. "Look, if you want to talk, I can do that."

"I guess I do, or I wouldn't have called."

"Okay. What do you want to talk about?"

"I don't know."

"Well, if you did know, what would it be?"

Light laughter. Maybe Ryan wasn't too drunk for a joke. "I have a...a proposition for you."

"Yeah?" Jack was still sleepy enough to picture Ryan's all too Nick-like body poised naked over him. Sweat dripping from his brow while he—

"I'm willing to let your company take the job if you let me work alongside you."

Earsplitting feedback destroyed the cheesy porn sound track in Jack's inebriated fantasy.

Despite the fact Jack never worked in the field anymore, despite the fact he would normally send a two-man team out to clean that scene, Jack had planned on doing the job alone.

And he only just now realized that fact.

"That's not what I had in mind."

"I'm sure it's not," Ryan said wryly.

"A lot of people believe they can do this type of work, but when they get right down to it, they can't. I know you're a doctor—"

"I'm actually a nurse."

"A nurse?" *How do you afford that house?* "Okay. Well, you're probably used to cleaning up blood and things of that nature, but it's still different when it's someone you know."

"Which is why you're so anxious to do the job."

"I'm not anxious. But a team from Grime can get in there and erase what happened for you while you spend your time—"

"You weren't going to send a team. You were planning to do the cleaning yourself."

"I— What makes you say that?" *How did he know?*

"Is it true?"

Jack hesitated. "Yes."

"We both want the same thing, even if it's for different reasons."

"Do we? What is it you think I want?"

"I think you want closure." A long pause. "What do you think I want?"

"I..." Jack wasn't sure he should say it. "I'm not sure what you want."

"Come on." Now the voice was liquid sex. "It's easy to be honest in the dark, Jack."

God, isn't that the truth. "I think you want to punish yourself."

"What makes you think—" Fumbling noises. The sound of ice in a glass. Maybe a swallow or two and then a sigh. "Why would I want that?"

"So you could say you'd done everything you thought you should do?"

"Fuck you." Ryan cursed, then huffed out a laugh. "You're probably right."

Jack relaxed fractionally. "I know I'm right."

"Because you have a lot of experience with the bereaved?"

"Not at all." Jack took another sip of his water. He wished it were cold. He *wished* it were rum. "For obvious reasons, I'm the behind-the-scenes guy. Gabe is the face of the business. He's the client whisperer. Eddie does human resources, such as they are. We have a couple teams of cleaners. We're pretty small-time, but we stay busy."

"Why for obvious reasons?"

"What do you mean?"

"You said *for obvious reasons*, you're the behind-the-scenes guy. I guess it's not so obvious to me."

Jack made himself more comfortable against his headboard. "It's hard for me to navigate some of the scenes. When we get hoarders, it's impossible."

"You were injured in the Freeway Complex Fire, right?"

"Yeah." Jack took a deep breath. "That was me. I fell through a roof."

"That was some pretty dramatic shit."

"Not on my part. I was unconscious for most of it."

"I'm looking at the news article right now. It says here you had multiple fractures of the pelvis and legs. Some second-degree burns. Knee-replacement surgery. Both knees?"

Thinking back on all that made Jack's throat close up tight. "Just the left knee."

"It says three other firefighters were injured. Burns, major head trauma, awful stuff. Everyone survived, though?"

"You Googled me?"

"I'm using Nick's laptop. He had all the related articles bookmarked."

Jack's heart lurched erratically. "He did?"

A thump on Jack's bed made him jump out of his skin until he realized he'd left the bedroom door open for Skippy's cat. She positioned herself on his lap and kneaded his thigh muscles to tenderize him before making herself at home.

Before he knew it, he was stroking her weirdly blue fur.

Time passed before Ryan spoke again, but it was comfortable. Like sitting with a friend, watching a game. Jack didn't feel required to say anything, but it was nice knowing someone was out there listening. Ryan must have felt the same way, because he didn't seem in any hurry to end the call.

"I don't think Nick ever stopped being your friend."

"Right." Jack paused midstroke to feel Tasha's low purr against his fingers. "I didn't stop being his."

"Didn't you?"

"I guess that depends on your definition of friendship." *I kept his secrets.* "You stuck by him."

"Not really. He used to come to AA meetings at the hospital annex, and I saw him there. He was pretty down. I thought I could help."

"Did you?" Jack asked. "Help, I mean?"

"No, I didn't. I probably only prolonged things by letting him move in with me."

"You're being a little hard on yourself."

"I'd been down that road before. In the end, nothing you do matters. You can't will someone to live if fate has other plans."

"But you didn't exactly cause his death either."

"No. But maybe if I'd told someone—his wife or his mother—how desperate things had gotten..."

"You don't think they knew?"

Ryan exhaled harshly. "He was such a phony with the rest of the family. He was so glib, and—"

"We're talking about a drug addict here. No one puts up that good a facade. Don't you think he stole from them too? They knew."

"They knew he had problems. We...we all knew." Soft sobbing accompanied the sounds of Ryan's breathing. "But not how bad they were. God, *why* didn't I tell someone who could help? Why did I think I could help when no matter what I do, it's never enough."

"Whoa. Time-out. Don't do this to yourself." Jack glanced at the clock again: 3:15. "Look, you're not at the house alone, are you?"

"No. Someone's here, and I guess my outburst just woke him up. Wait a minute."

"Okay." A few seconds passed. Jack heard another male voice. The words weren't clear, but the tone was...coaxing.

Ryan came back on the line. "I have to go."

"Wait, were you serious about doing the job together? Is that what you want to do?"

"Do you?"

"Yes." Jack closed his eyes. "I can be at your place with my equipment by nine."

An audible sigh. "Make it ten. I haven't gotten any sleep."

"All right. Ten." Jack ended the call.

He waited a few minutes to see if he was likely to fall asleep again. When sleep seemed out of the question, he rose from his bed and headed for the kitchen to put on some coffee. The cat followed him, threading her lithe body between his leg and his cane to get his attention. Did she sense his turmoil?

"Might as well get some work done." Jack told himself he wasn't talking to Skippy's cat.

He. Was. Not. Talking. To. A. Cat.

"Got to make sure I have everything we'll need on the van, including an extra Tyvek suit and boots big enough for Ryan."

He tapped his fingers on the counter while he waited for the coffee to brew.

When it was done, he took a hot, black mugful to the front window and looked out on the empty street while he waited for it to cool enough for him to drink.

A cop car crawled by. Otherwise he could see nothing but the sulfur-yellow glow of streetlights.

Tasha twined around his feet and attacked the bottom of his sleep pants. He had to grab the waistband to keep her from pulling them down.

"Stop." She used her paws like hands to trap his foot and then rubbed her face along his toes. "No. Would you stop?"

He dragged the cat along with him as he sought out a small flashlight he kept in one of the entertainment center drawers. Once he focused the beam of light onto the hardwood floor, she pounced on it, stalking and chasing it around for several long minutes. He amused himself by making spiral patterns while he sipped his coffee.

When he turned the light off, then on again, the cat went apeshit.

"This isn't playing," Jack told her. "I'm just occupying your time so I can make up my mind in peace."

He couldn't get Nick's sad little room out of his mind. For all Jack couldn't lay claim to any sort of artistic sensibility, his parents' old furniture had the lived-in look of any thrift-store-and-spool-table decor. He still had pictures of family on the walls. He kept boxes of get-well cards from people who'd seen him through some of the worst months of his life.

There was even a row of stuffed animals on the mantel, monkeys with messages like *"Hang In There"* and lions that featured sayings about pride. Dumb stuff, but when he looked at it, he knew people cared about him. Family and friends were there in the background, waiting like a safety net.

What did Nick have to cling to in those last days? A cousin he'd disappointed like he'd disappointed so many people before. A crucifix from a church that made him feel guilty. Suits he was never going to wear, a bed he couldn't share.

Christ.

In Jack's mind, he replayed the hours he and Nick had spent in his old bedroom upstairs during the months leading up to graduation. Spring sunshine on the south-facing window made his room so hot their naked bodies dripped with sweat as they rolled and writhed against each other. Winter nights they'd lain there shivering, huddled together for warmth, whispering secrets and lies.

Sacred time spent discovering each other's bodies.

Their affair began in freshman year. They'd satisfied themselves with frottage and blowjobs, but Nick always had to push things further. One day he'd penetrated Jack stupidly with no

preparation, and Jack had cried from pain and anger and something he couldn't name. Fear of the unknown. Loss of the fantasy.

Something that made him ask himself, *Is this all there is?*

Nick made promises every time, and Jack believed them. Jack
always believed Nick, no matter how much he put Jack off, no
matter how many excuses he came up with for hiding what they
were.

Jack was in love. Why wouldn't he believe?

Nick said he felt the same way, but the time wasn't right to
tell the world. He said it might be a kick to shock people, but
coming out had to wait until later—until they were ready to move
on anyway in case the world wasn't ready for them.

He'd said maybe when they were seniors, they could go to
prom together. He'd promised they'd apply to the same colleges,
room together, come out as a couple, and be open about things
with their families. What reason had he given Jack to doubt him?

Of course now, Jack understood. A man says anything he has
to in order to get off, and as little as possible after.

*Why didn't I see how he turned every spoken word into fore-
play? Why didn't I see that sex always led to sleep or aban-
donment?*

Why didn't I see how manipulative he was?

How could I be so stupid?

Jack found out the truth at the bottom of a pile of vicious
bullies, and after that he'd never given his heart to anyone again.

Until now he'd believed it was because he'd learned his
lesson, but in Nick's room in Sunny Hills, Jack had learned a
different, more awful truth.

Jack had never gotten his heart back from Nick, and now he
never would.

It's probably time to cry now.

When Jack started to sob, Tasha jumped into his lap like she
was trying to distract him. Jack couldn't have stopped crying if

he'd wanted to. He swiped at his seemingly endless tears and the snot that streaked his cheeks, and asked himself all the questions he still couldn't answer.

First he cried like a man without a safe place to vent his rage, and then he cried like a man who'd been horribly betrayed.

Finally, he cried like a boy who'd lost his first love.

Jack had three choices.

He could back out and let Ryan do the job alone. Ryan would understand if Jack told him he wasn't up to it. If bitter memories and a sleepless night—if his physical infirmity—made doing the job impossible for him.

Or Brothers Grime could send a team to help Ryan clean. His guys would realize that Ryan needed closure. They'd help him suit up, and give him some job to do. Eddie was a good guy. He'd make it work.

Or Jack could put aside his unhappiness, swallow his pain, and find a way to move past Nick Foasberg once and for all.

Tasha head-butted him in the breadbasket hard enough to get his attention.

"What?" he growled at her.

Her reptilian eyes shone in the darkness. She watched, sphinxlike, as if to warn him life's lessons could come at a high price. Jack had dodged most of the really hard lessons so far, yet he'd learned two very important things tonight.

One, pain mortgaged to some future date comes due with interest; and two, cats—even snotty, damp, *cried-on cats*—smell way better than clean, dry dogs.

CHAPTER 7

JACK TOOK a cab to pick up his van. Gabe was already in the front office with three of their employees: Paco, Jerry, and the only woman in the firm, Kim, who referred to herself as "Token Chick" and talked in the third person.

Eddie Vasquez, Grime's third owner, was all ready to lay on the sarcasm. "Nice to see you looking so well rested."

Jack adjusted his sunglasses unnecessarily. "I'm taking one of the panel vans."

Gabe and Eddie glanced at each other. Gabe wore his khakis and a uniform polo, but Eddie was dressed in a pair of slick black trousers, a fancy red dress shirt, and black tie. He had big, broad shoulders and narrow hips, and when he moved, it seemed impossible someone his size could be so graceful. He must have been the bastard offspring of a gangster and a dance instructor. He looked like a deadly tango master or a grim-faced mambo ninja.

"Where are you going dressed like that?" Jack asked.

"My sister's kid has a thing at school."

"Right. No way you're going to a kid thing dressed like that unless you're hot for teacher."

Eddie colored furiously. "Shut it."

Gabe looked Jack over. "You sure you gotta do this, coz?"

"I'm sure."

Eddie wrote something on his magic clipboard and held out a set of keys. When Jack reached for them, Eddie drew them sharply away. "Don't go parking in dark places with boys, and be sure to fill it with gas before you come back."

"Yes, Mother." Jack snatched the keys and followed Gabe to the warehouse out back to check over his equipment.

"Like your mother ever gave you car keys."

"You're right. She knew me better than that."

Years with the fire department drilled a particular sense of pride into a man. Jack insisted the trucks be kept spotless. Every team checked equipment off on a manifest, then *re*checked that against the needs of each individual job, making certain they'd have everything they'd require when they got to the job site.

The warehouse space housed three white Nissan panel vans all emblazoned with the Brothers Grime logo and URL, their phone number, and the slogan, "Life is not a fairy tale." Two box trucks they kept parked in the lot completed their fleet. Jack got there just as someone rolled the heavy metal door up.

Bright sunlight streamed into the work area, blinding Jack, reflecting off the sides of the vehicles. Glare washed color out of everything inside and made it hard to see.

Jack was glad for his sunglasses, and not just because he didn't want Gabe and Eddie to see his red eyes.

Everyone seemed to be watching him. Maybe because he rarely spent time in the warehouse, and when he did visit, his employees expected a white-glove inspection.

"Token Chick is doing her job, oh mighty Payer of Wages." Kim smiled from behind her tusklike lip piercings.

He smiled back at her. "Hail, worthy minion. The wage gods smile on you this day."

"Not on you," Gabe guessed. "I bet Dave a hundred bucks you're doing the job for free."

"You'd lose. But I admit I gave it away cheap. It's just—"

"Something you have to do. I know." Gabe sighed.

Jack checked through his supplies. "I'll need a basin wrench and some basic plumbing tools. The bathroom has a claw-foot tub."

Gabe took a toolbox down from one of the shelves. "You have to move it, huh?"

"Only if I want to clean around it."

"I could send one of the kids with you." He gestured toward Paco. "We've only got the one other job this morning."

"No."

"C'mon, Jack. You're not being reasonable. You've only been in the field a couple of times in the last six months."

Jack closed the van's back doors with a bang. "I'll see you later."

"It's not a crime to call if you need help. Drive careful."

"I will." He climbed up into the driver's seat. Before he shut the door, he said, "It's going to be okay, Gabe."

Gabe muttered something else, but it was lost to the noise of the engine. Jack pulled out of the warehouse carefully, then waved.

Whatever Gabe said, it was probably closer to *You're a fucking dick* than *I guess a man's gotta do what a man's gotta do.*

On the way to Ryan's place, Jack turned on the radio for the noise. He stopped to get a couple of coffees in case Ryan didn't have any made, and pulled up in front of Ryan's house at almost exactly ten on the dot.

There was a car in the driveway that hadn't been there the day before, but the house looked quiet—until a man Jack didn't know stepped out the front door.

Whoever he was, he turned, and then Ryan appeared behind him. They stayed pressed together, hip to hip in the doorway like lovers, saying good-bye.

Jack waited in the car, trying to look like he was busy with something—writing or taking a call. He didn't want to intrude, yet he couldn't tamp down his curiosity. He was absolutely not trying to see what they were doing when Ryan motioned for him to come up to the porch.

Jack grabbed his cane and got out. The way up the walk seemed miles longer than it had the day before.

Jack had dreams like that all the time, where seemingly short distances lengthened out before him—where hallways grew longer and destinations pulled away even as he struggled and struggled, trying to close the gap.

Jack felt Ryan and his friend watching. He couldn't help wondering what they were thinking, if they were judging him. If they were losing patience with each slow step he took as he made his way to the house.

"Jack," Ryan said. "This is Kevin."

Jack lifted his chin to acknowledge Ryan's words, then took a look at Kevin. What he saw surprised him. Whatever he'd imagined Ryan's boyfriend would be like, this man with his sharply defined features and thin, angular face wasn't it.

Kevin's eyes were overly wide, and his mannerisms too intense for the early hour. Jack had seen plenty of drug users before, and it looked like Kevin was one of them. He wasn't circling the drain by any means, but he was pretty obviously riding the waves in the basin. Jack guessed cocaine.

"Pleased to meet you," Jack lied. He held out his hand anyway, just to man up.

"You too." Kevin shook Jack's hand, but not before assessing and dismissing him as a potential rival. He turned to Ryan.

"Babe, are you absolutely sure I can't talk you out of this? This is some freaky shit. I don't mind telling you—"

Ryan preempted the argument. "No."

Kevin danced on the balls of his feet, turning to Jack to shore up his argument. "You don't think Ryan should do this, do you?"

"No, I don't," Jack answered honestly.

"I know, right?" Kevin's head bobbed. "He sees enough sick shit at work."

"I agree."

"See? Cleaning dude agrees with me." Kevin caught the belt loop on Ryan's low-slung jeans with his index finger and pulled him forward by his hips. Their groins rubbed intimately, and for a second Jack's gut tightened with longing. He couldn't remember the last time he'd shared that kind of intimacy with anyone in the light of day.

Currently, Dave was his go-to guy for sex, and Dave always left as soon as it was over so he could wake up in his own bed. *Period.* He showed not a whiff of interest in Jack where anyone but their closest friends—people like Gabe—could see.

It was clear Kevin had the right to morning-after familiarity with Ryan.

It wasn't clear exactly *why.*

"Stop." Ryan pulled away. "You need to go."

"C'mon, Ry." The man rubbed his lips over Ryan's. Whether Ryan didn't like it because Jack was there, or whether Ryan didn't like it at all, the act resulted in him standing on tiptoe as if to avoid being licked by a dog.

"Stop, Kev."

"Don't be like that," Kevin coaxed.

"I'll talk to you on Thursday if you stop by work at lunchtime."

"All right." Kevin frowned but dropped a last dry-looking kiss on Ryan's cheek. "I'll be there."

"Call your sponsor," Ryan ordered as Kevin headed for his car.

"Yeah. Got it. On it."

Ryan and Jack stood in some kind of limbo while Kevin got in his battered Jetta. It took him a minute to start the engine and back out. Talk about a walk of shame.

"Awkward silence." Jack pointed out the obvious.

Ryan folded his arms across his chest. "I had a crime scene in my house. I needed a distraction."

"I'm not judging you."

"That's good. I get enough of that from the voices in my head."

"I brought coffee." Jack motioned toward the car. "I could use some help carrying shit."

Ryan stepped out and headed down the path. He wore jeans and a faded T-shirt, but his feet were bare. Jack noticed they were nicely shaped with high arches and long, slender toes. Against the rough brick landscaping they looked oddly vulnerable. Jack was momentarily mesmerized by the desire to protect them.

"You should put on socks," he said as he followed. "I brought boots for you that I think will fit."

"Thanks."

"You're welcome."

Jack opened the passenger door and took the coffees from his cup holders. He handed one to Ryan and leaned against the door frame to drink his.

"Still steamy. Good. I didn't make any yet."

Jack snorted. "Kevin didn't need the caffeine."

"Meow." Ryan leveled a shrewd look at Jack over his cup. "Just saying."

"Sorry."

Ryan shrugged. "Kevin's a work in progress."

"Aren't we all?" Jack looked down at Ryan's bare feet again.

"Anyway, I spoke out of turn. It's none of my business. Nick was in my life for a lot of years, and maybe I get a little lost around you because you're so much like him."

Ryan stepped back, aghast. "I'm *nothing* like Nick."

"Wait." Jack tensed. "You look like him. That's all I meant."

"He and I couldn't even have a two-minute conversation without running dry."

"It's the physical resemblance I'm talking about. It's hard to wrap my head around." Jack put his coffee down and walked to the back of the truck where he opened the doors and started pulling out his gear. "He's dead. But here you are, and you look—"

"I like to think I'm more adaptable than Nick was, at the very least."

"I'm sure you are."

"Nick didn't give me the time of day until he needed a place to stay."

"I don't follow." Jack stopped what he was doing. "I thought you were cousins? You weren't close?"

"We may have been related, but Nick didn't hang around with his"—Ryan made air quotes—"'*homo cousin Ryan.*' Not unless I had something he needed."

"That's harsh." *And such self-loathing bullshit on Nick's part.* "I'm really sorry."

"I was used to it."

"And you still let him live here?"

Ryan pulled unhappily at the hem of his shirt. "He was family."

"That's mighty nice, considering."

"I do volunteer work with substance abusers and hospice, and I'm an ER nurse at a hospital called St. Jude. What can I say? I'm a magnet for lost causes."

"I apologize in advance if I'm a lost cause too. You sure you're up for this?"

"Well." Ryan lifted one of his eyebrows even as he heaved a dramatic sigh. "Even if the road leads nowhere, it's nice when the scenery changes."

CHAPTER 8

ONCE THEY'D DONNED their gear—hooded Tyvek coveralls, chemical-resistant work boots, gloves, respirators, and goggles—Ryan helped Jack carry his equipment and tools into the house.

Well, mostly Ryan carried the gear, and Jack cursed the fact he could only carry half of what Ryan could.

Curtains twitched open as some of Ryan's neighbors grew curious, but fell closed again when Jack glanced up to see who was watching. Across the street a woman in pajamas and a terry-cloth robe stared until Jack stared back, and then she picked up her newspaper and hurried inside.

"Is all this really necessary?" Ryan asked, looking down at his coveralls. "I feel like we're tracking an outbreak of Ebola virus."

"It's necessary," Jack answered.

In his kind of cleaning business, they handled human tissue, bodily fluid and waste, mouse and rat droppings, animal carcasses, and who knew what all. When Jack and Gabe started the Brothers Grime, they agreed the most important part of their business was keeping their employees healthy while their employees kept the public safe.

Did Jack *like* dressing like he was an extra on the set of the film *Outbreak*? No. Would he take any chances with his body, his employees, or God help him, Ryan Halloran?

Hell no.

"How did you even get into this business?" Ryan asked as he lugged a pump sprayer filled with disinfectant into Nick's room.

"I had to find something I could still do after the accident, and I had too many scars to go into porn."

"I think scars are hot." Spoken from behind a respirator, it was like getting hit on by Darth Vader.

Jack's face warmed up. "Yeah, but then I failed the flexibility test."

Despite the situation, Ryan laughed. That could be a good thing. Jack's kind of work required a strong stomach and a good sense of humor. Eddie, who trained new hires, had a wicked wit. His humor often made the difference between a trainee getting sick and quitting the first day out, and a valuable employee who could work and earn alongside them.

"Next, we'll put paper down so we have a path to and from the back door. There's a roll of tape in my bag."

Ryan left the disinfectant outside the bathroom door where they'd staged equipment. While Jack got out a roll of thick, plastic-backed paper, Ryan located the tape.

"If we're careful, we can use this paper and a small amount of low-adhesive tape without ruining your floor. Can you tape while I unroll?" Jack asked.

"Sure."

Starting at the bathroom door, Jack started spooling out brown paper. Wide as the doorway and a little unwieldy, the paper was tough enough to stand up to foot traffic. Jack was forced to admit he needed Ryan. There was no way he could kneel on the hardwood floor to tape.

No way he could have done this job alone.

"This reminds me of prepping for painting." Ryan tore a segment of tape and stuck it down. The long line of his strong back and the curve of his ass made Jack swallow hard.

Jack cleared his throat. "I thought of starting up a painting business. The physical labor wouldn't be any more intense, and the start-up costs were similar."

"But crime scene cleanup won out?" Ryan glanced up at him, blue eyes interested beneath long, coppery lashes.

"I guess I thought this would be more satisfying." Jack fussed with the paper roll unnecessarily. He had to stop looking at Ryan like that.

"How so?"

Jack shrugged off the attraction. God, was this ever the wrong place, wrong time. "Anybody can paint a house."

"Some painters are better than others."

"Painting is all about attention to detail. Same goes for cleaning, but this job lets me help people out of really traumatic situations. It's almost like I'm still with the fire department. We respond to a crisis and do what we can. I can stomach it. It's a good fit."

Ryan's gaze went from Jack's face to his knees and back again. "Seems like."

Jack felt his ears warm up. Was he telling Ryan his whole life story because he was nervous? Because he was putting off the horror that waited on the other side of the bathroom door? Or because the man intrigued and attracted him?

Was it because Ryan struck some familiar chord deep within Jack and he wanted to hear the music it promised?

"Thanks for taping." Jack pivoted abruptly on his good leg to start laying a paper path toward the back door. "I can't crawl like that."

"Your knee?"

"Yeah," Jack admitted. "Among other things. I've gone out on plenty of jobs, but usually I drive and oversee sorting and hauling at hoarding sites, or I spray and scrub walls. I do whatever I can do standing up, mostly."

"I'll keep that in mind," Ryan said with unmistakable sensual intent.

Jack glanced away. Apparently Ryan's go-to deflection was a sexual offensive. Humans always seemed to find a way to compartmentalize, even on a job like this.

Ryan's teasing wasn't going to make things easier. Jack's emotions teetered between elation and discomfort when Ryan looked at him with that warmth in his eyes.

"Okay." Jack's voice cracked. "Uh. Where were we?"

"Do you have chronic pain from your injuries?" Ryan touched Jack's knee lightly, then pulled his hand back when Jack jerked away as if Ryan's fingers burned.

Jack cleared his throat. "Complaining doesn't seem to pay the bills."

"Lots of guys would go on disability."

"I get bored easily." Jack normally used humor to hide, but Ryan's frank gaze kept stripping him bare. "Besides, guys dig this hazmat shit."

"Right. Make light." Ryan rolled his eyes and continued his crawl along the floor. He taped down the paper sheeting until he and Jack got to the door, and trimmed it off. He sat on his butt and let his gaze drift up Jack's body again. "And you planned to do this job all by yourself."

Jack set the paper aside. "I wanted to be alone with my ghosts. What about you?"

"I never really understood what that phrase meant until last night." Ryan shuddered. "Alone with ghosts."

"Stubborn," Jack chided gently. "I told you to stay somewhere else last night."

"Nick ripped me off enough while he lived with me. I wasn't about to let him take anything from me after he died."

"I understand." Jack laid his hand on Ryan's shoulder. "At least you had the sense to call Kevin."

"Only because every other person I called was busy or gone."

"I wasn't." Jack wasn't sure what made him say that. "I mean—"

"No. You weren't." Ryan rose lithely to his feet. Jack heard his spine crackle as he stretched the kinks out. "What's next?"

Jack felt caught under Ryan's pale-eyed scrutiny. "Now we put down a layer of disinfectant spray and let that kill anything we could come in contact with."

"Do you do this with everyone? Or just people you expect might have certain diseases? Because I'm pretty sure Nick was negative for hep C and HIV."

"I follow the same protocol with all biologicals, and I make sure the staff does the same. We never take chances."

"Good to know." Ryan nodded.

Jack primed the pump sprayer and took it into the bathroom. Nick's blood had congealed into thick, dark puddles in some places, had dried to reddish-brown stains in others. The acrid copper-penny flavor of it hung in the air. Maybe that was Jack's imagination. The smell was awful but easier to take from the inside of a respirator. He'd brought eucalyptus rub for Ryan, in case he started to look green.

"You want to spray? You just squeeze the trigger. Lay a cover down on every surface you see with blood. While you're doing that, I'll take out the trash. We'll leave for a bit to let the disinfectant do its job, come back and scrub, and that's it."

"You make it sound so simple." Ryan took the sprayer from Jack.

"It really is."

"It shouldn't be," said Ryan, softly.

Jack had to agree.

Ryan took the pump and started spraying the tub and the walls. Jack stood by the sink. There was no blood on the basin or the mirror above it, but being a nosy fucker, he opened the medicine cabinet just to see what Nick kept inside it. Nothing much. Aspirin. Condoms. Antacids and standard first-aid stuff. Jack figured Ryan was probably responsible for those things rather than Nick.

Jack threw away Nick's toothbrush, soap, and razor. The trash, toilet paper roll, shower curtain, and towels that had been hanging up when Nick ended his life—all of it would go into red plastic medical waste bags along with bloodied cleaning rags and used masks and gloves. Even their coveralls were disposable.

When they were done, those bags would be sealed into cartons and labeled as biological waste. Then they would have to be hauled to a designated facility.

That would be that.

"We're going to throw away the shower curtain, but spray it anyway," said Jack.

"All right." Ryan held the plastic liner up and hit it with the sprayer. It didn't take long to cover the small room with disinfectant. Respirators diminished the smell but didn't get rid of it entirely.

Jack got a plastic drain cleaner and shot Ryan a glance. Ryan's eyes widened behind his goggles.

"I've gotta pull hair clogs from the drain, because we're going to have to move this tub to clean behind it. This is usually pretty gross. You probably won't want to see what I pull out of there."

Ryan's eyes lit with challenge. "Bring it."

"No, really. I mean—"

"Don't baby me." Ryan's brows drew downward. "I can handle worse than a few hair clogs."

Jack started pulling hair from the drain, and there was a lot of it. A tub that old, it made sense, really. Who thinks to clean out the drains of a little-used bathroom? Most people didn't clean drains unless they backed up. Unfortunately, along with hair, Jack pulled up unmistakable bits of bone and a couple of teeth. They must have washed along a river of blood to the lowest point in the tub and slipped into the drain.

Ryan blanched. "Aw, *shit*."

Jack watched Ryan lurch out of the tiny room.

A man can prepare himself for all kinds of things. He can focus his attention, steel himself, and even do a really unpleasant job with the right preparation. It was always the unexpected that caught a guy in the gut, like the first hoarder house Jack had been to where the occupant had died alone, unmourned and unmissed, and her pets had half eaten her before anyone thought to check on her.

Life is a fucking mess. People only think they have a handle on their emotions until something weird enough comes along and they find out different.

It was true for Jack. It was true for most everyone.

Jack finished what he was doing so he could put it from his mind.

The gut-wrenching reality that those were Nick's teeth—Nick's *bones*—slowed his movement until it felt like he was swimming through glue. He had to treat the situation with the respect it deserved, so he separated the human remains from the trash and labeled them, although it didn't make much difference. They were going to the same place anyway.

This was the best way for him to mourn. To grieve for his long-ago lover. These last, stolen moments in Nick's physical presence, such as it was, were all he was ever going to get. He let that thought settle on his body and in his brain. Let it seep into his hands as he reverently collected what he could of someone he'd once loved.

When Jack finished, he sought out Ryan. Jack found him hosing vomit into the planter outside the back door.

Jack pulled his respirator off and pushed back his goggles and hood. "I should have warned you sooner."

Ryan didn't turn. "You tried to tell me. I didn't think I would react like that. It's not like I haven't seen all this before. Severed limbs. Gunshot wounds. People lose teeth in sports injuries and car accidents all the time, and I see it every day."

"This is different." Jack took the hose from him and turned the water off. "This is someone you cared about."

He leaned against the house so he could coil it back up—such a cliché, a firefighter reeling in a hose. When he was done, he motioned Ryan over to the patio chairs.

This is going to be the slowest job ever.

Jack gave Ryan's shoulder a pat before he sat down. Ryan looked young to him. For the first time, he appeared uncertain. He'd been a rock, tough and determined, up until he saw the garbage coming out of his drain. Poor kid. Most everyone had something that took the wind from their sails on a job.

"You must think I'm a joke," said Ryan.

"Don't be so hard on yourself." On impulse, he pulled off his gloves and took Ryan's hands in his.

Ryan stared at their clasped hands like he didn't know what he was looking at. "I need to do this job because it's Nick."

"Me too," Jack assured him. "It's my way of saying a final good-bye, but it's so hard. I'm so goddamn angry at him for taking the coward's way out like that."

Ryan pulled away. "Me too." He balled his hands into fists and covered his eyes.

"Of course you are. Especially after you did your best to help him. But we're also uniquely qualified to clean this scene with compassion." Jack took Ryan's hands from his face. "Do you still want to work alongside me? You don't have to."

"Yes, but"—Ryan hesitated—"I need to tell you something."

"Sure." Jack very nearly said, *Shoot*. God. "Anything."

Ryan gnawed his lower lip. The firm pink flesh looked painfully dented. "I wasn't honest before."

"About what?"

"I'm not sure I can do this." He closed his eyes. "This is so—"

"I don't know if I can either," Jack admitted. "But that's not going to stop me."

"I'm scared." Ryan closed his eyes and tilted his face up toward the sun. "I can't believe my own bathroom scares me, even though I've seen death a thousand times."

What a nice face.

In the slanted midmorning light, Ryan only bore a vague resemblance to Nick. His coloring certainly was similar, but Ryan had a kinder face. Even though he looked young, he definitely had a *wiser* face. Life had etched compassion there, not self-ishness.

Ryan's was a face a guy could pin his hopes on.

"I don't know why"—Ryan's Adam's apple bobbed—"but when I go in there, I'm afraid."

"Me too. There's a purely human dread of death that catches you in the gut and twists you inside out. It takes time to learn how to work around that."

"But I see death every day. I don't get why this is so hard."

"It's in your home. Your sanctum sanctorum. Of course it's hard. But Nick left us with this...job, for lack of a better word. What we're doing matters. This is like the coda at the end of a piece of music, or an epilogue that ties off all the story lines of a book. This is something that must be done, and for whatever reason, *I* need to be the one to do it. You come too."

Ryan's lips curved into a faint smile. "That's a poem."

"What is?" Jack studied Ryan's handsome face while his eyes were still closed.

"Never mind." When Ryan's lashes lifted, he looked so tired.

"Ready to go back to work?"

"Yeah." Ryan stood and stretched. "Yeah. Let's go."

They spent the rest of the afternoon scrubbing the ceiling, the walls, and the tile. By far the most difficult and time-consuming job was disconnecting the claw-foot tub to work behind it. Once the walls and floor were spotless, they reattached the plumbing and turned the water supply back on to check for leaks.

The work was stuffy and smelly—made ten times more difficult by the tight confines of the enclosed space, the gear they had to wear, and the weight of the goddamn tub. As the day wore on, Jack's physical limitations enraged him. Pain that nagged became a throbbing, aching nightmare.

A job that should have taken no longer than three or four hours ended up taking nearly seven, but finally they pulled up the paper and removed the trash, leaving the austere bedroom and bath tidy and impersonal.

Like nothing ever happened.

It was after four when Jack taped the last box closed, and he *ached* all over. For the first time in several months, he was going to have to choose between having a drink or taking a heavy-duty painkiller.

Ryan carried boxes and gear to the van while Jack texted Gabe to say the job was finished.

As they closed the van's rear doors and stepped back, Ryan seemed uncertain. They hadn't spoken much after they'd gotten things finished inside. Jack figured they were both too exhausted —physically and emotionally—for small talk.

Ryan gestured toward his house. "You want something to drink? Coffee or—"

"I can't," said Jack. "I need to get this van back to the warehouse." He also needed a shower in the worst way. He needed to sleep, maybe for a week or two.

Deep shadows underlined Ryan's eyes. "Nick's memorial service is tomorrow at Fairhaven."

"I—" Jack shook his head. "I won't be there."

Ryan nodded. "I didn't expect you to be. I thought I should tell you."

"Thanks." Jack held out his hand. "For everything."

Ryan shook Jack's hand, then pulled him in for an awkward hug. "Thank you."

"I'm sorry for your loss." When he stepped back, Jack put his hands on Ryan's shoulders. "Despite what happened when we were kids, I'm sorry Nick ended up like this. I wish I could have helped before."

"Me too." Ryan glanced back at the house.

"You're going to be okay, Ryan." Jack gave Ryan's shoulders a gentle squeeze. "You're going to be fine. You did everything you could, got it?"

"I know." Ryan's voice betrayed his doubt. "I'm glad we did this."

"I'm glad we did this *together*." Jack smiled. "You made it bearable."

"You too." Ryan's expression told a different story. He was clearly hanging on by a thread.

"Call your friends, Ryan. Take my advice and go somewhere else for a few days. Take some time off from work. See a grief counselor. Promise me."

"Yeah. Maybe." Ryan winced when Jack compressed his shoulder muscles again. "I'll think about all those things. I promise."

"Good." Jack got into the van and started the engine. He pulled away, keeping half an eye on Ryan as his image got smaller in the passenger side mirror. He hated to leave Ryan alone like that, but at some point every job ended. Survivors had to deal with the aftermath.

There was nothing he could do about that.

When Jack pulled the van into the warehouse parking lot, Gabe and Dave were waiting for him. It looked like they'd been having a beer.

"Hey." Jack rolled down the driver's side window. "Did you guys start without me?"

"Hey, coz." Gabe opened the van's door. "We've been waiting on you. Are you okay?"

"Sure."

"I had you under surveillance," Dave joked. "Mom called me when it looked like you were done."

Dave tried to help him, but Jack pushed his hands away. He grabbed his cane and let himself drop to the ground.

"I'm fine," he said curtly.

Dave frowned at him. "All right."

"Paco will be here any minute to haul the trash," said Gabe. "Leave the keys with me. I'll restock the van in the morning."

"I can do it." Jack turned to face his business partner. "Stop treating me like I can't do shit."

Dave put his hand on Jack's arm. "He's just trying—"

"I said stop." Jack pulled out of Dave's reach. "I don't need anyone's help to do my job."

"Drop the attitude, coz." Gabe's hands clenched into fists. "Just knock it off. I haven't seen you move this slow since right after you got out of the hospital."

Jack lashed out, aiming a kick at the van's tire. *Real mature.*

He only succeeded in smashing his good foot. "I'm tired, goddamn it, but I can still do my job."

"Look at me, Jack." Dave caught Jack's arm in a tight grip. His authoritative voice turned coaxing. "You've had a long day. You did work you're not used to doing. Would you let Gabe and me help you just this once?"

Jack sagged against the van. The metal was cool and solid next to his skin, and it felt so damn good to get even a little weight off his legs and back. Off his bad knee, into which someone seemed to be jabbing iron spikes.

"All right. Thanks." Grabbing a hot shower and then lying down for a couple of days would be heaven. He'd accomplished what he set out to do. He didn't have to torture himself. "I'm a dick. I'm sorry."

"Sometimes you don't take care of yourself," Gabe observed.

The way Jack felt right then, he had to agree. "I do some idiot shit, yeah."

"It doesn't have to be like that." Gabe forced the van's keys from Jack's clenched fist. "Go home and take a pill. Don't come back until Monday."

Jack sighed. "Thanks."

"I'll walk you out." Dave put his arm around Jack's shoulders. Jack let himself lean on him. They walked in silence until they reached Jack's truck.

"Thanks for checking on me," said Jack.

Dave studied him through narrowed eyes. "Thank my mom."

"You had your mother spy on me. That's just low." Jack laughed at Dave's discomfort. "Everyone in the neighborhood was watching. The curtains and blinds twitched the whole day."

"I hate that."

"At least I know your mom wasn't armed."

"She's worried about Halloran. She likes him."

"What we did there... That was harder than I thought it

would be," Jack admitted. "The physical challenges ate me alive. I was an idiot to think I could do it. Especially alone."

"And yet you did." Dave's expression was indulgent.

Jack grinned and Dave returned a lazy smile that made Jack's groin tighten. "I guess I did, at that."

CHAPTER 9

TWO THINGS WOKE JACK: the bed rocked because Dave sat at the edge, tying his shoelaces, and Tasha's slim, silken tail tickled his nose.

He pushed the cat gently away from the head of the bed. "I told you, not the pillows."

"You talk to the cat?" Dave turned and gave Jack's ankle a pat. "I worry about you."

"She's the smartest one in here." Jack checked the clock. *Two in the morning.* "You really have to leave?"

"Morning comes early for me."

"Morning comes here too. If you stay, you can make me breakfast."

"As tempting as that sounds, you know I like to start the day at my place." Dave's collegiate good looks were never more apparent than when he was trying to evade any kind of serious conversation.

"I do know that." Jack pulled himself up so he could sit with his back to the headboard. "What I don't know is why. You aren't married. We're not cheating on anyone. People know we're friends, and I'm most definitely out. Why the oh-dark-thirty walk of shame?"

Dave kissed Jack's neck, nuzzling him with his bristly cheek. "You really want to have this conversation now? We had a good time. Don't spoil it."

"Breakfast will spoil our good time?" Jack wasn't sure he was ready to have the conversation either, but here it was anyway. Waiting for them like death and taxes. "Things aren't like they used to be. In the FD—"

"The FD may be part of the family, but you're not a cop. I can't be a gay cop."

"What does that even mean? You *are* a gay cop."

"There's being gay and it's nobody's business, and being gay like it's a badge of honor. Get it?" Dave pointed to his head. It was a *Think!* gesture as if Jack were an idiot and Dave needed to remind him to use his head already.

"No, I don't get it." Jack folded his arms. The move was reflexive. It was defensive. "You were pretty proud to be gay when you fucked me just now."

"One doesn't have anything to do with the other."

"I beg your pardon?" Jack asked irritably. Sometimes Dave's attitude bugged the shit out of him.

"Fucking guys is just what I do sometimes. That doesn't mean—"

"So what, then? Are you going to get married? Have kids? Stop by my place between work and coaching your kids' soccer teams?"

"As usual, you're blowing things all out of proportion." Dave pulled his tie off the dresser knob and flung one end around his neck. He had to look in the mirror to tie it. Jack loved watching a man tie his tie. It was almost a kink for him. Desire tugged at his groin as Dave's deft fingers twined the silken strips into a Windsor knot.

"This thing between us…"

Dave stopped abruptly. "Whatever you think this is between us, it's not that."

"I don't think it's anything. It's so *not* anything, I'm wondering what we're doing here."

"Trust you to take a logical argument and make it sound like gibberish," said Dave. "You make my head ache."

Jack swallowed. "I'm not arguing. I guess I'm asking what your plans are."

"It's two a.m. I *plan* to go home and get some shut-eye." Dave sat beside him. He lifted his hand and gave Jack's short hair a scratch.

Jack lowered his gaze. Some things weren't easy to say. "I'm thinking about making other plans, Dave."

Dave frowned down at him. Some agonizing question hung in the air. Silence dragged out between them until Dave kissed Jack's forehead with tenderness he rarely showed. "I'll call you."

Jack nodded. Dave turned off the bathroom light and left the room.

Deep breath. Jack blinked several times to adjust to the darkness.

Dave's attitude wasn't unexpected. It wasn't exactly what Jack was hoping for either. Dave was a great guy. Jack enjoyed his company. Theirs was a true case of friends with benefits, but a sleepover now and again would be nice. Breakfast together. That wasn't going to kill either of them. A little more time spent in public places—dinner or a movie or a ball game would be heaven.

It wasn't love. But it wasn't lonely.

Christ. Am I lonely?

Jack pictured Ryan's happy smile and the warm feeling he'd gotten from working side by side with him. If he was honest with himself, he missed that. Missed working alongside men he saw as family. Doing the books and scheduling the jobs wasn't the same as sitting down to communal meals at the firehouse.

When they'd begun Grime, he, Gabe, and Eddie had worked out of his house. Back then, they'd shared meals, and often the guys stayed overnight in his guest rooms. When the business's growth forced them to move to the off-site office and warehouse space, things had taken a different, more impersonal turn. They had employees to go out on calls now, Jack's partners no longer ate over, and more often than not Jack spent the day doing the book work in his home office, alone.

Mondays when they scheduled meetings, and paydays. That was when he saw the guys.

Maybe I am lonely.

Jack could be with Dave without losing his heart. Without expectations and betrayal. What he and Dave had was good, but maybe Jack needed companionship as well. That wasn't too much to ask for, was it?

It wasn't a question of wanting things to change. Jack simply needed to know where the boundaries were.

That way, he wouldn't accidentally *cross* one.

And maybe now, I know.

Jack told Tasha, "That conversation didn't have anything to do with Ryan."

Jack was pretty sure he meant it.

He was certain he was in no way wondering about the man whose life had intersected with his in such a spectacularly awful way.

He wasn't worried Ryan might be alone in his house either. Ryan was what, thirty-one? He had to be if he'd been a freshman in high school when Dave, Nick, and Jack were seniors.

"I'm sure he found someplace to go so he isn't alone in that house by himself again," Jack told the cat. "Or he'll invite Kevin over."

Everyone has to learn to live with their ghosts, right?

Tasha meowed at him conversationally.

Jack gusted out a great, deep sigh. "Maybe I should tell Dave that when he sneaks out of here, I have a hard time going back to sleep."

Tasha the cat wasn't troubled by Dave's comings or goings, but she was nocturnal, wasn't she?

Dave's headlights fanned over the window as he pulled away from the house.

Jack grabbed the remote off his nightstand. The flat screen chimed and lit up.

"I like the food channel. How about you?" He idly scrolled through the guide, reading the evening's offerings. "Or *Deadliest Catch*? That's about fish."

The cat settled herself close to Dave's pillow—or what Jack normally thought of as Dave's pillow—but not on it. *Good cat.*

"Hey, look at that. *Lions*," Jack said. "Your homeboys."

The cat watched him. Jack didn't think of Dave or, God forbid, *relationships*, or even the way Ryan's broad shoulders and pert ass looked in scrubs, at all.

Eventually, sleep claimed him for a second time.

The phone rang early again, which seemed unfair considering Jack hadn't fallen asleep until late. He thought about letting the call go to voice mail. It was still practically dark on Saturday morning, after all. The phone stopped ringing, but then it started right up again.

Jack remembered the way his conversation with Dave had ended the night before, and cursed. Maybe it was Dave, checking in. Maybe he was feeling their connection waver, wondering if Jack noticed how he'd dodged his questions and backed away.

He took his phone from the nightstand and spoke. "Masterson."

"It's Ryan."

"Hey. What are you doing up so early?"

Ryan let out a shuddering breath. "I never slept."

Jack sat up. "How come?"

"I should have taken your advice and gone somewhere."

"What about Kevin?"

"I didn't call Kevin last night. I don't want him to think he's got a chance with me right now, or ever, really. It was a mistake calling him. I should have thought that through before."

"Isn't there anyone else?"

"There are people who'd let me stay over, but I don't want to leave my home. I can't let what happened drive me away. I love this place."

"That's a mighty fine house," Jack agreed. "I can see why you wouldn't want to leave the comfort of a place like that to stay on someone's couch."

"It's not what you think."

Jack lay back down to listen. And he smiled. Maybe it was true you could hear a smile over the phone, and he wanted to be sure that Ryan heard his. Ryan sounded like he could use a smile.

"What is it, then?"

"I don't really care where I sleep, but this place... It's...it's just..."

When Ryan didn't continue after a while, Jack asked, "Your place is what?"

"It used to be my grandmother's house." A whistle sounded— a teakettle, maybe—in the background. Jack heard footsteps and clattering before Ryan spoke again. "She left it to me."

"I wondered how you could afford that house on a nurse's salary."

Ryan snorted. "I can't. But I inherited money. Mom's side of the family had the car dealership, but the men on my father's side were all medical professionals."

"Is that why you became a nurse?"

"God no." Ryan gave a light laugh. "Becoming a nurse was the final straw. My parents don't speak to me anymore."

"That's their loss." Jack tried not to sound shocked. "You know that, right?"

"Of course."

"But your grandmother was on your side?"

"When things started to go really bad between my parents and me, they had an awful fight with my grandmother, and she threatened to sue for custody. I think they'd just washed their hands of me by that time. To be fair, I was a troublemaker."

"How bad could you have been?"

"Bad enough my parents boarded me at St. Catherine's Military Academy from the sixth grade to the eighth. They were looking to send me farther away for high school. I think my grandmother may have saved my life."

"So her place is where you feel safest."

"I did. I *do*." Ryan corrected himself. "No one is taking my home away from me."

Jack hurt for Ryan. For the owner of a house, a crime scene could be like a diseased limb. People like Jack—firefighters, cops, first responders—learned to live with the pain. They turned all feeling off—the pain and the pleasure. Maybe Ryan hadn't perfected that yet. Maybe he hadn't lost the ability to feel.

Jack hoped he never did. If Ryan lost his empathy, an important part of who he was would be lost with it.

"Nothing can take your peace unless you let it. Did you look into grief counseling like I said?"

Ryan was silent for too long.

"Ryan?"

"I'm here. God, what happened? I had everything under control, and then it all went wrong."

Jack tightened his grip on the phone. "I don't understand. What do you mean?"

"I told you. I'm familiar with lost causes. I knew what Nick was capable of. I knew how hard things were for him. I told myself there was nothing anyone could do if he couldn't get past his failures."

Jack swung his feet over to the floor and stood. The first fingers of light had begun creeping through the miniblinds. He opened them and watched his sprinklers water the lawn, such as it was. Did it still count as lawn if you just mowed the heads off a patch of weeds?

God, Ryan. "Are you saying you feel like what Nick did was somehow your fault?"

"No. *Yes.* I'm saying I thought I understood how I'd feel if—"

"Listen to me, Ryan. Someone who is really determined to kill himself will get the job done. You're not going to get any warning, and they won't take any chances things will go wrong."

"I know." Tapping. Ryan's fingers on a table? Nerves? Anxiety?

"I don't think you should be alone right now. Why don't you try calling Kevin?"

"Kevin." Ryan sighed. "Talk about hair of the dog that bit me. My dance card is all filled up with sick people who can't help me and addicts who don't know how. What about you?"

Jack hesitated. "What about me?"

"Did you sleep?"

"Some." Paws thumped onto the rug at the end of Jack's bed. After a few slinky steps and a stretch, Tasha executed a couple figure eights around his ankles. He guessed that must mean *Fetch my food*, in cat. "I had a secret weapon."

"Pain meds?"

Jack huffed out a laugh. "A cat."

"Seriously?"

"I'm cat-sitting, and she purrs. Keeps my feet warm. The pet experience is growing on me."

"Pets do lower blood pressure."

"I guess." Jack followed Tasha to the kitchen where he put his phone down on the counter. "I'm putting you on speaker because I need to open a can."

"Canned cat food? Is this cat spoiled?"

"I didn't buy the food. It came with the cat." Along with litter box scooping, which he did after filling Tasha's food and water bowls.

He came back into the kitchen just as Ryan said, "Hello, are you still there?"

"Still here. I was on kitty litter patrol."

Several beats of silence went by before Ryan spoke again. "The memorial service is today."

"I know. You said."

"Are you sure you don't want to go? You probably knew Nick better than I did. We were never close, even as kids. It seems so wrong for me to go while you're—"

"I said my good-byes years ago." Jack's heart tightened painfully.

"No, you didn't." Ryan pressed the issue. "If that was true, you wouldn't have come yesterday."

"That was my job." Even as Jack said it he knew it was a lie.

"That was your love," said Ryan, low-voiced and earnest. "Come with me. I don't want to go alone. My parents will be there and—"

"If I do, will you contact a grief counselor?"

"I told you, I'm not grieving. Nick and I weren't even close. He was just the most recent in a long string of lost causes I got myself involved with."

God, if Ryan didn't even know he had a problem... "Look. Why don't you come to my place, and I'll cook up some breakfast. We can talk, okay?"

A pause. "I don't know if I can handle that right now."

"All right. But can I ask why?"

"You apologized in advance for being another lost cause."

I'm not that lost, am I? I'm not.

I know that, because I could lay Nick to rest with some of the love I once felt for him, despite what he did to me.

Jack's smile was shaky, but he forced himself to smile so Ryan could hear it. "I don't think I knew the entire truth right then."

CHAPTER 10

JACK ANSWERED the door and found Ryan standing on his stoop, suit bag in hand. Ryan smiled warmly, although he looked like he hadn't slept in days. Attractive and well-groomed but subdued, he waited until Jack invited him in.

"Welcome. Come on in. Kitchen's this way."

"I brought my funeral clothes." Ryan followed Jack. "I didn't know if I'd go to the memorial from here, or—"

"You can change here." Jack pointed him in the direction of the guest bath. "Hang your stuff on the back of the bathroom door, right through there."

"All right."

Jack poured himself a cup of coffee and waited for Ryan to return. Tasha stayed close to his feet, suspicious of the newcomer. "What do you like to eat?"

"Anything's fine." Ryan came back to the kitchen and looked around. "Is that your borrowed cat?"

"Yeah." Tasha played it cool, peering out from between Jack's leg and his cane. "Her name is Tasha."

"She's a Russian Blue, so she should be *Na*tasha." Ryan knelt to coax her out. "Natasha Badinov, the spy with nine lives."

Jack tried to watch Ryan interact with the cat without imagining Ryan on his knees for a very different reason. Christ, was he a horndog or what?

He cleared his throat. "Are you in the mood for protein or carbs? I've got eggs and bacon, or I can make pancakes."

"I have to choose?" Ryan teased gently.

Jack took a step back and bumped the counter. "Not really. I can make both."

"I'm kidding. You don't have to go to any trouble for me." Ryan rose fluidly with Tasha in his arms. "I smell coffee."

"I'll get you a mug." Jack pulled one of the larger mugs from the cupboard. "Make yourself at home."

Ryan didn't appear to need telling where things were. With Tasha content in the crook of his arm, he found the sugar on the counter and helped himself to half-and-half from the fridge. Jack moved around him to get out eggs and bacon along with butter, milk, and pancake mix.

Jack worked while Ryan played with the cat.

As they had when working at Ryan's house, they said little unless there was a question that needed to be answered.

"Waffles or pancakes?"

Ryan glanced up. "I love waffles."

Jack smiled like an idiot. "Waffles it is."

"I can help, if you need me to."

Jack relaxed against the sink where he'd been rinsing off a pan. "Unless you really love to cook, I've got it. Breakfast is easy."

"I don't like to cook at all." Ryan set Tasha down on the floor. "What does that say about me?"

"It says you should date firefighters." As soon as the words were out, Jack tried to backtrack. "I mean, you know. Guys who can cook."

"As opposed to guys who are too high on coke to eat?"

"I didn't mean it like that."

"When I met Kevin, he'd been sober for two years. I thought —we both believed—he'd never use again."

"Sometimes people backslide." Jack held a glass of orange juice out for Ryan, and their fingers brushed when he accepted it. A small thrill, electric and intense, passed through Jack at Ryan's touch. "Nature of the beast."

"I need to stop trying." Ryan sighed. "It's fucking exhausting."

"Maybe you only need to stop trying the same thing." Before Jack returned to the stove to finish up the bacon, he plugged in the waffle iron. He glanced back at Ryan. "But I'm hardly one to give advice."

"How come?"

"I don't really do relationships."

"That's a little bleak."

"It's just been my experience I do better on my own." He closed a scoop of batter in the hot waffle iron and then removed the bacon to the oven to keep warm. "Other people probably do okay."

Between finishing the eggs and baking several more waffles, ten minutes elapsed without another word. Jack searched his little-used emotion-deciphering faculties and discovered the wholesome routine felt pleasant.

He was cooking a man breakfast, and it was *pleasant*.

While Jack worked, he sneaked occasional glimpses of Ryan. He liked Ryan's hesitant smile and the way he watched when he thought Jack wasn't looking. He liked the way Ryan played with the cat.

When Jack turned, he could feel the weight of Ryan's gaze on him like balmy air. When he shot a quick look Ryan's way, he saw warmth suffuse Ryan's lightly freckled cheeks.

Ryan's resemblance to Nick brought a new awareness with it, both pleasurable and painful. Nick had been Jack's ideal of physical perfection. Ryan—by a coincidence of genetics—shared his good looks. Nothing was dearer, nothing more physically attractive, nothing could flip Jack's switch the way Nick, and now Ryan did.

How wrong was that? To compare the two men or, God forbid, let desire for one manifest with the other.

But oh, my. Ryan smelled so good. *Uniquely* good, like soap, cut grass, and limes good.

The scent was entirely Ryan's own. He smelled of clean and spring and new things, while Jack spent most of his time with men who smelled of smoke and whiskey and sometimes fairly pungent sweat. Ryan's scent made Jack want to press his nose into Ryan's neck and take in a deep, deep draft of air. To hold it inside him until he was dizzy with it. Until he felt new again too.

Ryan helped Jack put plates on the table. As they moved around the small kitchen, Ryan brushed Jack's shoulder casually with his. Jack's whole body tightened. He looked behind him and found Ryan watching. Ryan's gaze swept down his body and back up to his face like a physical touch. Jack's body heated in response.

Ryan's pupils bloomed, eclipsing his pale irises.

"Here." Jack handed Ryan a plate of waffles. Ryan's fingers brushed his. Lingered.

Desire crackled between them. Jack's chest tightened, and his cock twitched. He turned away, murmuring something about pot holders and bacon.

Ryan followed him and stood a little too close. Jack had trouble breathing. He squeezed the handle of his cane with one hand and the oven door handle with the other.

"I'll just wash my hands first." Ryan's breath warmed Jack's ear.

Ryan crossed the room to the sink. He had long, powerful legs and broad shoulders. A long neck. There was a certain grace and economy to his movements that drew Jack's eye and stole his breath. He took his time washing up, using hand soap and making a thick, foamy lather. Bubbles floated into the air.

Jack got the bacon out of the oven. When he walked it to the table, he couldn't help but notice the way Ryan's jeans stretched over the muscles of his fine, firm ass.

Jack went to the counter to pick up some napkins and stood there, his back to the kitchen, catching his breath.

"Jack?" The word stirred the hair on the back of Jack's neck.

All Jack's blood rushed south, and his knees threatened to buckle. "Yeah?"

"Can I kiss you?" Ryan's lips brushed Jack's skin so lightly Jack wasn't sure he felt them at all.

Ryan was standing so close. So goddamn close.

Instead of saying the first thing that came into his head—*I don't know, can you?*—instead of overthinking things like always, Jack simply turned and met Ryan's lips with his.

Ryan cupped Jack's face to deepen the kiss, and Jack cooperated, shamelessly opening for Ryan's tongue, allowing him inside, letting him explore teeth and gums and soft palate around Jack's low, helpless groan.

Jack tasted orange juice between them, familiar and sweet. Beneath Jack's hands, Ryan's body felt like all good things, like excitement and novelty and strong man and coming home.

Jack tilted his head to make room for noses and air.

Ryan's kisses transmitted urgency. Jack met him with shivering desperation. Sublime, heady need ignited a fuse in Jack's body. He moaned into Ryan's mouth, begging for more.

Ryan shifted his weight to push Jack against the counter. Of a similar height, they fit together perfectly. Jack parted his feet for balance, and Ryan stepped between them. Jack felt Ryan's cock against his, hard and hot and ready.

Jack's surprise and his harsh, panting breaths mingled with Ryan's.

For a time, Jack reveled in the rasp of Ryan's freshly shaved cheek against his. Then Ryan found the column of Jack's throat with hungry lips. Ryan pressed so close the quickening beat of his heart thudded against Jack's chest.

Or was that his heart, racing in response?

Ryan slid his hips into Jack's, not quite grinding—not yet— but pushing against Jack's answering length. Hovering on some precipice, teetering between desire and restraint.

Will we? Won't we...

Ryan's cock pulsed against Jack's as he claimed another kiss. All the breath left Jack's lips in the form of another groan.

Ryan paused. "Sure you want to eat right now?"

Jack swallowed hard. "I—"

The half-moon of Ryan's pale lashes lowered over his flushed cheeks. His breath ghosted against Jack's throat as he kissed a path toward his collar. "We could take this someplace more comfortable."

Oh, my God.

"*Wait.* I-I didn't expect anything like this." Jack took hold of Ryan's shoulders and pushed him gently away. "I had someone over last night. My bed's still unmade, and it's probably... You understand? I can't just go from—"

"I see." Ryan stepped back, still flushed, still panting and hard.

"God, I'm sorry." Watching Ryan's slick tongue move over his freshly kissed mouth made Jack's groin tighten further still. "You have no idea how sorry."

"You're with someone?"

"I—" *Am I?*

This was why he wanted to know what his boundaries were. He didn't want to hurt Dave, but it was pretty clear Dave wasn't interested in anything but fucking him behind closed doors.

It was also pretty clear Ryan was carrying a direct ticket to Jack's happy place, and their attraction was mutual. Did Jack *have* to have scruples when Dave and he were just friends with benefits?

Had he ever?

Not until Dave had a *mom* who'd said, *"It was a pleasure meeting you."*

Aw, fuck.

"It's complicated," Jack said finally.

"Not to me." Ryan adjusted himself, ruefully acknowledging the elephant in the room. "If you're with someone, this would be what people call cheating."

"I don't do that." Jack turned away. "I guess what you have with Kevin isn't—"

"I don't have anything with Kevin. I don't *do that* either."

"Could we just eat?" Jack asked. "Would that be okay for right now?"

Ryan didn't look at Jack like he'd nearly dry humped him and then shut him down before the big finish. That had to count for something, right? He appeared disappointed but not angry.

"Sure." Ryan picked up his plate and headed for the table. "No hard feelings, okay? Nice kiss. No sale. It's all good."

"Thank you." Jack was having some hard feelings, all right. An uncomfortably hard ache of the most primitive kind. He was carrying his plate to the table when the doorbell rang.

"Expecting someone?" asked Ryan.

"I don't think so. It's probably someone selling something." Jack put his plate down and started toward the door. He didn't get three steps before Gabe burst past him into the kitchen.

Why did I give him a key?

"Hey, coz. Smells good. You making breakfast?"

"Yeah." Jack waited for Gabe to notice Ryan. Since he helped himself to coffee without looking around, Jack added, "I have a guest."

"Well, why didn't you—" Gabe turned and saw Ryan sitting at the table. "Shit. You must be Nick's cousin. That's an amazing resemblance you got there."

The color faded from Ryan's face, but he stood up and held out his hand. "I'm Ryan Halloran."

"Gabriel Masterson, Jack's cousin." Gabe shook his hand. "I'm sorry. I should keep my mouth shut sometimes."

"Most of the time," Jack murmured.

"Am I interrupting something?" asked Gabe.

"We were just sitting down to breakfast." Jack motioned toward the table. "You're welcome to join us. There's plenty."

Ryan returned to his seat, a troubled expression on his handsome face. "Do I really look so much like Nick?"

Gabe and Jack exchanged a glance. Jack shrugged. "At first, yes. I don't see it as much now that I know you. Your mannerisms are different."

Gabe nodded. "I only really knew Nick as a kid. You're what I imagined he'd look like as a man. I'm surprised to see you here. I expected—"

"Waffle?" Jack asked. Gabe's mouth snapped shut. No doubt he'd been expecting to find Dave at Jack's table. Maybe he didn't know Dave didn't *breakfast*. Or if he did, he didn't do it with the men he fucked.

"How're you feeling, Ryan?" Gabe asked, and thank *God* he did.

Now Jack wouldn't have to make awkward small talk. They didn't call Gabe the client whisperer for nothing. He and Ryan could talk about their feelings while Jack picked up a forkful of eggs and savored them. The bacon was crisp, exactly the way he liked it, and the waffle was superb for something he'd thrown together from a mix. One of the guys at the firehouse used to make waffles with bits of bacon or chunks of pecans in them. Those were pretty delicious too.

"What do you think, Jack?" Gabe asked.

Jack's brain came back from food thoughts with a thud. "I'm sorry?"

"I came to ask you if you wanted to shop for cars with me."

"You're getting rid of your truck?"

"I'm thinking about it." Gabe eyed Ryan again. "I'm sick of trucks. I've been wanting something sleek and powerful, like me. I'm thinking of getting one of those new Camaros that look like old Camaros."

Ryan shot a questioning glance Jack's way.

Jack said, "I'm going to Nick's memorial with Ryan."

"*Jack.*" Gabe's fork clattered onto his plate. "That has to be the worst idea I ever heard."

"I'd be going for Ryan, not Nick. Memorials are for the living."

"Correct me if I'm wrong." Gabe turned to Ryan. "But won't Nick's parents and the rest of his family and friends be there?"

Ryan nodded. "Yeah. I guess."

"So won't Jack's presence at Nick's memorial remind them of things they'd prefer to forget while they bury their son?"

Ryan pushed his chair away from the table and rose. "I don't think—"

Gabe continued, "I mean, he offed hims—"

"Gabe." Jack stood abruptly.

Gabe got up and stepped toward Ryan. "Nick wasn't one of my favorite people."

Ryan spread his hands out—a placating gesture. "Look. I know what he did."

"You don't know the half of it," Gabe taunted. "If you had any idea—"

"Gabe, for God's sake." Jack grabbed Gabe's shoulder to hold him back. "It's not your story to tell."

Gabe jerked out of Jack's hold. "Then tell it, Jack. Tell your new friend here how—"

"I said shut up, Gabe." Jack pinned Gabe against the kitchen wall. One of the pictures—an old five-by-seven of Jack and his mother—fell to the floor. Fortunately, the glass didn't break, but Tasha fled in terror. "Shut the fuck up, or you and me? We're *over*."

"You mean that, coz?" Gabe and Jack glared at each other, breath coming fast.

"Right now I do."

"*Dick.*" Gabe pushed Jack off him, and Jack let him pass. Gabe didn't turn until he got to the kitchen door. "You're protecting the wrong guy, you idiot. You always did."

"Goddamn it, get out. I'll talk to you when you cool down."

Gabe shot them both a last angry scowl and took off, leaving Jack stunned and alone with Ryan. Before Jack said anything about what happened, he picked up the photograph. He couldn't look at Ryan until he hung it back up where it belonged. He was about to turn when he felt Ryan's hands on his shoulders. Instead of gripping him hard like Jack expected, instead of forcing him to turn and spill his whole story, Ryan wound his arms around Jack's chest. He pressed his lips against the side of Jack's neck. Jack felt jerky huffs of breath as well—and the hot moisture of tears.

"I'm sorry, Jack." Ryan pulled him close. "If you need someone to be sorry for what Nick did to you all those years ago, accept that. Accept *my* apology. I'm so sorry he hurt you. Please. Forgive us."

CHAPTER 11

JACK TURNED with every intention of keeping his hands to himself. He truly did. But Ryan's face was streaked with tears, his lips and eyelids swollen, and his lashes lay spiky and damp against deep shadows etched by total exhaustion.

He is completely irresistible.

At least, that was what Jack told himself when he gave in and pressed a fresh kiss to Ryan's salty lips. That was what he told himself when Ryan pushed him back and stepped between his legs. When he felt the heat that flared instantly between them.

Ryan wrapped his hand around the back of Jack's neck and took his surprise-parted lips in a kiss so dirty and determined, Jack gripped Ryan's shirt with both hands to keep from falling when his knees buckled. Their earlier kiss—the one that made him almost speechless with desire—seemed tepid compared to the roiling, boiling need that bubbled up inside him now.

"Yes," Jack whispered. "God, yes."

Ryan hauled Jack's hips against his, and Jack winced. "Careful. I'm fragile."

"Sorry." Ryan loosened his grip.

"Rough is good," Jack grated out. "Just be careful what you're rough with."

"I'll take care of you." Ryan pulled Jack forward again, this time with more care, and their hard lengths met and brushed lightly, straining under their clothes.

Ryan's smile was slow to bloom but warmer for the wait. He tasted like bacon and maple syrup, salty and sweet, and he kissed like he had all the time in the world. He clasped Jack's hand and, taking some of Jack's weight on his firm forearm, drew him to the couch in the living room.

"This okay?"

"Yeah." Jack breathed a sigh as he allowed Ryan to push him down onto the ancient vinyl sofa in his parents' living room. If Ryan was comfortable taking the lead, Jack planned to enjoy every minute of it. His usual frantic couplings held very little in the way of tenderness. This promised to be different, and Jack wanted what Ryan offered him. Every languid, unhurried kiss.

Jack's vinyl couch blew out a flatulent gust of air when Ryan knelt between his legs. Jack cringed with shame. Maybe it was time to get better furniture. "Sorry."

"That was hilarious." Ryan grinned and took Jack's mind off things by nuzzling him, lips and tongue searching out all the places Jack hadn't been kissed in so goddamn long—the hollow of his throat, the juncture of his neck and shoulder, the ticklish shell of his ear, his temples, his eyes. Jack pulled Ryan's attention back to his mouth for another taste and then another.

Brief kisses were interspersed with quick catches of Jack's breath, until Jack wasn't sure he was breathing, wasn't sure he *could* breathe unless Ryan gave him breath—like life, like CPR, like he planned to resuscitate all the sensual longing Jack had forgotten he possessed.

Ryan smoothed his palms over Jack's chest and then undid the buttons of his shirt one by one, kissing each new inch of Jack's skin as he uncovered it. He lapped at the sensitive nub of Jack's nipple, curving the flat of his tongue over and around it, and then he blew on it to make it pucker.

"Ryan." Jack arched beneath him with a soft moan. He lifted himself to help when Ryan made an impatient noise and gripped the hem of Jack's shirt to pull it off over his head. With a light laugh, Ryan trapped him for a minute inside the warm cocoon of fabric while he blew a raspberry on his stomach.

Oh, my God.

Jack remembered how playful sex could be with the right partner.

Midmorning sun gilded Ryan's blond hair as he explored every scar, every freckle, every crisp, furry bit of Jack's bare chest with his fingers and lips. Jack carded his fingers through its silken softness. Ryan's hair was slightly springy, somewhat wavy, and as they ground against each other, it plastered the damp skin of his forehead.

Jack chased Ryan's lips for kisses even as he pushed his hands between their bodies to unbuckle Ryan's belt. Ryan slipped off him to make things easier. He pulled his T-shirt over his head and undid his belt and zipper, impatiently shoving both jeans and shorts to his thighs. He urged Jack to lift so he could rid him of his clothes. When they managed to free their cocks, Ryan lowered himself onto Jack's body with a satisfied sigh.

God, the fit was just right—a sweat-slicked glide of skin on skin with just enough hair to make things interesting. Jack put his mouth on anything he could reach. Ryan's meaty shoulder was his favorite target, strong and well muscled; it smelled like soap and fresh cotton but tasted of sweat and salt. Ryan's whole body tightened when Jack gave the freckled flesh a gentle bite. He arched his back, his cock digging into Jack's with more friction. More force.

"Oh, yeah." Jack stretched up to kiss him again. *"Yeah."* And again.

Ryan's palm warmed the back of Jack's neck, and his grip felt like iron. Jack's cock poked into the crease between Ryan's leg and thigh, into his stomach. It nudged happily alongside Ryan's rigid shaft, leaving damp trails on his skin even as it made the going easier for both of them.

Jack wrapped his arms around Ryan's neck and let him control the pace. His body hummed with every rise and fall of Ryan's hips. His cheek warmed when Ryan's moist breath caressed him.

Ryan's kisses bathed him like sunshine, like the light that wavered in from the miniblinds. Jack couldn't remember the last time he'd felt such contentment.

Every spontaneous, delicious. movement of their bodies was intimate and arousing. Deeply personal.

Each wave of sensation reminded Jack of things he believed he'd lost forever. In Ryan, he caught brief illusory glimpses of those long-ago days with Nick, even if he wasn't sure he wanted the memories back.

Ryan hovered above him, his expression transformed by ecstasy or oblivion, by horniness or happiness or simple completion. He was fierce and yet so tender Jack wanted to memorize every feature, every freckle, every line, every bone and hollow. Ryan closed his eyes and stilled, his body so rigid Jack held his breath.

Jack strained upward to press his lips to Ryan's. Jack wanted —maybe he even needed—the simple emotional connection before he could let his body go wild. Ryan kissed him back without restraint, without any artifice. The pressure and pleasure of Ryan's lips on his touched off the electric tingle of imminent climax in the base of Jack's spine.

Jack canted his hips in the frantic clamor for satisfaction, then spasmed all over as his orgasm swept him away. Ryan's low cry of triumph got trapped inside their frantic kisses. A spatter of hot release warmed Jack's belly.

Ryan held him through a rush of exquisite sensation, exchanging laughter and kisses for Jack's helpless grunts of pleasure. They landed back on the couch together, sweaty and sated, a loose-limbed, sticky mess.

Jack felt Ryan smile against his skin as he unfurled on top of him, a sinewy, long stretch of man and muscle.

"Oh, my God." Ryan picked up his T-shirt and gave a couple cursory swipes between their bodies. He tossed it to the floor next to the couch and relaxed.

A second before Jack could warn Ryan, Tasha sprang from the back of the couch. She landed on Ryan's back and made herself at home in the curve of his spine.

Ryan jumped and writhed pleasurably on Jack's body, wringing more spunk and new waves of delight from him when he'd thought he had nothing left to give.

Ryan gave a shout. "Oh, *Christ*, that scared me."

Good kitty.

Light laughter burst from both of them like a dam broke, and Jack found himself holding someone entirely unexpected. Someone irrepressible and happy and inexplicably radiant. Ryan ducked his head under Jack's chin and sighed.

Jack stroked Tasha while he waited for his heart rate to even out. Ryan bumped Jack's chin when he lifted his head again. "Wait."

"Ow."

"Sorry." A slow blink of light lashes. "I need a quick nap. Can you set an alarm?"

"I've got my phone, somewhere." Jack stretched his arm to capture the jeans he'd shucked off at some point. It would have been easier to move Ryan off him, but he didn't want to break the seal of their sweat-soaked skin or disturb the cat.

A few Cirque-worthy feats of contortion later, and he was able to set his phone alarm.

"Eleven thirty's good, right? A quick shower and clothes. We could be at the cemetery by one?"

Ryan nodded against his neck. "You're coming with me?"

"I said I would."

"I thought you said it to get out of car shopping."

"I did. But I'm a man of my word."

Ryan nodded again. "God, you're right. Tasha's warm, and she purrs. Secret weapon." Ryan nipped at Jack and closed his eyes.

After a while Jack heard Ryan's breathing even out—soft intakes of air with no discernible snoring or high-pitched nose whistling.

As he fell asleep, Ryan reached out. His fingers traced the features of Jack's face with deft curiosity. When Jack caught his hand and kissed each finger, Ryan reacted with a sleepy smile.

Jack tightened his hold.

While Ryan slept, Jack eyed his living room critically. Eighties peach-colored paint and wallpaper border. Rickety glass tchotchke shelves. Dust fluttered, confetti-like along each beam of light slanting from the blinds. It floated down to blanket the furniture and floor.

His house was shabby, filled with things either left over from his parents or handed down from friends. It looked the same as it had since he'd been born, only older. He'd played no active part in choosing anything he owned, even the relatively new big screen, which he'd won in a charity raffle.

How come he'd never noticed he'd been living by accident, accepting anything that came his way, letting anything he might want slide because he was too lazy or indifferent to go out and get it?

Ryan shifted his weight, forcing a groan from Jack and some fancy footwork from Tasha.

Jack lay on the same old wilted couch with Ryan, who was undeniably *new*. Undeniably delectable.

Fearless, and possibly free to enjoy a lover in the light of day.

The thought forced Jack to come to an uncomfortable conclusion. *Change is inevitable.*

Whether the seeds of change had been planted during the years-long recovery from his accident, or whether they'd been sown inside the tiny bathroom at Ryan's house, Jack was changing, and it was bound to hurt some—at least at first.

Ryan had come his way like everything else; he'd stumbled into Jack's house from some wreckage of his own, and for now that was okay.

But Jack might have to make some changes if he wanted to keep someone like Ryan in his life. He'd have to do more than accept; he'd have to *invest*.

Frowning, Jack closed his eyes and let the ache of evolution pull him into sleep.

Chimes?

Jack reached out from under Ryan and Tasha to turn off his phone's alarm. Tasha scattered when Ryan rose from the couch. He got up like a man who was used to rising at the last second every morning. He stood over Jack like a redwood tree, unselfconsciously stretching the muscles of his perfect upper body while Jack watched with deep satisfaction, cock stirring at the attractive sight.

"I'd give anything in the world to avoid going this afternoon." Ryan sighed.

Jack was less assured as he lifted his knees. Less assured and stiff as hell. Ryan sat back down at the end of the couch and picked up Jack's foot to massage it.

"That's *great*." Jack groaned with delight.

"I wish I could stay here and massage your feet all day."

"Ah, God. Me too." When Ryan pressed his thumb into the ball of Jack's foot, the pain was instantaneous and at the same time arousing. *Wow*. That had possibilities. "Do we have to go?"

"I'm afraid I do. Yeah. You promised you'd come with me."

Jack pulled his foot away and sat up, grimacing as his spine crackled into place. "Then let's go. It's like ripping off a bandage. Let's just get it done."

"Easy for you to say. Your family won't be there. I'll have to face mine."

"It'll be all right," Jack said, even though he worried it might not be. "Your family's probably classier than mine is. Our get-togethers are like *The Best of Jerry Springer*."

Ryan blew out a deep breath. "Mine's *All My Children*, and today's episode will be the one where the openly gay cousin that got disowned but still inherited all the family's old money comes to his drug-addict cousin's suicide funeral with the boy the dead cousin nearly got arrested for assaulting as his plus one."

Huh?

"I don't have to go if it will make things worse for you." *In fact, I'd kill to stay home.*

"I've got this image in my head where we go and you hold my hand." Ryan smiled sadly. "But I'll let you off the hook if you don't feel like you can do it. I'd understand if you can't."

"I said I'd go." Jack didn't want to see any sadness on Ryan's face because of something he promised and then reneged on.

"No. I mean it. Breakfast was great. So was"—he gestured between them and the couch—"this, you know? But I said no strings, and I meant it."

"Would I blow the chance to wear a suit and carry my

dashing fancy cane? Not a chance." Jack stood and offered Ryan his hand as a preview. "Take my hand now. We'll practice while we shower together."

Relief etched itself on Ryan's face. "You're one of the good guys, you know that?"

A wave of panic caught Jack by surprise. When had he ever been a good guy? Reflexively, he squeezed Ryan's hand. "I'm really not."

Ryan lifted their joined hands and pressed a kiss to the back of Jack's. "Then keep on pretending. That's all I need right now."

CHAPTER 12

JACK'S first thought was Ryan wore a suit really, really well. The black, slim-cut designer deal he'd brought with him seemed engineered for his broad shoulders, trim waist, and long legs. By comparison, Jack's "funeral suit" fit him tolerably but did nothing for him. Where Ryan wore a silky black hand-tailored shirt with French cuffs, Jack wore a new white shirt from a discount store that still had the creases in it from the manufacturer. Ryan's subtly patterned black tie was silk, where Jack's navy and red came from a thrift shop.

Despite the differences between them, Ryan's eyes gleamed with genuine appreciation when he looked at Jack. They held a warmth Jack could feel inside his gut and deep within his bones.

Before they left the house, Jack filled Tasha's bowls with food and water. He switched out his everyday cane for the fancy one Gabe had given him for Christmas. He didn't fill the flask concealed inside because it only held a swallow of alcohol, and Jack was pretty sure he'd need more than that. Instead, he got his dad's old silver flask down from the kitchen cupboard and filled it with bourbon, slipping it into his coat pocket as insurance against imminent emotional disaster.

Ryan rested his hand at the small of Jack's back while Jack locked the door behind them. Ryan put his shades on like a movie star and then escorted Jack down the walk as if they were heading for prom. He was careful and solicitous enough to make Jack grind his teeth.

"You don't have to hover. I won't fall or anything."

"I like touching you." Ryan frowned at him. "I'll stop if you don't like it."

"It's not that I don't like it." Jack examined how he felt about having Ryan's hand on him. It was nice. It was supportive. It bolstered his sense of well-being as they headed for an event he was dreading. He couldn't come up with a single reason to stop him—in fact he had a hundred reasons why he wanted it to continue. "Actually, I'm just not used to it."

"Why aren't you?"

Jack didn't have an answer for that.

Instead of heading for Jack's truck, Ryan led him to a sleek black hybrid. He opened the passenger door and then walked around to the driver's side to get in.

The car smelled new, and Ryan obviously kept it immaculate. As they pulled away from the curb, Ryan's garnet cuff link winked like a red eye, peering from beneath his neatly tailored coat sleeve. Jack tried brushing Tasha's cat hairs off the sleeve of his coat. When that proved impossible, he gripped the head of his cane nervously with both hands.

"What's the matter?"

"Nothing."

"Not nothing." Ryan glanced over at him. "You're fussing."

"I can fuss if I want to." He got out his flask and took a sip. It burned going down but warmed the tightness from his chest almost immediately.

"Whoa, open container. Put that away."

"I'm sorry." Jack slipped the flask back into his pocket.

"Are you really that nervous?"

Jack stopped rubbing his face to snap, "What do you think?"

"What, specifically, makes you anxious?"

"My parents stopped speaking to Nick's folks after high school. I went out of town for EMT training and the fire academy." Jack tugged on his shirtsleeves so a half inch showed at his wrists like it did on Ryan's. "I came back when I got the gig with Fullerton Fire, but I never went to church or anything. By then, there was no reason we'd bump into each other unless their house caught fire. This will be the first time I've seen them since—"

"They got old fast, trying to keep Nick on the straight and narrow."

"I can imagine."

"Everyone was so excited when he married Amy. Their first baby came along six months later, and it was like everyone heaved a huge sigh of relief."

"Did that settle him down?"

"For a while."

Jack looked out the window as Ryan pulled onto the freeway. The memorial was to take place in the cemetery chapel. No church service for Nick. Jack tried to imagine how hard this must be for Nick's staunch Catholic family. The older Foasbergs were true believers. They'd be gutted their son had died by his own hand.

He tried to imagine the boy he knew with a gun in his hand and such desperation in his heart. He tried to imagine Nick hopeless. Empty. Seeking painlessness through the void of death over the life he could have had with his family.

"I never asked." Jack's lungs contracted with new fear. "Did Nick leave a note or..."

"Not that anyone found."

"So no one knows exactly what led to him—"

"Not exactly. No."

God. Nick. What were you thinking? How could you believe you had nothing left to live for? Even in my darkest hours, even when I lost my job and nearly my life, I never felt that bad.

The parking lot was half-full when Ryan pulled in—even thought they were late, thanks to traffic. Jack wondered if there would be a lot of mourners. Addicts usually burned through their family and friends before they died. If Nick had stolen from Ryan, he'd probably done it before, with others.

He'd probably isolated himself from his wife, his kids, but of course they'd be there along with his parents.

Ryan and Jack entered the chapel and took a seat at the back. Nick's family—his parents and his wife and children—were in the front row, far enough away that if even a ripple of indignation sparked among the people directly around Ryan and Jack, they probably wouldn't notice.

Some people turned away, taut-shouldered, because as he'd promised, Jack held Ryan's hand. He continued holding it as the memorial meandered along on its course, even though the woman in front of them glared and hissed something to her husband Jack couldn't quite make out.

Ryan stiffened and let go. He leaned over to whisper, "I'm cool. Don't worry."

Jack offered his hand again and whispered back. "I've been thrown out of nicer places than this one."

Ryan stifled a laugh, but he gripped Jack's hand tight.

Noticeably absent from Nick's service were those mourners who would normally speak on the deceased's behalf. No one spoke for Nick except a nondenominational minister, and when he was done, Nick's immediate family got up dry-eyed and exited the chapel. Everyone except Nick's kids seemed relieved.

Am I relieved? Jack closed his eyes. *Is there a name for what I'm feeling right now?*

Everyone filed out after the family, and by then holding Ryan's hand was second nature. Ryan took Jack to greet his parents. The light frost of their general demeanor turned into a blizzard of icy disdain as soon as they caught sight of their son. It was over in a few brief seconds, with barely twenty words exchanged. They turned away from both Ryan and Jack and closed ranks to keep them away from Nick's parents, his ex-wife, and their kids.

"That's pretty much what I expected," Ryan said as his parents walked away. "I did what I had to do. When my folks stop circling the wagons, I'll go make my condolences to my aunt and uncle."

As far as Jack was concerned, the cold shoulder was a big win. He was about to tell Ryan exactly that when he turned and —*oh, Christ*—found Dave Huntley standing right behind him.

Dave's gaze traveled from Jack's eyes to his and Ryan's interlaced hands, then back up again in a microsecond. He gave a polite nod. "Jack."

Jack felt the blood drain from his face. "Dave."

"Detective Huntley." Ryan dropped Jack's hand to shake Dave's warmly. "Nice to see you."

"Nice to see you too." Dave glanced between them, still smiling his most pleasant smile. He wore a suit that fit his thickly muscled physique perfectly and—Jack knew—still left room for a concealed weapon.

Jack tried to interpret Dave's expression without success. He might have been wearing mirrored shades for all Jack could read him.

"Your mother's been so nice. She gave me a freezer full of food." Ryan looked around, presumably to see if Dave's mother was there with him. "I didn't expect to see you here."

"I knew Nick in high school," Dave answered, staring straight at Jack.

You came for me? Jack turned away, eyes burning.

"Are you all right here?" Ryan asked Jack. "I need say something to Amy and the rest, and then we can go."

"I'll be fine. Go ahead."

Jack and Dave watched Ryan walk away. Dave arched an eyebrow. "I guess you weren't kidding when you said you were thinking about making plans."

"It's not like that."

"What's it like?" Dave asked. "You're holding hands with Ryan Halloran at his cousin's funeral. Can't get more out than that."

"If you recall, I've never been *in*." Heat crackled in Jack's words. Did they have to have this conversation here?

"You've never been with someone, out," Dave countered. "Are you two in a relationship now?"

"Wh-what?" Jack sputtered. "Really?"

"Were you planning on telling me? Or—"

"There's nothing to tell." Jack felt his cheeks burn and looked down at his shoes. *Smooth.* "I've known Ryan for three days."

"God. You must think I piss my days away wearing the McGruff dog suit. I am a detective, Jack. I detect things. I didn't get my badge from a cereal box."

"We can talk *later*."

"Sure." Dave put his hands in his pockets and glanced around. "Chilly reception with this crowd, huh?"

"Yeah."

"You tell Ryan the truth yet?" Dave whispered. "About your *relationship* with Nick?"

"No." Jack lifted his gaze to Dave's eyes. "I don't out my friends."

Dave's face darkened. "Your loyalty is commendable, but don't you think he should know, if you two are—"

"We're not." At Dave's snort, Jack clenched his fists. "Look, I can't just blurt out the truth, not now. Maybe not ever. It isn't my truth to tell."

"The hell it *isn't*." Dave took Jack's arm and led him away from the others.

"Hey." Jack had to move his cane quickly to keep his footing.

"I get this, the thing with Ryan, and I'm glad for you. He seems like a good guy."

Jack eyed Dave for signs he was hurt or felt regret. "He is."

Dave's gaze pierced Jack's cool. "You know things with me are never going to be like this. It's what you want, though, yeah?"

"I—" Jack nodded. "Yeah."

"So." Dave nodded back. "You give me one good reason why Ryan shouldn't know what Nick did to you and why he did it."

The burn in Jack's eyes intensified. He closed them before hissing, "Because I'm ashamed, goddamn it. There. Are you satisfied? I'm ashamed I let Nick use me, and I was stupid enough to believe—"

"You're not the one..." Dave pressed his lips into a white line. He might have had more to say, but Ryan returned.

"Everything okay here?" Ryan wore a worried expression when he took Jack's hand in his. The move was possessive, even if Jack didn't think Ryan meant it that way. It was claiming. "Jack, your hand is freezing."

"We're good," Dave answered. He took a step back and said, arrogantly, "What about you, Jack? You doing okay?"

"I'm fine."

Ryan said, "I need a drink. Dave, will you join us?"

Dave shook his head. "I'm afraid I can't. Maybe some other time?"

Ryan smiled warmly. "Sure."

As Dave walked away, Ryan spoke, "Dave seems nice. He's good to his mother."

"He is." Jack fairly itched for the bourbon in his flask. Ryan gave a last long look at the crowd behind them before he headed for the parking lot.

While they walked, Ryan confessed. "I knew it was selfish asking you to come today. I knew it, and I did it anyway. I'm sorry I put that kind of pressure on you."

"It's all right."

"No, it's not. I was only thinking about myself, about what I wanted. I was thinking how much bringing a date would piss off my parents."

"Yeah?" Jack grinned.

Ryan studied Jack, his gaze troubled. "Yeah. I'm pretty much a prick where my parents are concerned."

"But you were so civil."

"You thought that was civil?" Ryan slipped his hand into Jack's pocket and removed his flask. "May I?"

"If you let me drive." Jack wasn't about to let Ryan drink and drive. His small sip earlier wasn't enough to impair him. He had a feeling Ryan wanted to get a swerve on.

"Yeah. Sure." Ryan tipped the flask up to his mouth. Jack watched Ryan take a healthy swallow, then two more. The muscles in Ryan's shoulders relaxed visibly before he handed Jack his flask back. Ryan sighed. "Okay. That's better."

"Define *better* so I can play the home game."

Ryan grinned at him. "My parents are such assholes. They act like it's all my fault we don't talk."

"Nothing's one-sided."

"Well, in a way, they're right. If only I'd done everything they ever wanted me to without asking questions, we'd be fine."

"I suppose that includes becoming a heterosexual."

"That's part of it. *'My God,'* they say. *'He's a nurse, he doesn't*

go to church, he's gay, he's a liberal Democrat, he drives a hybrid...'
The list goes on and on."

"What's wrong with driving a hybrid?"

"That hybrid proves I've been duped by the global-warming-conspiracy fearmongers." Ryan rubbed his temples. "I don't get along with anyone in my family. The last time Nick and I talked, we had a huge argument about gun control."

"Looks like he had the last word." The words were out before Jack could stop them.

Ryan's eyes bulged. "I can*not* believe you said that."

"I wish I could tell you I'm sorry."

Ryan groaned. "You're hilarious. I mean that. I can't believe you've been able to make me laugh while—"

"Don't make it something it's not. I use humor like Nick used drugs."

"No, you don't." Ryan stopped when they got to his car. "You use humor to make things bearable, not to escape. People like Nick don't know how to do that."

"Maybe because you grew up with *that*." Jack jerked a nod toward Ryan's family. "How would you ever learn to laugh? Your family's ice-cold. They don't have two emotions to rub together for warmth."

Ryan didn't get into the car right away. Instead, he leaned against the fender and regarded Jack thoughtfully. "And you're a hothead who only lets his emotions show for laughs. Is that it?"

"Like an episode of *Jersey Shore* without the accent, baby."

"Now's the time to tell me what I've stepped in here." Ryan toyed with his keys. "I know there's something between you and Dave Huntley. What is it?"

"Dave was...last-night guy." Jack avoided Ryan's gaze. How should he say something like this? *Sex should be like a freeway. On-ramps and off-ramps. Smooth transitions. No braking, no intersections.* "He was at my place. He..."

"I see." Ryan was silent for a while. "Wow."

"I didn't lie to you. I don't cheat. What Dave and I have isn't like that. We never made any promises or anything. We don't even go out."

"If I asked him, would he say that?"

"God, I hope so," Jack said fervently. He glanced back toward the chapel where he'd been talking with Dave. "Dave doesn't do this daylight shit. He said he can't be a gay cop, and he'll never, ever...but I would hate it if I hurt him. So maybe I'm stupid, and maybe I misread things. And now I...I feel awful for a lot of reasons."

Ryan studied him hard. Finally, it seemed like what he saw on Jack's face passed inspection.

"Here." Ryan handed his keys over. "You don't need the key to drive. It's just...symbolic."

"Then you'd better take this." Jack handed over his flask.

"You know it's illegal to drive with an open container no matter who's carrying it."

"Yeah, well," Jack told him. "I guess that's symbolic too."

I guess we're in this—whatever it is—together.

CHAPTER 13

JACK PUSHED the On button to start up Ryan's hybrid, and nothing happened. Well, the dashboard lit up. Since there appeared to be no way to tell if he'd started the car up correctly, and Ryan was taking another not-so-discreet swig from his flask, Jack studied the controls.

The gas and brake pedals seemed to be where they were supposed to be, but he had to look around for a way to get the car to move. Instead of a stick shift, the car had a toggle, like something you'd find on a golf cart. He put it into reverse without any problems and discovered Ryan's hybrid had a backup cam, which was handy when it came to leaving the parking space without mowing down their fellow mourners. The car made a whizzing sound like a golf cart too, but then it growled to life when he shifted into gear and got underway.

By the time they hit the freeway, Ryan was asleep. Jack heaved a big sigh of relief and tried to put Nick's memorial behind him. He was probably going to close his eyes that night, maybe for a lot of nights to come, with the image of Nick's mom and dad behind his eyelids. They'd left the chapel ahead of him, stunned and unhappy. After the service Jack had felt their eyes on him like shards of broken glass. Nick's family—even Ryan—had long memories, and it seemed they traced Nick's problems back to the trouble he got into as a result of his attack on Jack.

Which most everyone believed was entirely Jack's fault.

Now, with Gabe and Dave pressuring him to tell the truth, all Jack's emotional scars were tearing open. They were invisible next to his physical scars, but they hurt in a way time had never healed.

The afternoon traffic slowed to a crawl, and Jack had plenty of time to relive every moment of the service. To recall every face. Amy, the pretty wife in her black dress and headband. Jack's kids, a boy and a girl—blond, blue-eyed replicas of their father with just a dash of their pretty mother mixed in to keep things interesting. Ryan's parents, who didn't even bother hiding their disdain for their only son.

Cousins, aunts, uncles. A scattered handful of others, the stalwart few who'd still been in touch with Nick, or those who were curious, and Jack, who'd loved him. Who'd been mourning the death of the Nick he'd loved for nearly fifteen years.

Jack got to the cause of the traffic problem, a fender bender on the access road. Police and fire were on the scene. He gawked as much as everyone else. The sight of a fire engine still made his heart skip a beat.

Nick might have been his first love, but those big red trucks and the men and women who worked on them were his true love, and he'd lost both.

Someone unrecognizable beneath the blank anonymity of the uniform—grimy mustard-colored turnout gear and helmet—waved him by.

Jack had to swallow down several gulps of hollow unhappiness.

For God's sake. It was time to put his disappointments behind him.

Unless you want *to end up like Nick.*

Finally, he made it to the off-ramp by his house. "Ryan?"

"Hmm?" Ryan rubbed his eyes. His warm, sweet smile caught Jack right in the gut.

"Hey, Sleeping Beauty. We're almost back at my place."

"I was really out of it." Ryan sat up and discreetly wiped the drool from his chin. "Have I been asleep long?"

"You've been out since we got on the freeway. There was an accident, so traffic was backed up. It's taken us about an hour to get this far."

"Was it bad?" Ryan asked.

"I don't think so. Mostly it was gawkers causing the problem."

"I'm hungry."

"I could cook something at my place."

Ryan looked down at himself. "All dressed up and nowhere to go."

"Okay. Yeah. My place probably does seem like nowhere if—"

"I didn't mean that," Ryan clarified. "I meant we should go out. Somewhere nice, my treat. Not a celebration, but maybe...consolation."

"All right. Name the place."

"There's a pretty good steak house in downtown Fullerton."

"I'm in. Lead me to it."

While Ryan gave directions, he hooked his phone up to play music through the car's radio. "What kind of music do you like?"

"I don't know. Most music. Not a big fan of techno or dubstep."

"But you don't have a preference?" On the dashboard, Ryan scrolled through his playlists until he came to one that read *First Date.*

"Wait. Is that what this is?" Jack shot him a quick glance. "Did we just go to a *funeral* on our first date?"

"Doesn't it feel like a date?"

"How would I know?" Jack pulled at his tie and loosened the first button on his collar. *Is it hot in here?* "I don't exactly do relationships."

"All right. Since you're a beginner, I'll tell you how this goes." Ryan leaned back into his seat. "First, I put on my playlist. And then you make fun of my taste in music."

"What's the point of that?" Jack listened for a second. *Oh, my God. Is that Taylor Swift?*

"The point is you tell me you hate my tracks, and then you say what you like to listen to. We talk, ergo we learn about each other."

"So you choosing a Taylor Swift song is some kind of test? Like, if I go along with it, you'll know I'm an idiot?"

"*Exactly.* My first-date playlist is a musical minefield. I'll know by song nine whether I want to sleep with you. And that's Carly Rae Jepson, not Taylor Swift."

"You already want to sleep with me. And I don't care if that's Kylie Minogue. That is not music for a first date with a man."

"Ding, ding, ding." Ryan laughed out loud and advanced to the next song. "First round goes to you, Jack Masterson. But now the game gets tougher."

"Okay. I accept your challenge. Do I know this song?"

"Maybe?"

The tune was an oldie, not something he'd heard lately. "Rolling Stones?"

"Got it in one. That, my friend, is 'Brown Sugar.' What do you think?"

"Well." Jack wondered how he should phrase his thoughts. "The first song says I got my niece's iPod by mistake, and the second says *Grandma, can I play with your record player?*"

"Oh, you're going to get tough, eh?" Ryan appeared delighted.

"It's not that I dislike either song on principle." Jack stopped the car at a light. "But we're talking first-date music here."

"Okay, how about this."

Uh-oh. Smooth jazz. *What the hell do I know about jazz?* "This is a trick, right?"

"Not really." One of Ryan's eyebrows rose like Mr. fucking Spock's.

"Okay. See, I like this. It feels like beach music. Playing volleyball in the sun all day. Bonfires and brews at night. Fish on the grill and slow dancing and sex up against the brick wall by the bathroom. How's that? I say, *yes*. That's first-date music."

"Gzzzzzt." Ryan tilted his head to an odd angle. "*Wrong*. That's not how first dates go."

"That's how my first dates go."

"You said you don't do relationships."

"I don't, but I've been on a shitload of first dates."

Ryan's gaze could have lit Jack on fire. "Moving right along."

Ryan advanced the song again.

Jack wagged a finger at Ryan. "Okay now, that's just cheating."

"There's no cheating on the first-date playlist. I made the first-date-playlist game up, and there are no rules except what I say, and this is perfectly legit."

"But this can*not* be first-date music," Jack reiterated.

"Just because you've never heard it, or it's different, doesn't mean it isn't first-date music."

"I've heard it." Orchestral music swelled in a way particular to fifties films. Horns and harps and strings and percussion that clip-clopped along in a western cadence. "I know exactly what that track is."

"The hell you do." Ryan relaxed back against his gray leather seat and crossed his arms. His expression fairly crackled with doubt. Someone behind them honked, and Jack realized he should be paying more attention to the signal and less to Ryan's goddamn narrowed blue eyes.

"The hell I do indeed, my slightly shit-faced friend." Jack pushed down on the gas pedal. "That's the music from the movie *Shane*. I'd know it *anywhere*."

Ryan flung his hand out and gripped Jack's knee. "Oh, my God."

"*What*." Jack braked and glanced around frantically. There were no imminent collisions, no oncoming cars, thank God, but now they were getting way more honking from angry drivers. "*Shit*, don't do that to me. You'll get us both killed."

"But you're the first person I've ever dated who's recognized that track." Ryan's grip was like iron. "*Ever*."

"I ought to recognize it. That's my grandfather's favorite movie. I must have seen it a hundred times."

"You watched it because your grandfather made you?"

"Hell no. I watched it the first time for Pop-pop. After that, I watched it because of that scene where Alan Ladd and Van Heflin are chopping wood. I watched that with—" Jack stopped himself. The first time he realized *why* he couldn't take his eyes off Ladd and Heflin in the stump-pulling scene was when he'd watched it with *Nick*. "I like a man with an ax. It's a firefighter thing."

"Oh, my God. I can't believe you know that track." Ryan sighed dramatically. "That scene was how I knew I was gay."

"That film's older than both of us put together. Where'd you even find the sound track?"

"I had to rip it from my DVD."

"Okay, that's not weird or anything."

"The movie *Shane* is the litmus test as far as I'm concerned.

We can skip the rest of the songs now and go straight back to my place."

Jack laughed. "I thought you were hungry. You were taking me someplace nice, remember?"

"Okay, we can eat. But you could probably eat with your feet and still get laid tonight." Ryan turned off the radio. "Turn right at the next intersection, and you'll see a parking lot on the left. We'll have to park there and walk. Downtown gets busy on Saturday afternoon."

Jack covered Ryan's hand with his. "I want to know what the other first-date tracks are. Maybe I have a test of my own."

"Oh, hello. If you've got a test, I'll pass it." Ryan laughed lightly. "But I don't suppose it will come to that."

"Are you so sure?"

"I'm not getting my hopes up." Ryan's smile was stalwart, but his eyes were slightly sad. "You said yourself, you don't do *relationships*."

Jack's breath caught. "I suppose I could rethink that at any time."

It took a while to find a free space, but the hybrid turned out to be remarkably easy to park.

CHAPTER 14

THE HOSTESS GREETED Ryan by name and told him to wait while she'd see if she could seat him at his usual table.

Jack looked behind him. Was there was another, more famous Ryan she was talking to? Ryan Gosling or Nolan Ryan or someone else named Ryan besides his "date"? They were the only ones standing there.

Most people Jack knew didn't have their own tables at steak houses, even casual dining steak houses like this one. Jack and his buddies from Station 2 were pretty well-known at the local fish taco place, and they got preferential treatment at their favorite watering hole, but seriously. No one had their own "table."

Except Ryan, apparently.

Finally Jack had to ask. "You have your own table?"

"I do. The reason is eyes only. Top secret."

"Huh?" Jack realized Ryan's words were intended to be flirtatious.

That's what people do on dates, you idiot. They laugh. They tease. They build excitement. Ryan knows what he's doing, and you keep fucking things up.

He played along. "Come on. You can tell me."

"Sure, but then I'd have to kill you."

"That's a cop-out. You need to come up with a really good reason. Tell me you saved a guy from choking on a bull testicle. Tell me a guy *died* at that table, and you brought him back using nothing but your steak knife, a lemon, and your Zippo lighter. Or wait. You created an emergency potato battery and—"

"I'm hurt you think my superspy comeback is pathetic."

"It's not. But I know you can do better. I'd like to see you try harder next time. People should evolve."

"And I should add in a prairie oyster or two to make things interesting?"

"The word *testicle* always gets my attention."

"I see."

"Just trying to help out." Jack winked. *Take that.*

Ryan pinched his ass. "When I need your help, I'll ask for it."

They turned when the hostess asked them to follow her. "Come right this way, sir." By then, Jack's heart felt lighter than it had in a decade.

Maybe Ryan had the right idea. Jack could learn to enjoy going out with a guy to break the ice. He could get comfortable with a date and still build up a hunger for his body. If things didn't work out, he could probably just say so. Not run away into the darkness. Not leave his heart caught in a vise.

Dating might not be such a bad system after all.

Who knew?

The hostess seated them at a round red vinyl booth behind the kitchen, way off to one side, with a nice view of a tiny courtyard. They were well away from prying eyes. Jack guessed a lot of marriage proposals took place in this booth.

"This is the chef's table, but they let me use it when they're not doing a tasting. Want to know how I discovered it? The real reason?"

"Sure." Jack took a menu from the waiter, who blatantly eyed Ryan as if he were on the dessert menu.

"Your usual to drink, Ryan?" the waiter asked. Ryan nodded.

"I'll take a cola, please," said Jack. The waiter turned without answering.

Guess Ryan has a table and *a waiter*.

"If you want to get a drink, I'm pretty sure we could catch a ride from someone here. I know pretty much the whole staff."

"I could call the local FD, and someone would pick me up." Jack knew people. He could get them a ride too, but he didn't feel like drinking just then. "So tell me, why do you have your own table at a restaurant?"

Ryan's lips quirked into a genuine smile. "When my grand-mother got sick, it wasn't as easy for her to eat. She spilled things on herself sometimes, so she liked to put her napkin on her chest. After a while she was too embarrassed to let me take her out, so I finally called the owner and asked if he could seat us somewhere private. He was very accommodating, and in my enthusiasm I overtipped. Now they just seat me here for old times' sake."

"Aw, now. That's—" Jack played with his forks. "That's the kind of thing I'd never think of. That's so thoughtful."

"Yeah, well. This table hasn't hurt me on dates either. I've canoodled right here in this booth in front of God and everyone."

"Have you?" Jack leaned back. "But you seem like such a nice boy."

Ryan slid his foot over and bumped Jack's. "It only looks that way."

"Careful, you're about to mingle my man-made materials with your oh-so-nice leather shoes there."

"Speaking of which. I need to get comfortable." Ryan stood and held Jack's gaze with a teasing lift of his brows while he removed his jacket and tie. He threw in a lot of extra flourish so in the end, Jack felt like he'd gotten a brief private striptease.

Jack took his jacket and tie off as well, but he wasn't about to make a show of it. That was all Ryan, whose strong, lean body held a sinuous grace his cousin Nick couldn't have hoped to possess.

Goddamn it.

Jack had to stop looking at Ryan and seeing Nick.

"What's the matter?" Ryan slipped back in beside him, concern etched over the frown he wore.

"Nothing," Jack lied.

Things were too quiet while Ryan slipped his cuff links from his cuffs and rolled up his sleeves. Jack did the same, then tapped his fingers nervously on the tablecloth.

"What looks good to you?" Ryan asked.

"Everything." Jack couldn't help settling his gaze directly on Ryan. "*Everything* looks really good to me."

Ryan colored faintly and pressed the menu out flat between them. "You can't go wrong with the steaks here. Most everything else"—he glanced around and whispered—"is okay."

The waiter came to the table with their drinks. "Jack and Coke for Ryan, and plain Coke for you, sir. Have you had a chance to look over the menu yet? Can I interest you in any appetizers this evening?"

"What do you think?" Ryan asked Jack.

"I'm new here. Order what you like." Jack took his soda and relaxed back into the booth.

"Let us have some stuffed mushrooms and maybe a shrimp cocktail to share?" Ryan included Jack in the question, so he nodded.

"And may I have some lemon for my soda, please?" Jack asked, just to be an asshole.

"Certainly, sir. I'll get that appetizer order for you right away and come back with your lemon."

"Lemon for your soda." Ryan laughed as they watched the waiter walk away.

"Since I still don't know the rest of the tracks on your first-date playlist," Jack reminded him, "how do I know I'm not out with a guy who has Justin Bieber's 'Baby' on his iPod like some kind of musical time bomb?"

"Well, what can I expect on your playlist?" When Jack would have spoken, Ryan put his fingers over Jack's lips. "Let me guess. 'Fire' by the Ohio Players, 'Burning Down the House' by the Talking Heads, 'Set Fire to the Rain' by Adele."

"Are you saying you think I'm a one-trick pony?"

"I'm saying..." Ryan's teeth caught his lower lip for a second, and then he smiled again. "I think firefighters are hot."

Jack did something he couldn't remember ever doing in a restaurant before—he wrapped his hand around the back of Ryan's neck and brought him in for a kiss. Ryan was still smiling when their lips met. His warm skin was soft, and his breath smelled pleasantly like bourbon. One brief touch of lips between them led to two, then a deeper kiss; then Ryan sent his tongue out to play, and Jack opened up to him like he'd been waiting all his life. He tilted his head to give Ryan access. Ryan cupped his cheek to delve even deeper.

The sweet spell that wove between them was broken by the sound of a plate hitting the table with a thud.

"Your lemons, sir." Their waiter turned and walked away before they could say anything else.

Jack pulled back, slightly dazed. "I think you just broke a couple of hearts."

Ryan frowned. "What do you mean, a couple?"

"The waiter has a crush, and mine..." Jack licked his lips to savor the flavor of Ryan on them. "I think my heart just stopped for a second."

"I'm a nurse." Ryan ran his thumb along Jack's jawline. "I can tell you that's not likely."

"You have no idea what you do to me."

"Of course I do." Ryan deflected. "I'm all that. That's how I know if you had a first-date playlist, I'd pass your test without breaking a sweat."

"I think I have..." Jack took out his phone and searched his playlist. "Yep. 'Closer.' Nine Inch Nails. *Pow*."

Ryan gave a shocked gasp. "What will the neighbors think?"

"I don't know what your neighbors think. Mine think I don't do enough lawn care."

Ryan leaned in for another kiss—a sweet, chaste brush of lips that ended quickly. When he backed away, he said, "For a guy who doesn't date, you do it really well."

Jack smiled. He doubted he could sustain any kind of charm, but as long as Ryan was feeling it, who was he to contradict the man? The waiter came back with a shrimp cocktail in a large glass goblet and a plate of stuffed mushrooms. They were still steaming, oozing cheese and crab, speckled with fresh herbs.

Jack watched Ryan cut one into manageable bites. Ryan surprised him by picking up a forkful and holding it out so Jack could taste. "Here, blow. It's still hot."

Jack's gaze locked with Ryan's when he puckered his lips to cool the garlicky bite with a *whoosh* of breath. He let Ryan slip the morsel into his mouth and began chewing. God, the mushroom was delicious—juicy and fresh, filled with blue crab and bread crumbs and cheese, broiled to molten, gooey perfection.

Ryan licked the butter from his lips, and Jack moaned. Each stroke of Ryan's tongue went directly to his cock.

How is Ryan not taken?

How has Ryan roamed the streets of north Orange County without being captured already?

How has he escaped being snapped up and married and

strapped into a baby Bjorn by the first gay man he brought to this very table?

"I'm so clearly not in your league," Jack blurted.

Impatiently, Ryan raked his hair away from his face. Jack followed the motion with his own fingers. Ryan's hair felt better, softer and finer, than it looked, and while Jack had thought it was plain pale blond, in the daylight he'd seen it was actually made up of about a hundred different shades—from the finest wheat to glistening gold to copper.

"Can I tell you something?" asked Ryan. "I have the worst taste in men."

"I guess that explains a lot."

"No, don't be like that. You seem great. I mean that. I'm worried I'll blow my losing streak here." He picked up a shrimp and dipped it into cocktail sauce. "I'm counting on that thing you have with my neighbor's son to scotch the deal."

Jack decided not to pursue the subject right then, because Ryan held a shrimp between his teeth and lifted it, giving Jack access to a bite. Jack sampled the shrimp, getting spicy cocktail sauce all over his lips. Ryan took take care of that, laving Jack's lips with his tongue, causing Jack's cock to stir restlessly under the napkin he'd placed on his lap.

Breathless, Jack lost himself in the flavor and scent and feel of Ryan's tongue on his lips. When Ryan broke the kiss, Jack let out a shuddering sigh.

Wait. I'm going to blow his losing streak?

"What did you mean when you said—" Jack's phone rang, and the moment was lost. Jack searched his pockets for his phone after Ryan gave him tacit permission to answer.

"Masterson."

"It's me," said Eddie in his usual easygoing voice. "I'm calling in a favor."

"Tell me."

"I know we said you should take off until Monday, but can you go check out a job?"

"Where?" Jack glanced at Ryan. *Damn. It looked like it was going to be a good night too.*

"The Angel Motor Lodge. Sam called me on my personal cell, but I've got tickets for Tango Argentina at the Performing Arts Center, and Gabe's working another scene."

The Angel was a dank little place that reportedly catered to the hourly trade in one of the worst areas of Anaheim. He and Gabe had a long-standing arrangement with the owner. Between overdoses and violent crime, the Angel brought them enough business to make Sam a VIP. "Now?"

"As soon as you can. They're going to need a board-up, because one of the windows got shot out. Kim will meet you there with a truck. If she can find him, she'll bring Jerry."

"All right. I'll text her. I'm at an early dinner, but maybe in an hour or so, give or take drive time?"

"Perfect. Thanks."

"You're going to *Tango Argentina*?"

"Don't say it like that. It's hot."

"Have fun." Jack ended the call.

"You have to go?"

"Not until after dinner, but yeah." Jack took a sip of his soda. He relived the memory of Ryan's tongue licking sauce from his lips. "Sorry."

"Too bad."

"I need to supervise a board-up and write up some paperwork."

"I could go with you," Ryan offered. "We don't have to end the evening. We could go back to my place after you're done."

"I don't know. It's likely to be an ugly scene. There was a shooting."

"I'll be fine. It's not like I don't know what I'll see. I'll get the waiter. What do you want to eat?"

"Loaded question." Jack leaned over and raked Ryan's earlobe with his teeth. Ryan smelled so goddamn good it should be illegal. "I want to eat *you*, of course. I want to start with your toes and nibble my way up your calves and munch on the backs of your knees, then move up so I can lick your balls and take your dick in my—"

"Maybe I should drop something under the table and let you go after it," Ryan whispered.

"Uh..." *Right*. The image that conjured was dazzling. "Okay."

"I'm kidding." Ryan patted his hand. "Even I probably wouldn't go that far."

The conversation wasn't doing anything to soften Jack's inconveniently hard cock, and considering they were in a public place and he had to go to work, he ought to be thinking with his big head and not his little one.

"Later, I promise."

Ryan nodded and rephrased. "What *food* do you want the waiter to bring?"

"Surprise me."

"That ought to be easy." Ryan's smile was sinister, and Jack responded to it the same way he responded to everything about this unexpected, flirtatious side of Ryan—with a quick intake of breath and a nervous laugh.

"On the contrary. It's not easy to surprise me at all," Jack told him, "but somehow, you always do."

CHAPTER 15

JACK PULLED the hybrid past the manager's office and into the parking lot of the Angel Motor Lodge. The place was a standard-issue motor court with two stories of small, nondescript rooms surrounding a parking lot with an empty fenced-off pool. In the gathering darkness, the only source of light came from yellow security lamps on the ground floor and whatever light cracked through tears in the rooms' ancient drapes.

"Ah, shit." Ryan's dress shoes crunched over broken glass as he surveyed the scene. "What the hell happened here?"

"Guy caught his wife cheating." Sam spoke from ten feet down the motel's upstairs gallery where he didn't have to look into the room. He had the clipboard Jack gave him and was busy filling out paperwork. How he could see what he was writing in the gloom was anyone's guess. "He broke through the door and started shooting, and the wife's boyfriend returned fire. Blew out the window. Police cleared the scene over an hour ago."

Jack didn't ask what had happened to the victims. The blood told its own story. All three had probably been hit, and from the way things looked, it was hard to imagine they'd all survived. Maybe someone had.

"The course of true love ne'er did run smooth," Sam added. "That's Shakespeare."

"Yep." Jack glanced down at the blood-spattered glass beneath his feet, then over at Ryan. "Nothing's better for my business than true love."

Maybe the call was a timely intervention. Jack had allowed himself to start a little fantasy at the restaurant, but hadn't he figured love out already? Hadn't he told himself a hundred times?

Nothing comes from getting attached to people but pain.

"Anything I can do, Jack?" Ryan's nearness startled him.

"No, thank you." Jack turned to measure the window for Kim and Jerry, who waited next to the truck on the ground level. He turned to reassure Sam. "We're going to get this boarded up and take care of the glass and blood out here tonight. Eddie said he'd call and schedule a team for the interior as soon as possible, all right?"

"Fine." Sam hugged the clipboard to his bony chest. "You know, when my folks bought this place, the neighborhood was so different. I'd hate to know what they'd think if they saw it now."

"Sorry." Jack wished he had more to offer.

"Not necessary." Sam shrugged and headed back to the office. "I'll get the rest of this signed and copied. Stop by the office on your way out. Thanks for coming."

"Anytime." Jack absently rubbed his aching knee. He had a high tolerance for pain—always had—but since he'd taken his career-killing fall, his pain was chronic. He thought of it like an unpleasant relative who came and stayed too long. Sometimes the bastard's voice got shrill.

Pain wasn't anything he couldn't live with. What choice did he have? He dealt with it every day. But he'd exhausted himself physically cleaning Ryan's place the day before, and today he'd been on his feet too damn long. The normal, low-level ache he lived with felt more like burning agony now. It reached deep into his muscle and bone, throbbing so insistently he could feel its pulse in his eyeballs.

Jack leaned against the railing overlooking the courtyard and pretended nothing was out of the ordinary as sweat cooled on his forehead. Since his accident, he'd become the world's best actor.

"Jack, you're awfully pale." Ryan put his arm around Jack's waist. His intent gaze bored into Jack, flaying him, making him feel exposed and defenseless. "Are you in pain?"

"Yeah." Jack grunted. He guessed even good acting couldn't hide his physiological response to pain. No fair dating a nurse. "It's been a long couple of days."

"Why didn't you say something? I have ibuprofen in my car."

"Ibuprofen would be good." Just then Kim and Jerry emerged from the stairwell with a broom and disinfectant spray. They both wore protective gear because of the blood spatter on the gallery floor. "I'll just get my guys started on this board-up and—"

"Yo. Token Chick is not a guy, oh Mighty Payer of Wages." Kim pulled the top of her Tyvek suit apart. Underneath she wore only a lime-green bra. "Behold, *breasts*."

"Sorry." Jack would have laughed if he felt better. "Very nice, although I'm not considered a connoisseur."

"I'll get some pain reliever for you," said Ryan. "Maybe I can find a bottle of water or something."

Kim pointed toward the stairwell. "There's a pop machine at the base of the stairs."

"Okay." Ryan tilted his head and spoke directly into Jack's ear. "Are you sure you're up to this? I can help out while you wait in the car."

"That's very nice." Jack leaned his head on Ryan's shoulder

and briefly let the man take some of his weight. "But I need to double-check window measurements."

"Kim can do it." He turned to Kim. "You can measure the windows, right? Jack looks like he's going to faint, and I'd be remiss if I didn't help him get somewhere soft before he falls and breaks his neck."

"I'll be fine, chief. Just go," said Kim. "Jerry will double-check me."

Ryan patted Jack's arm. "At least go sit in the stairwell for a minute?"

"I'd have to burn my only suit afterwards."

"All right, forget it. You're coming with me. You'll sit in the office and wait for the paperwork. Kim will find you if she needs anything."

Ryan's words made sense. Sometimes pain clouded Jack's thinking. Kim and Jerry were solid professionals. She'd probably measure the window herself again anyway. *Measure twice, cut once.* They knew what they were doing.

"Okay." Jack let himself lean on Ryan while they descended the stairs. He'd grown stiff just standing there. It took a while to get down that single flight because he had to take steps one at a time. Ryan bought him a soda from the machine and gave him a few pills. He took them while he and Ryan walked to the office together.

"I'd be worried about your blood sugar if I hadn't seen you eat."

"It's nothing. Yesterday was tough, and I'm achy."

"Given your color and the way you're sweating, that's gotta be the understatement of the year."

"Probably," Jack admitted.

"I deal with firefighters and cops all the time. You guys never do what's good for you."

Jack's laugh startled a boy slinking out of a ground-floor door.

God, he couldn't have been more than fifteen or sixteen. He took off running, but Ryan blocked his way.

"Hey!" Jack shouted when it looked like a collision was unavoidable.

The kid pulled up short and gave them an appraising look. "Hey."

"You okay?" Ryan asked.

Jack noticed how skinny the kid was. The uneasy way he stood on the sidewalk, trying to act tough.

"You guys want some company?" The kid's dark hair fell into one of his brown eyes, and he tossed it back in a gesture he must have practiced in a mirror. "Threesomes cost extra."

"How old are you?" Jack demanded.

Ryan put his arm on Jack's to calm him. "Knock it off, Jack."

That gave the kid some traction. He grinned at Ryan like they had a new private joke. "Yeah, Jack. Knock it off."

Ryan took out his wallet. Jack gaped at him. "You're going to give him money? Are you—"

"I know what I'm doing." Ryan offered the boy a business card and a strip of three condoms. "Look. I don't know you, but take these. If you want a safe place to stay, call the number on this card. Nobody asks questions. They're just there to help. If not, use the condoms."

The kid shoved the card and condoms into the pocket of his jeans. His chin jutted out. "I always use a rubber."

"That's good to know. How do you find your dates?"

"What do you think?" The kid laughed at them. They were obviously way too old and stupid to understand anything. "Old guys like your man here love my ass."

"I would never—" Jack sputtered. "Kid, that shit is dangerous. You let us—"

"Gotta bounce, Gramps. Places to see, people to do." He turned away, but Ryan caught the sleeve of his hoodie.

"Keep the card," Ryan urged. "You never know when you'll want something different."

The kid yanked away and took off running. Jack and Ryan watched him disappear beyond the oddly yellow light. "Whose card was that?"

"A friend of mine from Children of the Night."

"Shouldn't we do something?" Jack wasn't at all happy. He was conditioned to rescue people even if they didn't necessarily want to be rescued. "He's underage. We should call the police."

"He's long gone. If we try to force him, we'll only get ourselves in trouble."

"But he was just a kid." Jack's chest felt tight. He wanted to bang on the door the kid came out of and seriously fuck up his john.

"There are hundreds, thousands more just like him out here every night trying to get enough money to eat or score or bed down somewhere warm."

"We had the chance to take one off the street, and you offer what? A card and some condoms?"

"I'm sorry I didn't do what you think is right," Ryan said quietly. "I've been down this road before. You can only give a kid like that the chance. You can't make him take it. If he calls the number on that card, it gets him off the street. The decision has to be up to him."

"What if he wanted help and was afraid?"

"If he'd even hesitated for a second, I'd have made the call for him. I'd have waited until someone came, or taken him to the shelter myself. Did he seem like he wanted help to you?"

Jack snorted in disgust. "He seemed like a little shit."

"I know it's hard." Ryan took Jack's hand. "I give all the help I know how to give."

If Ryan hadn't sounded so wounded right then, Jack might have reminded him that for a guy who had everything to offer,

Ryan seemed pretty lacking in the hope department too, with his talk of lost causes and losing streaks.

Jack shook his head. He didn't say anything, but he wondered if maybe some people just didn't know how to let themselves believe in something. Maybe some people needed a little push.

"I thought I was going to get laid tonight?"

CHAPTER 16

BY THE TIME Ryan pulled Jack into the foyer of his house, the ibuprofen was taking the edge off Jack's pain. Desire took him the rest of the way. At the moment he felt nothing but the throb of his dick as he followed Ryan halfway up the stairs and pushed him against the wall. Ryan kissed like there was no one else in the world but Jack.

"*Jack.*" Ryan lifted his mouth from Jack's and backed up a stair. Jack had to stretch on tiptoe for another kiss. While he did that, Ryan unbuttoned Jack's sleeves. Jack brushed Ryan's hands away. Ryan would have to wait, because Jack needed to explore every inch of his body. Jack tussled with him, mindful of his unsteady legs and the possibility of a fall.

If they made it to the top of the stairs, the situation was sure to become a heated battle they could both win.

Ryan grew impatient. "Just let me get this—"

"Oh, all right." Jack's shirt finally fluttered over the railing to the foyer below. Hands now free, Jack was able to thumb Ryan's light brown nipples, to breathe hot, moist air on them while he watched them pebble up. He licked his lips before diving in.

Now let's see how they taste.

"Ah, Jack." Ryan wrapped both hands around the back of Jack's head and arched up into his caress. They rubbed their hips together in shuddery confusion. Jack groaned against Ryan's neck as the evidence of Ryan's arousal came to rest snugly against his own hard cock. Ryan moaned his name again. "*Jack.*"

Ryan raked Jack's spine with his trim fingernails. Jack reached for Ryan's belt buckle, ready to tear it open with his teeth when it seemed uncooperative. Ryan helped him, opening his belt and zipper without comment. White-hot passion rode Jack as he kissed his way down Ryan's tight abdomen to the elastic of his underwear, tugging the fabric off to kiss the dusky skin of his groin.

Suddenly it wasn't enough, and Jack pulled Ryan's pants and shorts down over his hips. He gave a happy gasp when Ryan's cock sprang free. To taste it, Jack had to fall to one knee on the carpeted stairs and stretch his bad leg out behind him. As far as positions went, it wasn't the worst he'd ever been in. Discomfort took a backseat to desire any day. Once settled, he pressed his face into the musky, damp skin of Ryan's groin and nosed around, delighted by the nest of curly hair he found there. *Red* hair—a tangled brush of glittering, coppery strands—a secret treasure.

Ryan's cock bobbed, glistening and needy. Jack pushed his whole face into the jumble of curls and breathed in Ryan's essence—the musk of his private scent, which competed with the soapy smell of clean skin and something uniquely Ryan, sharp and warm and slightly sweet.

Jack tasted Ryan's skin, licking into the hollow places of Ryan's groin with the tip of his tongue like he'd lap the sweet cream out of a pastry. He drew his mouth over the crease of Ryan's leg, back into the soft, hidden places behind Ryan's dick. He nudged Ryan's balls aside and urged him to open his legs while he traced the delicate skin between them with his tongue.

He wanted to press his mouth into the very center of Ryan's being and breathe him in like the scent of newly mown grass or fire or rain, or any scent Jack wanted to take inside him and hold onto forever.

"Hey." Ryan's knees parted, and Jack caught the briefest glimpse of his tightly puckered hole. It was there and gone again, because Ryan pressed his knees back together. It seemed odd that in this one thing—being on display—Ryan seemed shy.

"C'mere," Jack coaxed, reaching up to catch Ryan's cock. He gently chafed the delicate skin between his palms and then took Ryan into his mouth with reverence. He got a muffled curse and a tremble of Ryan's thigh muscles in response, but Ryan didn't pull away.

Time spun out while Jack explored the feel of Ryan's firm, cut cock as it slipped against his tongue, his cheeks, and his soft palate. He mapped the shape from spongy head to ridged glans and all along the veins pulsing down its shaft. God, how sweet, taking a man like that. In control, and at the same time, so very much at his mercy.

Allowing Ryan's deep, rhythmic thrusting required practice and patience, both of which Jack drew on. He got a familiar rush of satisfaction when he heard Ryan groan with pleasure. Pure lust took Jack out of his broken body, away from his odd little life to somewhere only he and Ryan existed. Where it was so very good—he could be good—and Ryan would shatter like glass, like a shower of stars, all around him.

Jack had desire, and Ryan pleasure, and now that they were together, they were all that was necessary in the world.

Ryan cried out when Jack bobbed down over the tight length of his cock. Jack rested his hands on the backs of Ryan's thighs and relaxed to let Ryan know control was all his if he wanted it. Ryan caught on quick, driving deep into Jack's mouth, into his throat, giving him time to find rhythm and breath between strokes. He tangled his fingers in Jack's hair while he tested Jack's limits, but after the first three or four long thrusts, Jack was so desperate, so eager, he wasn't sure he had any limits at all.

Ryan slid into Jack's mouth slowly, all the way to his balls. Jack held still for him, relaxing his throat around the blunt head of Ryan's cock, then caressing it with his throat muscles. Hot tears stung his eyes as Ryan pulled back and thrust again, hunched over him, crying out his pleasure. When Jack was able, he hummed around Ryan's thrusts. He warbled like one of Ryan's stupid first-date tracks, like a love song in a way, because he surely loved everything he was doing right then.

"God, Jack." Ryan shot his hips forward again, and though Jack's eyes burned, he took every inch Ryan had to give. His own cock throbbed like a bass drum, pounding its deep rhythm through his belly and chest, hammering in his ears and behind his eyes. He licked the swollen veins on the underside of Ryan's cock, and as he did fresh flavor flooded his mouth. The glistening essence of Ryan's precum washed over his tongue like foamy seawater.

"Oh, Christ, Jack." Ryan nearly whined. "So *goddamn* good."

Jack cupped Ryan's balls and snaked his index finger out along the hidden damp stretch of skin between Ryan's legs. Ryan's muscles clamped down hard when Jack fingered the puckered skin of his anus. Jack met Ryan's jolt of genuine surprise with a skip of his heart. He pressed the delicate ring of muscle again. The brief spasm of Ryan's glutes and thighs felt like both a warning and a promise.

Jack backed off enough to ask, "Okay?"

Ryan opened his eyes, on his face a mixture of ecstasy and urgency. His disoriented expression preceded a garbled cry of gratitude as he surged forward again, none too gently. This time Jack was ready. He was ready to feel Ryan Halloran—attractive, enigmatic Ryan—fly apart in his arms. Jack was *eager* to earn one of Ryan's brilliant smiles or, better yet, the helpless confusion he'd seen on Ryan's face after they'd gotten off that morning.

Jack circled Ryan's tightly wrinkled skin, massaging the muscle, giving the delicate flesh little more than baby kisses with the tips of his fingers, even though he longed to kiss that deeply personal part of Ryan's body, to tongue it and invade it with his mouth and cock as well. Ryan thrust into him, but now his ass clenched and quivered with every stroke.

Ryan's fingers tightened in Jack's hair, and his balls pulled up. Jack swallowed in anticipation, pressing a finger against Ryan's hole, pressing just enough to make him feel it, just to the first knuckle. Ryan's hips bucked. He took Jack's mouth almost roughly, then spasmed, coming in gushes, calling Jack's name, muttering curses and praise—a blissed-out litany of sex words and gasping and breathy sighs. Ryan's hips and legs juddered wildly as he poured every last drop of his essence down Jack's throat.

Jack held him through his release, feeling oddly protective, oddly tender. Even though he was on his knees on the stairs of a strange house, blowing a man he barely knew, he felt intensely connected.

Maybe Ryan wanted to lose himself in sensation. Maybe Jack wanted to forget the part of the house where Nick had died. Maybe it was chemistry or physiology or just plain luck, but at that moment Jack couldn't think of a single place he'd rather be than right there, licking Ryan's softening cock clean while Ryan held his head and stroked his hair.

Ryan collapsed two stairs above the one where Jack knelt, exhausted, and Jack stretched out along the risers to rest his head on Ryan's thigh.

Ryan sighed deeply. "God, that was incredible."

Jack closed his eyes as Ryan's fingers described lazy circles on his back. He could have died happy just then, despite the hard-on leaking damply on his trousers. Died happy and gone to heaven—whatever that was.

Ryan leaned over and pressed a kiss to Jack's temple. "Give me a minute, and I'll return the favor."

Jack lifted his face toward Ryan shamelessly. *More kisses, please.* "My head says no one is keeping score, but my dick says gimme."

"Gimme?"

"Yeah. That's the most sophisticated word my dick knows."

Ryan snorted. "I've got you covered. I want that dick of yours in my mouth every bit as much as I wanted my dick in yours."

"Oral, are we?"

"Among other things."

"Am I going to find out what those *other things* are?"

"All in good time. Hey." When Jack opened his eyes, Ryan loomed over him. "How are you feeling? Need anything stronger for pain?"

"Ibuprofen worked well enough. Thank you. Endorphins will kick in later, I hope." Jack caught the hand on his chest and kissed it. "I don't want to get sloppy."

Ryan didn't seem ready to move, and Jack was just fine with that. If it weren't for his cock, which was still fully erect and pounding against his belly like a landlord after overdue rent, he probably could have fallen asleep right there.

The quiet of the empty house. The way Ryan was stroking his chest. It all conspired to relax him until he felt like he was floating on some carpet-scented cloud.

Ryan finally moved. "My bedroom is the last door on the left. There's an attached bath. Go make yourself comfortable while I open a bottle of wine."

"Sounds nice."

Ryan slid out from beneath Jack and stood, pulling his trousers up just enough to zip them. As he stepped down the stairs in his stockinged feet, his pants hung precariously low on his bare torso. Jack watched him go with his heart in his throat.

God. Jack had never, ever blown a guy like that. He'd never simply given it all up, never gone buck wild. His throat ached and his body was sore, but he'd gotten more than he'd given just then.

Way more.

The memory of Ryan's smile and the happy little circles he'd drawn on Jack's skin, the tenderness he'd shown... Jack wanted more of that. As much as he could get.

Even if beyond the stairs, beyond the kitchen, and down a little hallway there was a room that reminded him of why he should exercise extreme caution.

It's just sex, right? Hot guy. Nice night. Just sex.

Jack walked up the stairs and found the room Ryan called his. He didn't plan to explore it, at least not at great length, but he discovered right away it held as many clues to Ryan's personality as Nick's small room had lacked with regard to his. Hardwood floors formed a foundation for all different shades of brown: rich mocha walls, beige linens, pillows as dark as coffee and as light as cream.

Behind the bed a picture window looked out over an amazing garden. From where he stood, Jack could see a pergola covered with wisteria vines and beyond that, a gently rising slope crowned with fruit trees. The other walls held framed panoramic landscape photographs, and they added color and drama to the room. There were several pictures of a forest in all different seasons. There were some of the ocean. A couple Jack recognized as Iceland.

Just looking at the pictures gave Jack gooseflesh. He felt as if he could fly into one of them and hover between the vast green pastures, or soar out over the cobalt-blue water and look down at the way sea foam eddied around volcanic rock formations.

He could almost feel the chill of ice or the warmth of

sunshine coming from behind the glass.

Ryan returned, carrying a bottle and two glasses. "I picked a white. Okay?"

Jack shrugged. "I'm no expert."

"I'll just put them on the nightstand." Ryan set the glasses down without a sound. He turned and walked toward Jack, skin still glistening from their rendezvous on the stairs.

"I—" Jack had no idea what he'd been about to say. Ryan's fair skin bloomed with a deep flush while his swollen lips begged for kisses. His eyes glittered with faint fresh longing.

Jack's feet felt glued to the floor. He nodded toward the bed. "Maybe we could—"

"Sure." Ryan stepped forward and placed his palms flat on Jack's chest. Jack shivered when Ryan slid his hands down Jack's torso. Ryan undid the button on Jack's trousers and carefully lowered his zipper.

Jack closed his fingers over Ryan's "Wait."

"Wait?" Ryan's absurdly pale lashes lifted. They were longer than Jack had realized and distracted him for a second or two.

"I'm covered in scars. No surprises, okay? It's not pretty, some of it."

"I think I can handle it." Ryan smiled as he pushed Jack's trousers and shorts down over his hips and braced him while he stepped free of them. While Ryan got rid of his socks, Jack closed his eyes. He didn't have to look. The image of his lower body was burned into his retinas. Scars from surgeries on the broken bones in his legs. Scars from knee replacement, scars over his lower torso where they'd had to stabilize his pelvis.

He had scars on his back and arms too, but they weren't as unappealing. They were the normal wear and tear of doing business as a boy child who liked a little thrill. He'd earned them the old-fashioned way, falling off skateboards, surfing, and rock climbing. They didn't bother him.

In his mind, those surgical scars were directly linked to his mortality, and Jack had a hard time looking at them. They should make him feel resilient, he knew. But somehow, they only made him feel ugly.

"They're not so bad, patchwork man. Just some surgical graffiti. It says, 'Dr. Huesos was here.'"

Jack laughed. "Easy for you to say."

"Easy for me to see past too. So what? You use a cane, and you've got some scars. You're a hot guy with a terrific body. Did you think a few scars would make me want you any less?" Ryan palmed Jack's hips. "Cause it's all good. You're a fine man, Jack Masterson."

"All right." Jack's dick reacted predictably to Ryan's hands. The cock that had barely flagged from their encounter on the stairs grew positively, painfully erect while Ryan felt him up. "You're killing me here."

"I plan to rescue you"—Ryan practically purred—"as soon as you tell me how you want me."

"Any way. Every way." Jack hooked his fingers in Ryan's belt loops. "Can we get these off?"

"Sure." Ryan stepped away, then slipped his trousers and shorts off, giving Jack a tantalizing view of his firm, well-muscled ass in the process. Fine golden hair dusted his body. It caught what little light there was and winked like sparks off his skin.

Jack nudged Ryan up against the bed and kissed the back of his neck right below his hairline. He planned to lick and kiss every vertebra, to caress and massage every muscle, until Ryan poured like liquid gold in his hands.

"Can you get up on the bed?" Jack asked, and Ryan complied, climbing up onto his bed and kneeling with his back to Jack's chest. Jack continued kissing down Ryan's spine, down to the top of his ass crack. Jack thumbed the dimples on either side of Ryan's ass, kissing each in turn, secretly naming them

Frick and Frack, because he was never going to forget that, was he?

Frick, Frack, and the crack in the middle. Sounds like a children's book.

The good thing was Ryan seemed to like it when Jack laughed against his skin.

"What are you doing?" Ryan slipped away, laughing. "That tickles."

"Nothing," Jack said in a way that made it sound like it wasn't nothing at all. "Kneel up, and let me get at you."

"No." Ryan dissolved into squirming fits. "This is embarrassing."

"I'm *serious*." Jack turned Ryan around to give him a good, hard kiss. He let his cane fall and braced himself against the bed. "I'm not flexible enough to be Mr. Smooth, baby. Why don't you put your ass where I need it, and we'll see how embarrassed you feel with my tongue in it."

"Why didn't you say so?" Ryan started to turn around again, but he glanced back. "As long as we're entering into negotiations, do you plan to slap my ass?"

Jack hesitated. *Is this another test?* "Would you like me to?"

"Hell yes. I'd be insulted if you didn't." Ryan shifted and put his ass right in Jack's face. "'Bout there, you think?"

"Yeah, that's good." Jack couldn't believe he was about to give Ryan's ass a nice firm slap. *Ker-smack!* "How's that?" Jack didn't give Ryan time to answer before he swiped his tongue over Ryan's tight sphincter. A loud gasp let him know he was on the right track, and Ryan didn't move, not at all, except to push back against Jack's mouth.

Jack pushed his face in between Ryan's ass cheeks to flick and tease the wrinkled bud, and then he thumbed his way into the cleft for a better angle. Ryan leaned forward, letting his head drop to the bed with a thud.

"Ah, *God*. Yeah. Just like that."

Jack tongued along the pristine white skin between Ryan's pucker and his sac. He licked at Ryan's balls from behind. The flavor, salt and musk, the man-smell and earthiness of private places never failed to make Jack's mouth water, and he hummed when he went back to teasing Ryan's hole.

"Shhhhit," Ryan hissed.

When Jack didn't think Ryan could take more teasing, he speared his tongue and pushed it against Ryan's hole, fucking right into him with everything he had, gliding into the spit-slicked aperture, and feeling the tense muscle tighten around him.

There was nothing like that, like being inside the heat and need of a man, feeling his most essential, helpless desire against a cock or a tongue, or probing with fingers until all will left his body and he was nothing but sensation and greed.

"Ah, God, Jack. Please," Ryan begged. "More. I need more."

Jack pulled back and gave Ryan's ass a few solid slaps, knowing he would feel the reverberations of each in quick, percussive bursts of fire against his hole.

Ryan shivered. "Shit... *Shit*."

Jack slapped him again and then once more, loving the way Ryan moaned his name each time.

"That's mine." Jack stopped Ryan from rubbing his darkly engorged cock over the duvet cover. His slaps left red ghosts that warmed and sweetly stained the skin of Ryan's ass. Jack laved each pink print with the flat of his tongue and blew a breath to cool the reddened skin.

Ryan begged for more. "Please, Jack. *Please*. I need your goddamn cock."

"Lube and condoms?"

"In the nightstand." Ryan gasped for air. "Please, now."

Jack got what he needed and rolled a condom over his cock.

He slicked Ryan up and worked him open until first one finger, then two slipped inside him easily.

When Ryan responded by hissing and pushing back against Jack's hand, Jack replaced his fingers with the blunt head of his dick and poised himself at the entrance of Ryan's tight channel.

"Here we go," Jack said as he pressed forward. "Let me know if I hurt you."

"You can't hurt me. I just need—" Ryan's voice was ragged, and his words slurred. "Yeah. *Yes. Ah, God.*"

Ryan's ass was a hot vise that made Jack's nerve endings jangle like ten thousand volts of electricity rushed up and down his spine. He started with short, sharp strokes and let himself glory in the exact claiming moment when his balls came to rest against Ryan's softly furred thighs, and Ryan was open, exposed to him all the way.

The first pull out was pain and bliss as their bodies adjusted to invasion and penetration. Then they played out the drama and electrifying animal pleasure of fucking at its most primitive. Jack lost himself in the grip of powerful sensation as Ryan met his thrusts with desperate cries. They heaved and rose and fell, gripping and flexing until they found a perfect rhythm together. Until Jack's balls felt like they were climbing up into his throat, and he wanted to scream, to pour out passionate cries while he emptied his cock into Ryan's ass.

He took Ryan's cock in his fist, giving him pressure and friction, something to fuck into while he held Ryan's hips steady. He fucked Ryan's ass with everything he had. Jack's hips had a mind of their own, and he let them go, let himself buck and rock and plunge his dick into Ryan while Ryan practically screamed his enthusiasm.

"That's it. Come for me!" Jack shouted when Ryan's ass clamped down on Jack's cock. Jets of hot spunk filled the palm of his hand. "Oh, *yeah, yeah, yeah.* That's it."

Ryan trembled beneath him, crying out, "Jack. Ah, God, Jack."

Jack cradled Ryan's spent dick through the last of its spasms while he let himself finish, giving Ryan's ass one last shuddering stroke of his dick as his heat flooded the condom. Neither of them spoke. They lay frozen in time, locked together in the throbbing, watercolor lassitude of fucked-out repose.

At last, Jack pulled gently free. Some unexpected wave of tenderness made him lay the flat of his hand over Ryan's abused-looking ass to soothe it.

Ryan rolled over and shot him a smile so angelic—and at the same time so filthy dirty—Jack's heart did a happy flip.

"You look good like that."

Ryan stretched languidly and sighed again. "Well fucked?"

"Mm-hmm."

"How do you look when you're fucked? Am I going to find out?"

"Hell yes," Jack teased. "If you think you're man enough, you can go right ahead and start now."

Ryan smiled at him again, and goddamn if Jack wasn't ready to bend over and let Ryan give it a try. "I think I'm going to need a nice warm towel and a few minutes to recover first."

Jack bent over to pick up his cane. Every molecule in his body cried out that he'd done too much. Ligaments popped. Joints creaked. Bones ached. His dick felt like he'd left it out in the sun too long.

Is that going to stop me from enjoying everything Ryan has to offer?

Nope.

Jack gave Ryan one of his own less-than-angelic smiles. Ryan's face and upper chest turned a delicate shade of *aroused*. "I'll get that towel. You go ahead and recover."

CHAPTER 17

JACK ROLLED from the bed and rose slowly to his feet while every cell in his body sang its unique pain song. Hips definitely hurt. That made his back spasm. His thigh muscles and left knee felt like someone was tearing the muscles away from the bones. Things hadn't progressed to the place where he'd feel the pleasurable pain of a well-fucked ass, because he and Ryan had fallen into a sound, contented sleep. It wasn't likely to get that far either, as Jack had woken in agony a couple hours later. Even so, he'd lain there, debating whether he should wake Ryan and try.

Jack doubted very much he'd be able to get himself up for another round, no matter how tempting it was. The lower half of his body was so frozen if he tried anything, his legs would probably snap off at the hips like a GI Joe's.

He'd finally gotten up, because if he was standing, at least he could contemplate moving enough to find a solution—either showering to warm up his muscles or looking for more ibuprofen. Or both. But currently he was getting used to being upright, and the pain he experienced in his legs just from bearing the weight of his body took his breath away.

To distract himself, he looked out the window. He saw the whole garden from where he stood. Ryan must love his place. No wonder he wanted to do whatever he had to do to take it back and make it his sanctuary again. It was still dark outside, but landscape lighting cast pools of creamy illumination along the edges of a wide brick patio, where old-fashioned steel gliders with thick padding flanked a low glass table. Next to that, an old wooden wheelbarrow extended its usefulness as a planter, overflowing with a riot of pretty flowers in shades of red and purple and white.

Jack wondered if Ryan had planted it, or if he paid gardeners to keep the place up. It looked like a hell of a job, but Jack didn't underestimate Ryan Halloran.

Behind him on the bed, Ryan shifted beneath the covers. "Hey."

Jack turned. "Hello, Sleeping Beauty."

Ryan's smile was wry. "What a line."

"It's pretty cheesy, yeah." Jack did like looking at a sleepy Ryan, whether he meant the line or not. Ryan was attractive. He had nice bones, good skin. A face that could actually be called beautiful. "But in your case I meant it."

"Thanks." A slow blink, and then a lopsided smile. Jack saw Ryan's hand creep to his dick under the covers. "Hey, how about you get back in this bed? We could get that whole me-fucking-you thing underway."

Jack let his head drop forward onto the windowpane. "God, I wish."

"You have to go?"

"Not exactly. I just can't move," Jack admitted.

"Muscle or joint pain?" Ryan sat up and dropped his legs over the side. When he rose from the bed, Jack envied the fluid grace with which he managed it. At some point, he'd put on silky blue sleep pants. Jack was still bare-ass naked. "What hurts?"

"Everything."

"Are you stiff?"

"Yeah, and not in a good way, I'm afraid." Jack leaned against the side of Ryan's simple wooden headboard for support. "I need something for pain, and then I can stretch out. I'm sorry to be such a mess. Maybe you should just take me home."

"I'm no PT, but I can probably help. First things first, though. I'll get you another anti-inflammatory. Then we'll get you on my yoga mat, and I'll help you stretch out slowly. Okay?"

"I don't have much choice." Jack shot Ryan a rueful smile. "I'm too weak to fight."

Ryan went to the bathroom and returned with pills and a cup of water. "Take this."

"Ain't I smooth." Jack did as he was told. His sense of personal shame took a backseat to pain. "I'll bet you wish all your dates required medical attention in the middle of the night. Talk about taking your work home with you."

"Shit happens, so just knock it off. Didn't you ever get a charley horse right in the thick of things?"

Jack laughed. "Sure. But I never had a whole-body horse."

"Can you bend over just a little and put your hands on the bed?"

"Uh..." Jack gave that a try. "No. Back's spasming."

"We could try a couple of things." Ryan let his strong fingers explore a path down Jack's spine and feather out to the tops of his hips. Jack's muscles clenched like a vise, crushing his spine, shortening his breath. "Yeah. You're tight."

"Kinda," Jack choked out.

Ryan opened the drawer of his nightstand. "Kevin left a couple blunts. I don't usually smoke, but sometimes people like to, so—"

"What?" Jack wasn't sure he'd heard right.

Ryan held out a small box with three hand-rolled cigarettes in it. "I think you should smoke one of these, and afterwards I'll see if I can't get your muscles to loosen up."

"I..." Jack's mouth snapped shut. "Really?"

"Is there any reason you'd get in trouble if you do? Drug testing? Allergies? Are you likely to exhibit reefer madness and go on a crime spree?"

"Uh, no." Jack didn't think so. He'd experimented as a kid. Actually, compared to some of the shit he'd taken for pain after the accident, a little pot seemed pretty mild.

Ryan handed him a blunt and held up a lighter. Jack let Ryan light him up because he figured things couldn't get worse. He couldn't fucking move.

Jack took that first familiar drag and held it in his lungs—not until he was going to burst or anything, but long enough for the drug to start relaxing him—then blew it out in a thin stream.

"Thanks. God, it's been forever since I've done this."

Ryan handed him an ashtray. "Blow out the window, please, as much as you can."

Jack did as Ryan asked and tried to send his air outside. "Is Kevin going to be mad I'm smoking his stash?"

"I doubt he'll remember he left it."

"Is he going to be mad I'm fucking his boyfriend?"

"Are you fucking Kevin's boyfriend? I had no idea. Whoever he is, you can tell him 'Good luck' from me, 'cause I've been Kevin's boyfriend, and it's no picnic."

"You're not seeing him?"

"No." Ryan gave his head a shake. "The other night was desperation."

Jack nodded.

"What are you going to tell Detective Dave? Because he surely put two and two together at the funeral."

"It's fine. According to Dave, it's fine." Jack turned a worried look Ryan's way. "You can't let Dave know I said anything about him and me."

"He's in the closet. I get it."

"No. He makes all the closeted gay men I know look out and proud."

"There are other gay cops around here."

"Not according to Dave." Jack took another hit. He could already feel his muscles loosen up. His head felt light, as if his brain were distancing itself from his body on a long string, like a balloon. "How do you know that? About the other cops, I mean."

Ryan rolled his eyes. "How do you think?"

"Oh." The thought of Ryan sampling the local gay law enforcement buffet didn't sit right with Jack, but he couldn't exactly say why. Jack blew his smoke out the window again. The breeze blew some of it back in. Between tokes, he inhaled a deep, cleansing breath of fresh air. "Thanks for this. It seems to be helping."

"Take another drag or three, and we'll see if I can bend you a little."

Jack blinked slowly. He had to fight the urge to smile. God, Ryan's herb was working really well. He moved away from the headboard he'd been leaning against to test his body's limitations. It felt like he could finally get enough air. He might even be able to bend his knee without the fiery blast of pain he'd learned to live with. He flexed his toes and calves and lowered his shoulders one at a time. He took a deep breath and breathed it out in a long, relieved sigh.

"I feel better." Another hit, and a cloud of smoke came out with his next words. "Much better."

"Out the window, please." Ryan's smile was indulgent. Jack took one last drag, this time for pure pleasure, and held it for a few seconds before blowing a thin blue stream out the window.

He'd stopped fighting a grin. "Wow."

"Feeling it?"

"Yeah."

"What's it like?"

"I could probably do the splits if you put a bowl of crunchy cheese puffs on the floor."

"I'll get a mat, and we'll see how it goes." Ryan buffeted Jack's arm as he walked past. He went to the closet and brought out an honest-to-God yoga mat, which he spread out on the floor. "I'm going to lay this down here next to the bed. It's more cushioned than it looks."

"I don't stand a chance of getting down on the floor just yet." Jack ground out the blunt and left it in the ashtray. No point in overdoing a good thing.

Ryan got to his knees and smoothed the mat out. "In the absence of cheese puffs, I'll find a way to help you get down."

"Get *down*," Jack intoned. Weed made certain words taste more fun than others. *Get down* was not just fun but funky too. He was James Brown. He couldn't do the moves, but he could sure as hell say the words. "Good God, y'all. Ima get *doooown*."

"Take it easy, Sex Machine." Ryan's amused voice came from right next to Jack's ear. "I'll help you."

"How? I don't bend that way anymore."

"We're going to take it nice and slow." Ryan stood behind him. "Like a trust fall. Can you do that?"

"What's a trust fall?"

"You just let yourself go. Fall backward. I'll catch you and take it from there. Do you trust me?"

"I was going to let you stick your dick up my ass."

"This is going to be harder."

"Harder than your dick?"

"No." Ryan laughed. "Nothing's harder than my dick, baby. Maybe I should say this is going to be scarier. You just do as I say, okay? Lean back... Keep going. That's it. I've got you."

God, it was tough. Jack had to let his body go, lean back, and trust that he wasn't going to crash to the floor, even though for the briefest few seconds it felt exactly like that, like he was going to just keep falling and plunge over backward and break his neck.

But suddenly Ryan was there, just when Jack was most afraid. Right after he'd lost confidence in himself and faith in everything else, a pair of strong arms wrapped around his rib cage and slowed his fall. It stopped his descent and cushioned his landing, and then he was lying down with his back against Ryan's chest, panting hard, but no longer because he was scared.

Because he was relieved that his faith in Ryan wasn't misplaced.

"I've got you," Ryan said again, unnecessarily. "Okay?"

Jack's answer came out as a half sob. "Yeah."

Ryan helped him to his back and then crawled around him to sit by his feet. "I'm going to stretch out your legs. You know your body and what you can take. I'll need you to tell me where I need to stop here, all right?"

Jack cleared his throat. "All right."

Like he did it every day, Ryan lifted Jack's right leg and started putting him through range-of-motion exercises. Jack let him know what his limits were, but Ryan watched his face, taking his cues as much from Jack's expression as from Jack's words.

"There. Ow." Jack winced. Right away Ryan let up. He helped Jack bend his knee and pressed his whole leg down to stretch Jack's hamstring. "How come you're doing this for me?"

"It needs doing."

"I feel very disconnected from my body right now."

"That's the weed talking."

Jack snorted. "Weed talks like Al Pacino."

"You're a lightweight."

"Of course I am. I haven't smoked since high school."

"I guess you smoked with Nick."

"Yeah."

"So you have some good memories too, yeah?" Ryan didn't look up when he said that but kept his eyes down, focusing on Jack's knee, the left one this time. "Not just the bad, right?"

"Sure." Jack winced again. "That's enough there."

Ryan let up. "Do you feel like you can put your past with Nick behind you now? Did you get closure?"

"Yeah. Maybe." Jack didn't want to talk about Nick.

"Because I have to tell you. I thought I knew how you felt about Nick until his memorial. Now I'm not sure I know anything."

"That's... Stop. That's tender." Jack put his hand up to keep Ryan from bending his knee farther. His head hurt from thinking. "I don't know anything, but I don't suppose it matters anymore. I don't know what closure really is."

"I underestimated your damage. He wounded you. More than anything that happened after."

"Old headline." Jack took in a deep breath just as Ryan picked up both his legs and rocked his knees side to side.

"This should help unlock that clenching spasm in your back."

Jack's eyes watered, but he went along with it. In a way, it did help. His back felt looser. "Okay. Yeah. That is better."

If better *is the right word. For now, I don't feel so much like screaming.*

Ryan helped Jack let his legs down gently and crawled over to lie down next to him. He lay on his side with his head resting on his crooked arm so he could look at Jack, who stared up at the ceiling.

Jack was enjoying his fabulous flatness. He felt the whole length of his body along the floor with the gratitude of the newly unknotted. Just then he could have melted right there in marijuana-induced *happy* and disappeared through the floorboards.

"I guess what I need to ask is how much of this"—Ryan gestured between them—"is because I look like my cousin."

Ryan's eyes held serious concern. Jack could see that. It wouldn't be enough to blow the question off with a laugh. It wouldn't be enough to simply say he was attracted to Ryan and Nick's type, because while that was the truth, it was an oversimplification.

At the same time, Ryan's face was inches away. The faint light created interesting highlights and shadows, and the difference was obvious. Two different people lived inside similar shells.

When Ryan was engaged in something, when he was thinking, feeling, laughing, loving, his expression was open, generous, and tender. He couldn't have been more unlike Nick in those moments if he tried. It was as if an artist used the same medium to create two wholly different works of art.

Jack lifted his hands and moved his fingers over each of Ryan's features like a man reading Braille.

"Your features are the same." He thumbed the straight ridges of Ryan's pale brows, traced a line down Ryan's nose, and followed the Cupid's bow of his lips. "And your coloring."

"I know, but—"

"But Nick had a scar right here at the outside of his lip on the left that he got falling off a bike when we were eight."

Ryan's lips closed into a tight line.

"And his ears weren't pierced. Yours are, even though you don't wear earrings," Jack continued. "He had a scar over his right eye he got on a fence when we were sophomores. Your aunt had a fit, and they called in a plastic surgeon. He took that jagged laceration and left the finest, smallest white scar."

Ryan's expression was vulnerable now, and Jack's heart hurt for him. He wasn't sure he could come up with any words that would make things right. Certainly not while he was baked, but it wasn't the time for half-truths or platitudes.

"I loved Nick my whole life."

Ryan's Adam's apple bobbed, and his lashes swept down. A wry expression—a conciliatory, well-better-luck-next-time smile framed his words. "Thank you for telling me that."

"I'm not done." Jack cupped the sides of Ryan's face and gave it a small squeeze. "I have no illusions that I could replace Nick even if I wanted to, which I don't. But I have no trouble telling you apart. I may have loved him from my heart, from deep inside my gut, but I like you better. What I know of you, anyway. I'd like to find out more."

Ryan's intake of breath was as surprised as the flicker of sensual interest in his eyes. "Maybe we should go back to bed now."

"I'm not up to more than sleeping. I did enjoy falling asleep with you, which is...unusual for me." Jack wondered if Ryan knew how unusual.

"That's okay. I think I'll like waking up with you," Ryan admitted. "As unusual as that might be for both of us."

CHAPTER 18

JACK SAW Dave's SUV when Ryan pulled into his driveway to drop him off. It was still early Sunday morning, but obviously Dave had been there for a while. He sat on the porch, sipping a cup of coffee. He wore jeans and a V-neck T-shirt under a brown leather jacket. He looked casual and handsome, but his face was expressionless behind his shades.

Jack read unhappiness in the set of Dave's shoulders, but he doubted anyone who didn't know him intimately would see it. *He looks like trouble.*

Ryan asked, "Did you guys have a thing this morning?"

"No." Jack's heart sank a little. "We didn't have plans that I know of."

"Should I just let you off here?"

"I promised you breakfast after I feed the cat."

"It's all right. I can just go."

"We had plans. If I have a *thing* this morning, it's with you."

Ryan pushed his door open and stepped out with one foot. "All right."

Jack exited the car on his side and pulled out his cane. He

wished he'd filled his hidden flask after all. Dave remained silent and watchful as they walked up. Dave was a detective. He probably couldn't fail to notice Jack was wearing his funeral suit from the day before.

"Hey, Dave," Jack said as he got out his house keys. "Did you forget where I keep the spare?"

"No," Dave answered.

"Hey, Detective Huntley. Day off?"

"Yeah." Dave's face gave nothing away.

Jack looked him over. "Are you going undercover on *NCIS: Los Angeles*?"

"Very funny," said Dave.

"You do have that hipster LEO vibe today," Ryan agreed.

"Right." Dave got up from where he sat on the steps. He stumbled a little and reached out for the railing to steady himself.

Definitely trouble.

Jack eyed him warily. "We're about to have some breakfast. Want to join us?"

"Maybe a little more coffee. I'm almost out." Dave turned to Ryan. "Gabe said you were having breakfast here yesterday too. Did they close the pancake house?"

"*Dave,*" Jack growled in warning. "What are you doing here?"

"What do you mean, what am *I* doing here?" Dave's eyebrows rose above his shades. "Did you open a restaurant you didn't tell me about?"

Ryan stepped forward. "Jack is asking if you're always an asshole this early in the morning."

"Whoa there, Ryan. It's okay." Jack gripped Dave by the arm and led him up the stairs to his front door. "Everyone needs to eat something, starting with my cat."

"'S not your cat," Dave slurred. "You don't have a cat."

"She's my cat today." Jack keyed the lock and pushed Dave in ahead of him. Tasha came out of nowhere and danced around their feet, inviting disaster. "Don't step on her."

"She's a frisky little thing." Dave avoided her.

Ryan walked in behind them and picked Tasha up. "If you tell me where her food is, I'll get it."

"In the pantry cupboard," said Jack. "Can opener's in the drawer by the sink."

"Got it." Ryan walked past them with very much the same expression Tasha wore, slightly put out but willing to be mollified should Jack begin his groveling now and do it exactly right.

"What the hell are you doing?" he asked Dave as soon as he heard Ryan moving around in the kitchen.

"What does it look like I'm doing? I'm here for one of your *famous* breakfasts. I'll take one of those two-by-two-by-two-by-two things. Sausage, bacon, eggs, and pancakes. I like my bacon crisp. Like my men. Almost burned but not quite, and sure the hell not *twice*."

"I have no idea what you're talking about right now."

"I'm talking about what you're *not* talking about." Dave sat down in Jack's leather recliner and tilted it back slightly. He shook his coffee cup. "Have you ever heard of an Aqualung? That's coffee, coffee liqueur, chocolate syrup, and vodka. I'll have another one of those, please."

"You will not." Jack raked his hand through his hair. "Is this about Ryan? Are you fucking falling apart over him or what? Yesterday, you said—"

"I pick"—Dave's grin was almost cruel—"*or what*."

What the hell? Jack's eyes burned. "Who the fuck are you, and what have you done with my *friend*?"

"That's the million-dollar question, Jack. Do you even know who your *friends* are? 'Cause I do. We're the ones who stuck behind you when you were nearly killed on two separate occasions."

Jack glanced at the kitchen before speaking. "Dave..."

Dave thumped his chest. "Me and Gabe and Eddie are the ones who pulled you from the wreckage after Nick screwed you over. We carried you home when you were too drunk to fuck. We hauled puke buckets and made excuses to your family and your employers, and we stayed with you some nights because we were afraid you were so fucking depressed you wouldn't wake up the next morning."

Jack stood over Dave, both hands on the arms of his chair, pinning him in. "Now you wait just a damn minute. I was never—"

"*We're* the ones who sat in the hospital with you for months. We prayed and cried and begged God to let you walk again. We're the ones who drove you to PT and sweated every bullet with you while you were in agony."

"That is so fucking unfair. Have I not been grateful enough? Is that what this is? Wait. Are you jealous?"

"Jealous?" All the color leached from Dave's face. "Why would I be jealous? Because you've got a do-over with cousin look-alike, so it's all good?"

"I can't believe you even said that." Ryan stood framed by the kitchen door, pale as a ghost.

"This isn't about jealousy." Dave pushed Jack out of the way. Jack leaned on his cane while Dave faced Ryan down, hands on his hips. "It's about the truth. And it's time someone told it."

Jack tried to get between them. "It isn't your truth, Dave. How many times do I have to tell you?"

Dave shoved him aside again. Jack had to scrabble for balance, grabbing on to the recliner's cushioned backrest to stay upright. "I don't care whose truth you think it is. Someone's got to set the record straight."

Jack tensed, hand clenching into a fist. "I'm warning you, Dave."

"You can't threaten me like you did Gabe. You and me were over before we started, but Gabe? You broke his fucking heart. You're business partners. You're *family*, for God's sake."

"I'll apologize to Gabe." Jack knew he'd crossed the line with his cousin. "Go home, Dave."

Dave shook his head. "Not this time. This shit is not right. Someone has to say something, and if it isn't going to be you, it's going to be someone who loves you. Someone like me, who doesn't have anything left to lose."

"Please," Jack said brokenly. "Don't."

"You want to know why your cousin and his pals beat the crap out of Jack in high school?" asked Dave.

Jack moaned. "*Dave—*"

"Because he was an asshole," Ryan answered, sure of himself. "Because Jack outed Nick, and he didn't want to look gay in front of his jock friends. Nick and his friends beat and nearly—"

"Jack, you tell him now, or I will," Dave ordered implacably. "Last chance."

Jack couldn't speak. He couldn't breathe. His pulse drummed in his ears. He could barely hear what Dave said to him.

Dave's disappointment was evident from the set of his shoulders. He pierced Jack with his cold gaze, then turned to Ryan. "Jack and Nick were *lovers*. Nick made him a shit ton of promises he never intended to keep, and when it looked like Jack wanted to come out, Nick decided to teach him a lesson. Jack got played, man. He got used and shamed and beaten because he believed his *lover*, the boy who'd been his first and only for *years*."

Ryan's jaw dropped, and he turned to Jack. "Is this true?"

Jack's stomach roiled. He blinked the tears away to clear his vision. "It's not what—"

Dave interrupted, determined to tell the bitter truth at last. "Jack asked Nick to the prom. That's all. He asked his secret boyfriend to go to the prom, and what he got for it was..." He shook his head. "You know the rest."

"Oh, Jack," whispered Ryan.

Instead of making things better, this newly deflated Ryan, with his pity words and sympathetic eyes, made everything so much worse. Jack wanted to drop through a hole in the floor, to be swallowed up inside the ancient crawl space under his crappy house and die.

"Nick was furious," Dave continued, "because Jack humiliated him in front of his friends. They dragged Jack to the alley behind the Fox Theater and took turns beating on him. Someone had the brilliant idea to bring a broom handle along, and Nick said *nothing* in Jack's defense. They stripped some of Jack's clothes off him, but he fought for his life. If one of the busboys from Angelo's and Vinci's hadn't been outside smoking, if he hadn't shouted he was calling the police, Jack probably wouldn't have survived."

"God, stop." Ryan covered his ears, but Dave advanced on him like an avenging angel to peel his hands away. "Stop."

Ryan was tough and sure-footed. He danced away, but Dave was well trained, and he fought dirty. In no time, Dave had Ryan by the shoulders, backed against the wall. Dave forced Ryan to hear him out.

Jack remained frozen, cold fingers gripping the chair.

"It took months for Jack to heal from his physical wounds." Dave glanced at Jack. "He's nowhere near over the wounds you can't see."

There was no ticking clock to mark the time as Jack waited for something more to happen. His horrified silence lasted so long he had the chance to watch Ryan regain control of his breathing. Of his expression. Shock turned to pity—the last thing Jack wanted or needed.

"Just go, Dave," Jack said woodenly. "Just shut the fuck up and go."

"*No.*" The word burst from Dave. "You don't get to tell me to shut up this time. Nick hurt us all. Why the hell do you think I—" Dave's mouth snapped shut. "What Nick did to you hurt everyone around you. You just don't see that."

Jack could only stand there mute. He'd really underestimated Dave. He hadn't seen the truth behind Dave's behavior until now, how one hateful act could be a stone cast into a still body of water. Jack wasn't the only one to be rocked by its ripples, to be caught unaware years later and dragged under by the powerful waves that stone precipitated.

"I didn't know," Jack whispered.

"Maybe I didn't either." Dave swallowed. He glared at Ryan. "Funny how something can trigger a painful memory."

"I have to go." Before Jack or Dave could stop him, Ryan shot between them.

Jack damned his legs as he tried to follow. "Ryan. *Wait.*"

Ryan ran from the house and down the porch steps. He got to his car and slipped inside before Jack even made it to the porch.

"Ryan!" Jack called out.

Ryan slammed the door shut and, just like that, took off. Jack closed his eyes when he felt Dave's hand on his shoulder.

"Did you imagine I'd thank you for that?"

"Nope." Dave pulled out his phone and headed down the steps, leaving Jack standing on the porch by himself.

Jack watched Dave walk past his truck and down the street, watched until he turned the corner and disappeared from sight. He was probably calling Gabe for a ride. Whatever Dave was, he was always going to be a cop first, and he would never drink and drive.

Jack stared at the quiet street, at the view he'd looked at for the whole of his life.

That was it, then. His secret was out. Jack's secret. Nick's. Maybe Dave's too. Probably Jack's secret had built up and up over the years, creating a wellspring of darkness inside all of them.

Jack thought he'd been carrying it alone. But obviously not.

He turned and walked up the stairs.

Inside, he found Tasha waiting for him with big, unimpressed eyes. Her expression asked, *What did you expect? A happily ever after with the uncrowned prince of Sunny Hills? That you'd lay your private ghost to rest, and bibbidi, bobbidi he'd disappear in a cloud of lavender smoke like so much Disney magic?*

That you could go to sleep for once in your life and wake up with something good?

Twenty-six painful steps took him to his bathroom and the bottle of Percocet that waited for him there. He dry-swallowed as many as his doctor said he could safely take and then washed them down with a mouthful of water from the sink. After, he settled on his bed, and Tasha jumped up to lie in the crook of his elbow, her nose nuzzled right up to his heart.

Even Tasha was borrowed from someone else. She wouldn't be there in his empty future, where he'd wake up every single morning, alone.

Why had that empty future never bothered him before when just now, loneliness seemed so unpromising?

How did a couple days of uncomplicated fun with Ryan change things so much?

Jack closed his eyes.

First-date playlists. Dinner out. Driving a car with a man sleeping softly beside him. Hot sex. Playful banter. Even stretching out his sore muscles with company was fun.

Ryan was *fun.*

Jack smiled. Ryan was *play.* Ryan was unassuming and positive and lighthearted, despite being an acolyte to St. Jude and all the lost causes he attracted to himself. Ryan was happiness—at least he had the capacity for it. Just thinking about Ryan's smile, which seemed unlike Nick's enough to have come from a different man altogether, untwisted something inside Jack more than the drugs did.

He grabbed his phone off the nightstand.

Before he could forget exactly how he felt right then, before he let the drugs pull him into the painless oblivion of sleep, he needed to call Ryan to remind him of what he'd said the night before.

Dave had unloaded on them both. And even though Dave's words had been true, they were awfully goddamned harsh. Jack had told the truth the night before—or as much of the truth as he'd allowed himself to tell.

Jack rang Ryan's phone, and of course it went straight to voice mail.

Of course it did, because nothing good is ever easy.

Beep.

"Dave wasn't supposed to tell my truth like that. I don't know if I'd have carried it to my grave, but I like to think I would have. I like to see myself as the kind of guy who wouldn't out a man who is unable to respond. I like to see myself as a man who can live with his foolish choices and not ruin someone else's reputation more than they already ruined it, because I'm *better than that.* What Nick and his friends did to me, the punishment they did or didn't receive for it, the lies Nick did or didn't tell, *that's all on him.*

"I don't know how long this will let me talk, but I told you my truth last night. I buried my heart with my pride a long time ago.

"I could never, ever mistake you for Nick. I would cross the street to avoid him if he were still alive, but if I could have, I'd have run alongside your car, begging you to come back and listen to me all the way to that big house you live in.

"This isn't the last message I'll leave. That wasn't the last time you'll see me. I'm coming after you. I just go...slow."

Jack let the call end. He curled up around Tasha and let her purr him into a faintly pleasant buzz. This had to be the worst he'd ever felt in a lifetime of pretty bad shit. He closed his eyes and sighed as the medication began to separate him from his body for a while.

"Oh, Tasha. How low can we go?"

CHAPTER 19

DAWN CRACKED through the blinds in Jack's room when he woke up on Monday morning. He checked his phone. No calls from Ryan. He had the nagging feeling he was going to have to work hard for what he wanted. He was going to have to prove it was Ryan's heart, and not his face, that mattered.

Piece of cake, Jack thought wryly before he let his head drop back on the pillow.

He reached for his phone to call Gabe.

"Christ, it's early." Gabe answered on the first ring. "Does this mean you're speaking to me again, coz?"

"I'm calling, aren't I? Did you buy your new car?"

"Yeah, and she's awesome. I got the SS with the performance package in black. You should see her. Sweet."

"As a matter of fact, I've got somewhere I need to go, but I don't want to go by myself. You got time to take me for a spin?"

"Now? Yeah, even though you acted like a douche bag, I'm free as long as it includes coffee."

Jack wanted to chuck the phone against the wall. *Family*, you had to love it. "How'd I act like a douche bag?"

"You don't put your new squeeze before your old friends, Jack. Not ever."

"What are you talking about?" Jack asked. "I never—"

"The hell you didn't. You got pissed at me other day, and now Dave's all busted up. We aren't going to lie to Ryan for you, and we aren't going to shut up if we see you making the same dumb mistakes over and over again. You're family, but you crossed a line."

"All right. I know," Jack admitted miserably. "I was stupid to think I could keep the truth from Ryan. But in my defense, I didn't know how much I'd like him. "

"You've gotta ask yourself, do you like him because he looks like Nick? The mere fact that you refused to tell him the truth makes it seem like you got some fucked-up baggage."

"Of course it does. But I kept the truth from Ryan *because* he looks like Nick. I didn't want him thinking that's why I'm into him. Now he's going to believe his looks are the reason no matter what I say."

"That's what we were trying to tell you."

"You were right. What can I say?"

Gabe snorted softly. "This is one for the record books. Now I wish I'd taken Dave's bet you'd apologize. I didn't figure you'd ever get around to that."

"Right, well..."

"I'll be over in twenty minutes. You'd better have coffee. I'll bring my travel mug. Maybe we can grab breakfast before work while we're out."

"Okay." Jack disconnected the call. He sat up and let his legs down over the side of the bed only to find Tasha staring at him from the floor by his feet.

"What?" he asked her before he got up and headed into the bathroom. She was still waiting outside the door when he came back out.

"You're hungry, huh? Let's go do something about that." Tasha followed him into the kitchen where he opened a can of food to fill her bowl. She accepted the food as her due, not bothering to glance up at him in thanks.

Jack wondered if Tasha would even be there after he got back with Gabe. Skippy was supposed to be coming over to get her, wasn't he?

He was really going to miss that cat.

Jack hurried to get dressed. He had only seconds to spare before Gabe knocked on the door.

"Hey." Jack smiled at him. "That was quick."

Gabe shrugged and held out his travel mug. "Hey, coz."

"Thanks for coming." Jack took the mug to the kitchen and filled it. He shoved his keys and wallet in his pocket and picked up his cane.

The happily-soon-to-be caffeinated Gabe held the door for him. "Okay, so where do we need to go?"

Jack told Gabe where he wanted to go, and got into his new car, prepared to listen to whatever lecture Gabe was preparing to deliver.

When they pulled into the gates at Fairhaven Cemetery thirty minutes later, Jack was still trying to defend his attraction to Ryan.

"I don't know." Jack wrapped his jacket tighter around him. "It's complicated."

Gabe appeared bent on pursuing the subject. "You can't recapture the past. Even if things come out right this time."

Jack gave an irritated shake of his head. "I know that. Don't you think I know that?"

"Then why does it have to be Ryan Halloran?" Gabe asked. "Why can't you find a nice guy who has nothing to do with Nick at all?"

"I don't deny Ryan flips my switch physically," Jack argued, "but I don't see Nick when I look at Ryan."

"Seeing not-Nick is just as bad. Thinking *this guy is nothing like Nick* still puts Nick in the picture. Until Nick's nowhere near the picture, you need to be careful. That's all Dave and I were trying to say. We're sorry we ruined things between you and Ryan, but we're right about this."

"No, I'm sorry." Jack made himself own up. "Ryan deserved the truth. I should have told him myself from the very beginning. Now I have to fix things between us, even if he doesn't want to hear it."

"Fine." Gabe turned the radio on and tipped his chair back. "Wake me when you're done with your emo garbage. It's too early for this shit."

"All right." Jack got out and made his way across the damp grass, past rows and rows of markers to Nick's grave. The flowers from his memorial, a formal affair, stood on a tripod next to the grave.

Jack leaned on his cane there for a long time, thinking over everything that had happened.

Why had he kept silent all those years? Was it really to protect Nick? Or was it something more, something less admirable? Was keeping the world from learning the sad, sick truth about Nick simply Jack's way of copping an attitude? Was it some show of superiority?

Keeping Nick's secrets had been Jack's curse as well as a manifestation of loyalty Nick didn't deserve.

Surely after so long, Jack could loosen his death grip on the old news that Nick had abused him sexually and emotionally, that he'd abused Jack's trust and betrayed him horribly.

Jack took a long, deep breath.

"This is it, Nick." Jack was dry-eyed at last. Clearheaded. "This is the last time I look back. I hope wherever you are..."

Jack left the rest unsaid, afraid of what he might have said if he'd completed the sentence. He let the thought go. That was what *not looking back* was all about, wasn't it? Letting things go unsaid. Letting things go, in general.

Jack turned back to the car where Gabe waited, and was shocked to see Ryan heading along the path toward him. Ryan was dressed casually in jeans and a hooded sweatshirt, carrying flowers. Sunlight glinted off his hair, off the sparks of red and gold in his beard, making him appear lit from within.

Ryan gaped at Jack, surprise written on his features as he hesitated, then came forward.

"Small world," Ryan called out.

The sight of Ryan coming toward him caused a funny roiling inside Jack, like Ryan was sunshine and he made Jack bloom inside. Ryan did more than just lift Jack's cock. Jack craved his warmth.

Ryan had begun to fill something inside Jack that had been empty for way, way too long.

"Hey," Jack said finally when they were face-to-face.

"Hey. I brought these for Nick." Ryan placed a small bouquet of flowers on Nick's grave. He looked like he felt as awkward as Jack did. "I figured no one else would, except maybe his folks."

Jack nodded. He hadn't thought to do it. "Going back to work tomorrow?"

"No. I'm taking a few more days off."

"I'm working later. I just thought I'd visit Nick's grave since we didn't after the memorial." *Duh, Captain Obvious.* "You...uh... doing all right? At the house, I mean."

Ryan nodded. "I think so. I slept okay last night. Early days."

Jack nodded. At that rate, they were going to stand there like bobblehead dolls forever. "I suppose—"

"I wanted you to know—"

Jack laughed. "You first."

Ryan shrugged. "I want you to know, I understand why you didn't tell me the truth about Nick."

"I wish I had, now."

"I wish you had too. I'm not sure I'd have—"

Jack started to reach out for Ryan, but the unhappy expression on his face told Jack he didn't have the right. "I swear. You're not some kind of substitute for Nick. Dave was dead wrong about that."

Ryan seemed to search for the truth in Jack's eyes. "I don't know..."

Jack held Ryan's gaze, letting him look his fill. Jack had nothing left to hide. "It's possible being with you, thinking about Nick, reminded me of some things I'd forgotten. I won't lie to you about that."

"I'm sorry," Ryan said softly.

"Don't be. It wasn't all bad. I was a different person back then."

"Weren't we all? I was a Q-tip with braces."

"Yeah. I guess." Jack had been pretty goofy back then too. "But I thought about things differently. I believed in things. I didn't remember that until—"

Ryan lifted his hand and cupped Jack's face. His thumb brushed Jack's lower lip, causing a tingle Jack felt down to his balls. "You can't get back what Nick took, you know? Not with me, not with anyone."

"I know." Dave and Gabe might have to knock some sense into him about other things, but Jack knew that much at least. "But—"

"So that's good, anyway, right?" Ryan dropped his hand to dig impatiently in the pocket of his hoodie for his keys. "You learned something."

Jack saw what he hoped for start to spin away from him again. "Yeah. But I need to tell you—"

"Stop." Ryan laid his hand on Jack's arm. "I'm really sorry my cousin hurt you. Really. You will never know how badly I wish things could be different."

"Wait," Jack said stupidly as Ryan started to walk away from him. "Things *are* different."

"Take care of yourself, Jack," Ryan said over his shoulder.

Jack stood there, watching Ryan go. Again.

Jack's heart said, *Run after him.*

Jack's body said, *If you let Ryan Halloran leave without fixing this thing between you, whatever it is, you'll be sorry for the rest of your life.*

His body was like that. All or nothing.

Ryan walked away—at an awfully brisk pace, the bastard—and Jack knew it was futile to try to catch up.

It would be futile to try anything while Ryan was angry and feeling freshly insulted. While he was still fuming over the fact that Jack hadn't given him the entire truth, rather than focusing on how much fun they'd had together.

"Ryan Halloran!" Jack's voice thundered over the stretch of ground between them. Ryan had reached his car and had a hand on the door latch.

He turned with a frown on his face.

"So. I'll call you, okay?" asked Jack feebly.

Ryan gave an indelicate snort before he got in his car and slammed the door shut. Jack watched Ryan's sleek little hybrid drive away.

Gabe's new ride pulled up next to the curb where Jack stood. The window on the shiny black beast caught the light like the glint in a predator's eye. It rolled down as Jack heard the door unlock.

"That was real smooth, Jack," Gabe leaned over to tell him. "It's a wonder you're not happily married by now."

"I told you. It's complicated." Jack opened door and climbed back into Gabe's car. After he seat-belted himself in, he took out his phone and dialed Ryan's number.

"Don't tell me. Are you calling him again?"

"Yes," Jack said tightly.

"Stalker. You've either lost your mind or become the most annoying guy ever. Why don't you wait a week or so? Give the man a break."

"He doesn't need a break. He needs a reason to believe I like him for who he is, not who he resembles."

"How much clearer can you make things? What if he's just not that into you?"

"Oh, please." Jack ignored that possibility. "Obviously I just haven't said the magic words yet."

Gabe tried to take Jack's phone, but Jack clung to it like a limpet. "You're going to end up on the wrong side of a restraining order."

"Maybe."

"Just wait." Gabe pulled into an empty parking space where they could talk. "You don't do this, Jack. This isn't you. Where is all this relationship shit coming from?"

"I don't know." Jack finally let go of his phone. Gabe gave it cursory look, thumbing through his call logs. Jack felt embarrassment creep over him. Taken at face value, the number of times he'd called Ryan probably looked excessive.

"Holy cow." Gabe checked out Jack's unanswered text messages. "You really like this Ryan guy *that* much?"

"No." Jack shook his head, and then nodded. "Yeah. Well. I don't know, do I? We've only known each other for a couple days."

"So what is all this? Why the hell can't you let this go?"

"I had *fun* with Ryan, Gabe." Jack unclenched his fists and rubbed his palms over his thighs. "Real fun. Even though every time I looked at him, I remembered all the reasons why I shouldn't get involved and all the reasons I can't trust people."

"Are you kidding me?" Gabe frowned at him. "Then why—"

"It made me realize all the ways Nick marked me—not just physically, but all over everything I am. I haven't felt right, haven't felt trust, haven't believed in anything *at all* since he fucked me over. I think cleaning up that last mess Nick made helped me pull my head out."

Gabe peered right into Jack's eyes. "So. You feel like you're healing, finally."

"Maybe that. Or maybe not. It doesn't matter, because I'm moving on."

"And Ryan made you see all that."

"I like who I am when I'm with Ryan." Jack held his hand out for his phone. "It doesn't have to mean more than that. I only want the opportunity to find out."

"All right." Gabe handed Jack his phone. "But seriously. If you don't hear back from him in a couple days, cut your losses, all right? We'll go out, get drunk, get laid, and forget all about both Nick and Ryan. All right?"

"It's a promise."

Jack pressed the Call button and waited for Ryan's voice mail. "Ryan, this is Jack. You ran off before I had the chance to tell you I like you. I want you to go out with me. It has nothing to do with Nick and everything to do with how much fun I have when we're together. The problem is, I don't think I'm a lost cause after all. I think I'm well and truly not lost, and if you want to know what it feels like to go out with a guy like that, I'll be right here. Waiting. As long as it takes."

Jack hung up.

Gabe glanced over at him and back to the road. "That was good," he said grudgingly.

Jack shrugged. "It's funny how easy it is to say what you mean when it's true."

CHAPTER 20

BY WEDNESDAY, Jack had pretty much lost hope he'd hear from Ryan again. That was the way all the big drama in his life played out. Sometimes he had a breakthrough moment, and where there should have been cheering and a ticker-tape parade, there was only the eternal, endless *ticktock* of his mother's ancient analog clocks.

For some reason, he'd heard nothing from Skippy either, which meant Tasha still roamed free on Jack's kitchen tiles. She twined around his legs as he opened a can from a freshly purchased supply of cat food. He was her human. The transformation was complete.

"Skippy's not answering my texts, Tash. What do you suppose that means? I know he's been at work."

Before Tasha tucked into her grub, she gave Jack a look that said, *Skippy, who?*

"He'll show up tomorrow for sure, because it's payday. Then he'll probably collect you."

I'm gonna miss you like you were my very own vibrating, foot-warming font of wisdom.

Tasha's gray-blue tail waved like a flag.

A knock on Jack's front door interrupted his thoughts, and he went to answer. For whatever reason, he wasn't surprised to find Dave standing there, looking damn uncomfortable. Gabe probably put him up to coming over with an apology.

"Hey." Jack opened the door so Dave could enter.

"Hi." Dave stepped in. He wasn't the kind of guy to wring his hands, but the way he kept them in his back pockets, the way he seemed to make a study of the lettering on Jack's T-shirt, said he was probably feeling like an asshole.

Jack let him stew.

"I, uh"—Dave wrapped one hand around the back of his neck —"felt like I ought to come by here and apologize."

Jack nodded. "Thank you."

"It wasn't a jealous thing, or... You know. Me and Gabe figured telling Ryan about you and Nick would be a sort of intervention."

"Yeah?"

"And..." Dave swallowed hard. "Fuck it, Jack. Maybe I should have done things differently."

Jack toed a spot on the floor where he'd found a hair ball earlier in the day. "You're probably right."

"Anyway. I'm sorry." Dave finally glanced up, meeting Jack's gaze. "You want to go get a drink or something?"

"I—"

"I don't mean...a sex thing."

Jack took pity on him. "Maybe you can come in and have a drink here. Watch a game?"

"Yeah." Dave's smile looked relieved. "Yeah. Okay. What's on?"

"I was getting ready to find something."

"All right." Dave checked his watch. "It's dinnertime. Should I order pizza?"

"That would be awesome. I didn't even shop today, except for cat food. We could invite Gabe and Eddie over, if they're free. Play a game of cards later?"

"Perfect." Dave smiled happily at him.

"You get pizza; I'll call the guys."

The rest of the evening passed pleasantly. Familiarly. Going through the motions, playing cards, drinking, eating pizza and wings, seemed so normal. No one talked about work. No one brought up the past or the pain in it. Even though they were all aware Jack was changing inside, no one asked him about his plans for the future.

Even Jack wasn't sure what he planned to do after he said good night to his three best friends.

Jack only knew how glad he was to have good friends.

He could build the rest of the life he wanted from a solid place like that.

<hr>

At around two a.m., Jack's phone rang. He grappled for it in the dark, dry-mouthed and fuzzy-headed. The number was local but unfamiliar. "Masterson."

"Hey." Ryan's voice.

"Hey." Jack sat up.

"I have a trauma sch-scene I need cleaned up-p." Ryan talked too loud and slurred his words. Jack could hear ice clink in a glass. *Music and talking in the background.* "Guy hurled himself onto a bottle of Grey Goose. 'S a fucking mess, man. I need a cleanup on aisle— Hey. What aisle is this?"

Rust flaked off Jack's heart as it started beating again. Interested, Tasha crawled over to curl up in the crook of his arm. "How big a team will you need?"

"Just one guy with a cane and an inscrutable gray cat should do it."

"Cat's borrowed." Jack stroked the sleek fur between Tasha's ears.

"You've still got her, though? Cause the purring...that's gotta be in the contract. We're gonna need a guy with a cat and a cane, or a cat with a cane and a guy. How much for an awkward, unco-ordinated, fuzzy, and purring meow-nage of pure comfort right about now?"

"Who you calling fuzzy?" Jack smiled into the cat's reflective glowing eyes. "I'm fucked-up too. I can't drive like this."

"I see a tragic pattern forming."

"You are the patron saint of lost causes, after all."

"I *work* for a hospital named after the patron saint of lost causes," Ryan corrected him. "But I've decided to take a few days off. Do you have to work tomorrow?"

"You know what? I own my own company, and I can tell everyone to fuck off and die if I want. Especially after today."

"I sh-smell road trip." Ryan nearly choked with laughter. "Vdara in Vegas? It's a nonsmoking hotel attached to Bellagio. With a spa."

"I think—"

"*Aw, man.* Don't thiiiiiink," Ryan admonished. "Just this once. Don't think. Let's just—"

"Get a cab. I'll call the airport. We'll have to fly out of LAX, because SNA is closed."

"I don't have clothes."

"I'll throw enough into a duffel for both of us to get there. We can buy whatever else we need once we—"

"Christ. When you don't think, you really do it right." Jack heard Ryan's happy laughter. "How about I just come over to sleep, and we drive to Vegas in the morning."

"You could do that. By then Skippy will have picked up

Tasha, so I won't have to figure out how to make sure she gets fed."

"You'd have just done it, though—gone, without giving it a second's thought."

"With you? Yeah. Hell yeah."

Silence. *Maybe too much silence?*

Jack gripped the phone. "Are you still there, Ryan?"

"Won't I remind you of bad things every day?" Ryan asked.

"Nah. You remind me of *me*. How I used to be when I could still imagine good things for myself."

"Yeah?"

"You remind me of when I used to go on dates and make mixtapes. You remind me of when I could still *play*." Jack swallowed. "I won't deny I like how you look. I have a type, and Nick was it, ergo...you, my Irish-by-way-of-Viking-marauders friend, are *it* as well. But what you remind me of is...better days."

"That's good to know—" Ryan's voice broke, and he cleared his throat. "I'm going to like reminding you of better days."

"I'm going to Vegas, Ryan. I'm going to see a Cirque show and gamble away a whole roll of nickels. I'm going to order irreverent adolescent comedies to watch from bed. I'm going to eat cheese puffs until the sheets turn orange. What do you say?" Jack hoped he'd say yes. "Are you in?"

"Will we make long, slow, serious love during the commercials?"

"If you think that's possible, I'm willing to give it a try. You come too."

A long pause. "You said it again."

"Yeah. I have a confession to make," Jack whispered.

Ryan laughed softly. "Another one?"

"I've known that was a poem all along."

EPILOGUE

AN ARM WRAPPED around Jack's chest. Considering the first rays of morning light were slanting through the window, having an arm creep around him and a thick cock nudge at his ass was new.

And oh, so good.

Silken, lube-slicked fingers found his hole, and he grunted when they slipped inside. Lips nuzzled at his neck.

Jack rasped out his first words of the morning. "Ah, God. That feels so good."

"You like to get fucked?"

"Yeah." Jack sighed. "Love it. It's hard on the body, but..."

"Maybe we could rig you up a swing in here. Less bending and twisting. Easier on the knees."

"Is that my PT talking or my—" Jack pressed his face into the pillow before he could say it.

"Your what?"

A particularly fortuitous graze of Ryan's fingers made it impossible for Jack to think just then. "Boyfriend."

"Is that what I am? Am I your boyfriend?"

"You want to be?"

Ryan pushed Jack's leg forward a little, his good leg, the right one, and the blunt head of Ryan's cock entered Jack's ass. "Yes. I want to be your boyfriend."

"*Ah*...yeah...whatever. *Boyfriend.*"

"Tell me if I put too much pressure on your hips."

Ryan, you are clearly not engaged enough. Jack reached back and pulled Ryan closer. "C'mon, Ryan. I'm not going to break."

"Uhn...God." Ryan bit down on Jack's shoulder and pulled his hips in. Jack let him go as he pushed against Ryan with everything he had. He needed as much of Ryan's cock as he could get, and he tightened his muscles to squeeze him, even though his lower back protested a little.

Ryan's tongue came out to soothe Jack's bitten shoulder. He nosed beneath Jack's ear while he lipped Jack's neck. All the while the flat of his hand strummed Jack's belly like Jack was an instrument Ryan was mastering, and he'd found a whole new way to nuance his performance.

Ryan was fast becoming a virtuoso. In fact, he was an overnight goddamned sensation.

Ryan's hand covered the casual grip Jack had on his cock, lacing their fingers together. When Ryan's rhythm quickened, it forced Jack's cock through their entwined hands. Fresh floods of precum slicked Jack up when Ryan found the perfect angle, and then it was bliss, bliss, *bliss.*

A sob of pure relief fell from Jack's lips when the telltale tightening of his body signaled his point of no return. He let himself go, and Ryan took him over, holding him while he spasmed in Ryan's arms.

Right then, Jack had a sudden memory of what it was like to carry the immense weight of his gear. Back at the academy, he'd had to run up flight after flight of stairs as fast as he could, carrying everything until his lungs burned like fire, until his heart felt like it was going to explode.

Reaching the top meant piercing through all his limitations. He felt like he could drop everything and fly into the sky, into the stars. That day, there had been nothing that couldn't be his if he'd wanted it badly enough.

Later, after Jack's heart rate slowed to a mere gallop, he lay quietly with Ryan's body curved like a big spoon against his back. Jack reached behind him to pull Ryan's face alongside his so he could rub their bristly cheeks together. If Ryan felt the wetness of Jack's tears, he didn't mention it.

Jack reached for comfort, and Ryan gave it until he deftly turned it into tickling and more foreplay. Ryan declared he was going to monogram Jack's back with bite marks, and Jack let him because it was so goddamn good to feel Ryan smile against his skin.

"Stop," Jack said into his pillow. Ryan hovered over his back, panting hot breaths on his skin. "Were you serious about Vegas?"

"Sure." Ryan licked a trail from the hollow between Jack's shoulder blades up to his hairline, giving Jack chills.

Jack's whole body drew up tight. "Cut. It. Out."

"Oh, all right." A loud smacking noise accompanied one last kiss. Ryan wrinkled his nose. "Do you smell something?"

"What, like something burning?" Jack rolled out of bed and reached for his sleep pants before Ryan could get a hand on him to stop him. Despite his physical limitations, he was heading for the bedroom door before Ryan even had a chance to swipe himself clean.

"Wait." Ryan reached for his own sleep pants. "It's coffee I smell."

Alarmed, Jack followed his nose into the kitchen. He found

Skippy, Gabe, and Dave sitting at his kitchen table, coffee mugs in hand.

Jack slapped his hand over his heart when it seemed like it was going to burst from his chest. "What the ever-loving fuck is going on here?"

Skippy raised his hand like he was in school. "I let myself in 'cause it's payday. I came to see how you did with Tasha."

The little traitor was twined around Skippy's feet, purring. The least she could do was meow so Jack would know people were in his house getting comfortable, drinking his coffee. "Some superspy cat you turned out to be, Natasha Badinov."

Skippy smiled at that. "Maybe she's a double agent?"

"And what the hell, Gabe?"

Gabe shrugged. "Dave and Eddie's cars were here."

"And I need to apologize to Ryan." Dave glanced up at the ceiling. "I guess."

Ryan sauntered into the kitchen with his usual smile in place. He looked sleep-tossed and sexy. Freshly kissed.

"For what?" Ryan asked.

Four pairs of eyes—Jack included his own because Ryan wasn't someone he could easily take his eyes off—gaped at Ryan.

Ryan turned after he'd poured his coffee. "What?"

Dave was the first to speak. "I'm sorry I was an ass."

"Okay," said Ryan.

That was it. For a while no one spoke.

Dave looked over at Jack. "We good?"

"We're good." Jack wanted his own cup of coffee, but if he turned his back to get it, they'd see the bite marks still throbbing on his skin. "Me and Ryan are going to Vegas for a few days."

"Hey, I went to Vegas last weekend." Skippy beamed at them. "I won a thousand dollars at the Hard Rock."

"That's good." Jack nodded. *This is getting surreal.*

"We got some things we needed for the baby."

"Good." Jack kept on nodding. "Good."

"So..." Ryan trailed off. All five men glanced at everything but one another.

Goddamn it. Jack had to ask about the cat. He didn't want to, but he had to. "You'll be taking Tasha back now?"

"Uh." Skippy's gaze flew to Gabe.

Jack was going to miss that goddamned cat. "What?"

"See...the thing is, Tasha's not really mine." Skippy found something fascinating to look at in his coffee.

Gabe intervened. "What Skippy's trying to say is—"

"It was Gabe's idea," Skippy blurted. "He said you oughta have a pet, and then there was this cat at the scene we was working. Not the gorgeous scene, but the one two days before where the lady exploded."

"The lady what?" Ryan grabbed a piece of toast from the table.

Jack was pretty sure Ryan knew all about this sort of thing, but he explained. "Sometimes when a dead body is left in a warm environment unattended for a period of time..."

"Oh, God. Never mind. I know." Ryan handed his toast and coffee to Jack.

Jack smiled. That was one way to get coffee without having to turn around.

"The owner's daughter was allergic to cats and asked did I know anybody who could take care of her? See, I can't take her because Kelly Ann thinks cats steal the breath from little babies—"

"Wait, what?" asked Jack.

"Kelly Ann can be..." Skippy seemed to search for the word. Jack assumed *crazy* wasn't the word Skippy was looking for. *Crazy* was the word Jack would have used, but he kept his mouth shut. "Kelly Ann is old-fashioned. Anyhow. Gabe said you should have a cat, and if I left Tasha with you, she'd adopt you and you'd have to keep her."

"Gabe said that, did he?" asked Jack.

"He was right," said Ryan. "Jack is definitely now Tasha's *bitch*—er...human."

Jack rolled his eyes, but he was pleased. Delighted, in fact.

Dave muttered, "Seems like there's a lot of that going around."

"By the way. Someone has to take care of Tasha while I'm in Vegas."

"I'll do it," Skippy said. "Leave me a key."

Jack arched an eyebrow at him. "Since when do you need a key?"

"*Ahem.*" Skippy cleared his throat. "Detective Hungley is right there. Just sayin'."

"One of these days, Skip. You and I are gonna dance." Dave tried out his highly trained cop glare on Skippy. It could peel the average person like a grape, but Skippy was oblivious.

"Is that like, some gay thing?" Skippy's eyes narrowed. "On account of I don't swing that way."

Dave's eyes widened. "No, I—"

"Okay. So. Skippy will watch the cat while you're in Vegas." Gabe got to his feet, and Dave rose with him. He looked so anxious to leave Jack almost felt sorry for him. *Almost.* "I'm going to take care of the business, and Dave's going to keep his big mouth shut from now on. Meeting adjourned."

Gabe and Dave nodded to everyone as they exited the kitchen through the back door. That left Skippy, who blinked up at Ryan and Jack like he was expecting them to serve him breakfast. Jack sipped his coffee thoughtfully while Ryan got himself another cup.

"So you two?" Skippy used his hands to describe a pretty

filthy act into the air and then grinned happily at them. "It's like that now?"

Ryan nodded. "Yeah. Probably."

"I guess. Yeah." Jack glanced at Ryan, who shot back a smile that knocked the breath from his lungs. "Yeah. It's exactly like that."

SKIPPY'S BIG ASK

A BONUS SHORT STORY FOR YOU!

Skippy rolled down the quiet street in his piece of shit Mazda. As he drove, he pondered another night, another quiet neighborhood, and the "messages" he delivered in Jaime Ochoa's Escalade SUV.

That was forever ago—before he got betrayed by one of his crew. Before he met Kelly Ann. Before he'd come to Cali, and joined the Brothers Grime, and started a new life for himself as a whole different kind of cleaner.

He never forgot where he came from. And on nights like this one, missions like the one he was on now, it was obvious he never would.

Twice, he passed the house at a crawl with his lights off. He checked out the cars in the driveway. The owner was home, entertaining his business partners. Whether it was for work or play those guys always hung out together. Between them and Jack's boyfriend Ryan, it had proven extremely hard to catch his boss alone. Didn't look like there was any choice now. He'd have to take the chance when they were around.

He made another circle of the long block and its squat bungalow homes. Some were inviting, with porchlights and fancy gardens. Some looked dark and uninhabited, perfect for squatters and junkies.

As he drove, he asked himself whether he could do this. It was one thing when Jack was alone with Ryan. But if Eddie and Gabe were with him, or God forbid, Detective Huntley, who always looked at him like he smelled decomp...

He reached for the crucifix Kelly Ann had wrapped around his rearview mirror and glanced at the family pictures he kept in his visor. Kelly Ann and Baby Eduardo—nicknamed *Lalo*—were the most exquisitely perfect things in his life. What wouldn't he give, for them? What wouldn't he do?

On the fourth trip around, he parked his car in front of a vacant place four houses down from Jack's.

If it weren't for Kelly Ann, he'd probably still be visiting the squatters in houses just like that one, organizing runners and lookouts. Collecting cash from the kids his people trusted with their product, making trouble for anybody who broke that trust.

He was a world away from all that now, but being here like this brought memories back and gave him the shivers.

He'd grown soft. He liked his cushy life. He didn't want to fuck things up and lose it, ever. He'd weighed everything against what was most important, and he came to the inescapable conclusion that he had to walk up to Jack's house, knock on the door, and do what he'd come there to do. No matter what.

His footsteps sounded like gunshots on the concrete. His knocks, like bomb blasts.

The door opened, and a wedge of light spilled out. From inside, he heard music, and the low laughter of men.

"Skippy. What's up?" Jack asked.

"Can I talk to you?" Skippy shot a quick glance both ways. There was no one else on the street. A cat's eyes reflected Jack's porchlight from the bushes. Somewhere a dog barked. "Alone?"

"Sure." Jack stepped outside and closed the door behind him. Skippy had the weird urge to scold him for it. *You don't come out just 'cause I ask. You don't make yourself vulnerable to whatever's out here on my say so.* "Everything okay? Kelly Ann and Lalo—"

"They're fine."

"Okay." Jack waited. "That's good."

"I mean." Skippy's heart raced. How could this be so hard? "Maybe."

"Maybe they're fine?"

"I don't know." He scrubbed at his short hair. "Lalo's fine."

"Something up with Kelly Ann?" Jack gestured toward the bench on his porch. Maybe on account of he had a bum leg he needed to sit? Skippy stepped back so Jack could pass, and then sat down next to him.

"Maybe." He stared straight ahead.

Jack leaned forward and clasped his hands between his knees. "Is she sick or something?"

"Sort of." Why was a this so hard?

"Is there something I can help with? Do you need cash, is that it?"

"No. I mean. Things were hard, but now they're better. I just —" He wasn't sure he could do this, after all. Was it disloyal? Would Kelly Ann think he was an asshole for talking about things like this?

Jack waited him out.

"Kelly had that thing. Baby blues. And her mom knew what it was. She told Kelly Ann to ask the doctor for help."

"That's good. Did she?"

"Yeah. She has to take pills for it now and all. Seems like she's a lot better, except"—he glanced at his hands—"it's exhausting having a toddler. And she works so hard. Neither of us ever get any sleep."

"Doesn't Kelly's mom live at your place?"

Skippy glanced up. "Her mom kind of makes things harder."

"Really?"

"She's got some strong opinions, I guess you could say." He didn't want to speak ill of his mother-in-law. "She keeps Kelly Ann company but she's older, and she doesn't help a lot."

"So Kelly Ann is pretty much taking care of both of them. Maybe you could find Kelly Ann a helper or something?"

"I will. Only for now, I was thinking of something more...romantic."

"How can I help?"

"You're in a relationship." Skippy found something to look at on the street. "You got any ideas for something nice I can do?"

"Me?"

"Yeah you. Ryan looks at you like you're the last line of coke at a yacht party. What can I do for her that will let her know that she means everything to me?"

"You just went to Vegas, right?"

"Yeah, but her mom and the baby ended up going too."

"So you didn't spend any special time together?"

"Not really."

"So that's probably the first thing. You should go somewhere it's just the two of you. No distractions."

"Like where? 'Cause Vegas isn't that."

Jack frowned. "I'll bet Ryan knows a lot more about this stuff than I do."

"Yeah?"

"He's inside. You want to ask him?"

Skippy stuffed his hands in his pockets. "Who else?"

"Gabe, Eddie, and Dave."

He winced. "Detective Hungley."

"Don't let him hear you call him that," Jack warned. "I don't know how we'd fit his head back in his ball cap."

The door opened, and Ryan peeked out. "Jack? Everything okay?"

Jack gave Ryan a nod. "Come on, Skip. Let's put our heads together. I'm sure we'll come up with something."

"Okay." He let Jack talk him into it. "If you think that will help."

"Help what?" Ryan asked.

"Tell you inside." Jack shooed Ryan in. Skippy followed. They joined the rest in Jack's 80's era kitchen, where they had a poker game going. "Have a seat, you want something to drink?"

"Ginger ale, if you have it."

"Sure." Jack filled a glass with ice and handed that over, along with a can of pop.

"Thank you."

Dave rolled his eyes. "Polite for a guy who used to bust kneecaps for a living."

Skippy sipped his pop. "Says who?"

"Your rap sheet?" Dave baited him every single day, but he was going have to do better than that.

"No it didn't."

"Dave," Jack warned

"There is no proof of any illegal activity," Skippy said the words mildly, because he knew it made Huntley's head explode.

"No proof doesn't mean you didn't do anything."

"Doesn't mean I did."

With a huff of annoyance, Dave rearranged his cards. "Are we playing, or what?"

"The game can wait," said Jack. "We're helping Skippy right now."

Dave turned his chair to glare at them. "Now? Are you kidding me?"

At his vehement tone, Jack shared a look with Ryan. "I fold."

"Me too." Ryan smothered a laugh.

"You fucks, I finally had you." Dave threw down three kings. "I hate you, Skippy."

"Honestly? I'm not surprised to hear that, Dave."

Eddie asked, "What do you need?"

Skippy glanced at Ryan. "You guys just hooked up, right? If you wanted to treat Jack to a real nice time, what would you do? I mean something classy."

"This for Kelly Ann?" Ryan asked.

"Of course."

"Let me think."

"Let's all try to figure something out," said Jack.

Eddie asked, "Do you need time off?"

Skippy's face heated. "Maybe. I want to do this right. Kelly Ann deserves it."

"What about spending time away alone?" Ryan asked. "You could get a nice hotel room and take some time to reconnect. Maybe at the beach?"

"I thought of that, but it's like she has invisible ties to her mom and the baby and they don't stretch that far." The only way he'd gotten Kelly Ann to Vegas was to take her mom and Lalo, too.

"Maybe she'd go for a local hotel?"

Skippy thought about it. "If it's not farther from our house than Costco or something."

"I can work with that." Ryan took out his cell phone.

"That's it. Make a couple reservations at local restaurants, take some time to yourselves, and you'll be her hero," said Eddie.

"Will she leave the baby with your mom?"

"Yeah. Mrs. Higgins can watches the baby if we stay close."

"Wait. You call your mother-in-law Mrs. Higgins?" asked Dave.

"I wouldn't exactly call her *Mom*." That was one of his problems. "It's not that she isn't a nice lady. She just isn't real warm, is all. With me, I mean."

"And she lives with you?"

Skippy shrugged. You changed what you could. And Mrs. Higgins was not that.

"What days do you think you'll want to go?" Ryan asked, still typing. "I need to put in dates to look at the room rates."

"Uh…"

"What about weekend after next?" Jack asked. "Kim asked if she could have time off this weekend and I think Kevin's got hockey tickets for Sunday, but next weekend should be okay."

"That would work," Skippy agreed.

"So let's say you leave Friday afternoon…" Ryan thumbed something into his phone. "You could stay until Sunday. I'll see about getting you a late checkout."

"Wait, where?"

"Embassy Suites maybe? Rooms includes a breakfast buffet."

"By the mall?" Skippy asked.

"Right. It's close enough that if there's an emergency, you can be home in ten minutes."

"That sounds cool. Kelly Ann might actually go for that. She could even tuck Lalo in if she wanted."

"Sure." Ryan typed and typed. "*Yes.* I knew it. I have enough bonus points for both nights."

"You don't have to use—"

"It's my pleasure, Skippy." Ryan beamed at him. "I've had these points forever and I'm not going anywhere."

"Thank you." Skippy knew when to be grateful and shut his cake hole.

He loved his little family. He did. But when it came to his mother-in-law, things were complicated. He longed for just one day without the need to maintain a polite facade when he wasn't feeling it. One day with Kelly Ann, just the two of them, like it used to be.

Lalo was the love of their lives, but Skippy wanted his wife back from Mommyland. His heart beat faster just thinking about it.

As if Ryan read his mind, he said, "It's probably not going to be easy for Kelly Ann to let go."

"You think?"

"Taking two nights away will help. You'll need to get to know each other all over again. Redefine what you are to each other, now that you're Lalo's parents."

That was the problem. He wasn't jealous of the time Kelly Ann spent with the baby. He only wanted to make the most of their alone time. But it took changing gears. Sometimes they fell asleep before they said a single word to each other that didn't have to do with the baby.

He eyed Ryan. "How'd you get so smart?"

Ryan leaned against Jack, who slid an arm around his waist. "We all work the kind of jobs where you have to learn to leave things behind at the end of the day. If not, we couldn't have lives outside work. It's not easy and it takes effort. I have to decompress every time I leave work."

"I guess I do too, come to think of it," said Skippy.

"I know you do."

"That's why cops don't stay married," said Dave. "We can't leave the job at work. It changes you too much."

"Plenty of cops stay married, Dave," said Ryan. "I know some."

"Statistically, they're outliers."

"Maybe." Gabe glanced away. "But if only one does it, that means there's hope."

"I'll bet you play the lottery."

"Just poker," Gabe fired back. "With your loser ass."

Dave sniffed. "I had three kings."

"So I guess we all need to thank Skippy for stopping by, huh?"

Dave picked up his beer. "Not me."

Skippy got up to leave. "Thanks for your ideas."

"I'm not done yet," said Ryan. "Give me until the beginning of next week, and I'll have an itinerary for you."

"That sounds so sexy," Jack teased. "Itinerary."

Skippy frowned. "I don't think—"

"I doubt he wants you to plan every minute, there Ry."

Ryan blushed. "I'll pencil in sexy times."

Skippy said, "I'm just gonna go now."

Jack walked him to the door. "I think you've unleashed a monster."

"It's nice." He glanced back. "I can un-plan whatever he plans, right?"

Jack opened the door for him. "I'll tell him you have the power of veto. You can even cancel the whole thing, if you need to."

"I want to do this. The problem might be getting Kelly Ann on board."

"I'll book you out all that weekend, anyway. You need a little downtime."

"Thanks, again, Jack."

"You're a great employee Skippy. We're happy to help."

"Speak for yourself, Jack" Dave called from the kitchen.

"I'm not your employee, Dave." Skippy waved and made his way to the car.

He should have known Jack would be willing to work around a little time off. And Ryan. He was a class act. He probably knew all kinds of places he and Kelly Ann could go where the atmosphere was romantic.

Skippy wasn't the most brilliant guy in the world, but he

knew what to look for in a mentor. When a dude was going somewhere he wanted to be, he followed them.

From the way Jack and Ryan looked at each other, they were making something work. He'd take their advice and remind Kelly Ann that even while he was up to his eyeballs in crime scenes and disapproving in-laws, he remembered exactly why he'd fallen in love with her.

He owed it to her, even if he had to stretch everything in him to do it.

Bloody footsteps gave Skippy his next best idea ever.

He was laying down a layer of antimicrobial spray over the unfortunate scene of a terrible domestic battle that ended in murder, and he wasn't really thinking about anything in particular, except maybe he wished people wouldn't hurt each other so goddamn much. And then he saw it. A macabre sort of pattern that looked almost like a dance.

He followed the footprints with his eyes. If he used his imagination like detectives did when they were studying a crime scene, he could reconstruct how the combatants had moved around the apartment. Except for the blood spatter, they could have been dancing.

Would Kelly Ann enjoy dancing?

She watched all those shows on TV. Sometimes he caught her moving with the vacuum when she thought no one was looking. She hummed, and even beneath the sound of the machine he was so in tune with her, he usually knew the song. She liked old school music. Or Latin tunes, where she could go to town, shaking her hips.

If he caught her at it, he usually took over the chore and she'd act all shy and embarrassed that he saw. Maybe that was a little fantasy world he had no part in. But maybe he could learn to be her partner.

He knew just the guy to ask about that, even if he had to swallow a boatload of pride.

After he finished cleaning and restocking the van, Skippy entered the office and knocked on Eddie's door jamb.

Eddie sat in a fancy leather office chair big enough for his muscled frame. He held up a finger while he finished looking at something on his phone before waving Skippy in.

"You got a minute?" he asked.

"Sure." Eddie sat back. "What's on your mind?"

"I thought of something else. I know it's a big ask." Skippy took the seat opposite, which was smaller and made him feel like he was in the principal's office. "I'm hoping maybe it's not too much."

"I won't know until I hear it."

Skippy blew out a breath and forced himself to say it. "Could you maybe teach me a couple dance moves?"

"That's it?" Eddie's lips curved into a smile. "I love dancing."

"That's what Kim said. She said you've got all kinds of slick moves."

"She's seen me?" Eddie wrapped a hand around the back of his neck. "Probably on the Fourth of July last year, huh? Too much cerveza, I guess."

"She said you were great."

"When would you want to do this? We can go out into the warehouse and crank up some tunes. I can't make you a superstar overnight, but I can keep you from geeking out."

"That sounds great. I really appreciate this. The only thing is..." Man, this was going to be tough. But for Kelly Ann, he'd do anything.

"What?"

"I want to learn those couple dances. Like on Dancing With the Stars."

"Ballroom?"

"Can you teach me that?"

"Theoretically"—Eddie frowned—"I could teach you the moves to a couple types of dances, but it's complicated. You can't just wing it."

"Think it's too tough?"

"Nah. We'll figure it out. Nothings too tough for us, right?"

"That's just you being all positive and shit, right?"

"Yeah, kinda." Eddie smirked.

"If I learn one move where I can spin her around, I'm in. I want to make her feel like one of those Disney princesses, even though she got the frog."

"You're no frog, Skip. We can do this. It'll be like coaching your first wedding dance. Did you do that?"

Skippy shook his head. "We got married at the courthouse on account of her mom was real pissed at the time."

"I see."

"Kelly Ann deserved a wedding with a band and bridesmaids. She says it's fine, but I know her. There were a lot of things I couldn't give her before that I can now, and I just want..." He let the words die. Of course, he wanted. Kelly Ann was the perfect woman—the perfect wife—and he was pretty sure he'd die believing he didn't deserve her. Instead of saying the words and getting all choked up, he stood. "So if you could, that'd be awesome."

"Let's get started now." Eddie rose. "You got time now?"

Skippy nodded. "They don't hold dinner for me because I'm never home at the same time."

"I know it's long hours. If you ever need a break—"

"We're saving for a house, so I need all the work you can give me."

"Okay, well. If you ever need time, we're happy to accommodate you. You're a valuable employee, Skippy. We couldn't do this without you."

Skippy had heard those words before but this time he believed them. This time, he knew he wasn't going to get a knife in his back if he made a mistake.

"I'll meet you out there." Skippy ducked his head and hurried to the warehouse so Eddie could try to make a dancer out of him.

It wasn't going to be easy. He was built more for busting heads than for waltzing. He was Beast to Kelly Ann's Beauty. If he could dance one tenth as good as the cartoon character, he'd call it a win.

Eddie followed him out, head down, scrolling through playlists on his phone. There were Bluetooth speakers outside so they could have music when they worked on the vans. Mostly only Eddie and Gabe bothered, but when they did, the work seemed to go faster.

The speakers came to life on a latin station. Salsa music filled the massive building.

"That sound about right?" Eddie asked.

"Yeah. Kelly Ann likes this music." Skippy rubbed his arms where goosebumps made his anxiety visible.

"Salsa is great because it's fun and you can make endless combinations out of a few basic steps. You ready to try it?"

"You really think I can do this?"

"I know you can. It's just fancy walking. I promise."

Skippy wasn't so sure. "All right."

"Stand next to me and listen to the music. Hear that?" Eddie paused to let him listen. "I want you to listen and count to eight, like this: one, two, three, four, five, six, seven, eight."

"Okay."

"Keep counting in your head and watch me." Eddie moved. "I go forward then back together. Back then forward together. I pause on together."

As Skippy watched it seemed to make sense. Dancing really

was like walking. Step forward, back, pause, step back, forward pause.

Before he knew it, he was doing the move. They started on the left, step forward, step back, pause. The with the right, step back, step forward, pause.

That wasn't so hard. Why did he think this was going to be so hard?

"Let's do that step for a while. Get a feel for the music." Eddie smirked. "You can get your hips involved, you know. It's not supposed to be feet moving with a wooden body stuck on top."

Eddie got his hips involved. Then he used his whole body. He drew attitude around him like a bullfighter's cape. Skippy didn't know if he could swagger like that, but he tried to at least loosen up. He stopped looking at his feet. Let the move become natural to him. By the third song, he had it. Maybe he even sold it a little.

Eddie grinned at him. "Okay. Now, you learn to turn your girl."

"What's she doing while I'm doing all this?"

"We'll get to that later, once you have the steps. Basically, you're going to lead her. How you touch her will tell her how to move."

"Okay." That sounded pretty nice actually. He'd like to spin her around until she was dizzy, like in the movies. Maybe they could put the vacuum aside and dance at home, too. "Show me."

Skippy learned to turn. It was the same, really. Only where you put your feet was different. In fact, it was pretty easy. Eddie was a great teacher. He made it fun. They laughed so loud Gabe came out of his office to see what all the noise was about.

Once he knew what they were doing, Gabe got in on the action. He executed his own moves, copping an attitude similar to Eddie's only Gabe flung his head when he moved and his curly hair, damp from their exertions, flopped comically into his eyes. He also did faces—mock serious, snooty, over the top expressions. Sometimes he looked like a model even though he acted like a clown.

When Skippy caught a glance of himself in the window of one of the vans, he looked almost giddy. He froze, feeling extremely weird all of a sudden. He'd spent a lifetime projecting one personality—badass. Happy people were so vulnerable. Could he allow anybody to see *him* that way?

Maybe, for Kelly Ann.

After an hour they shut the party down. It killed him that he couldn't show Kelly Ann what he'd learned, but he had to save his new skill for a surprise. He wanted to give her a big reveal, like on the TV show. He wanted the moment to be perfect.

Like his dance attitude, he gathered patience around him. He could wait.

Kelly Ann deserved the best surprise ever.

A week later, Eddie told him it was time to work with a partner. Skippy dreaded this part. Somehow, he had to imagine dancing with his wife while Eddie stood in for her.

Hard enough holding a dude, although he could do a lot worse than Eddie Vasquez, for sure. It was the fact that Eddie was as big as him that was the problem. They couldn't stop laughing.

Gabe got in on the action. He took a seat in the corner as they tried, and failed, to dance together.

"Be serious," Eddie ordered.

"I'm trying, but it's weird."

"How do you think I feel, letting your tattooed ass lead like this?"

"Sorry."

"Again." Eddie let go so they could start over. "Don't forget to signal me where we're going."

"Okay. But take a hint, because you keep trying to lead."

"That's our Eddie," said Gabe. "I'm not sure he knows how to follow."

"Shut it, Gabe." Eddie winced when he started off on the wrong foot. "Sorry, Skip. Habit. Let's go again."

They tried again and got through one of the turns.

"Well, well, well." Dave stood beneath the warehouse door they'd rolled up to get some air. "What have we here? Dancing with the felons?"

"*Shit.*" Skippy missed his footing. "See what you made me do?"

Dave asked, "What on earth—"

"None of your business, Dave." Eddie spoke mildly, but firmly.

"Show's over, Detective. Move along." Skippy wanted to fall through the floor and die.

"Oh, no, no, no. I've got to see this." Dave sauntered into the warehouse like he owned the place. He didn't, but since he threw some business their way, he stuck his nose in all the time and nobody said anything.

"I should have known you'd find out about this," Skippy muttered.

"Don't let him mess with you," said Eddie. "You've got this."

"You're learning to dance for your big romantic weekend?" asked Dave.

Skippy sighed. "Maybe."

"Knock it off, Dave," said Gabe.

"I'm not even doing anything," Dave insisted.

Gabe pushed a second chair Dave's way. "Except acting like a dumbass kid. Sit down and shut up. He's trying to do something nice for someone he loves. Take a lesson, will you?"

Dave shut his mouth, but his expression remained stubborn. He hadn't gotten over Jack finding Ryan, yet. Skippy wasn't supposed to know about that.

"Again, Skippy. Don't pay any attention to them. Signal me when you want me to turn."

They went again, and again, and again.

Sweat dotted his forehead and dampened his T-shirt.

He did okay, but stayed clunky and self-conscious with Gabe and Dave watching. Every so often, Eddie stepped off with the wrong foot. They'd laugh it off because the problem was his size and his bulk and his tendency to lead. There was no help for that.

Eddie pulled away. "You need earth-moving equipment to get me to spin. Sorry."

"I think it's me."

"I wish we had more time."

The big weekend was coming so fast. He'd barely learned the basics of the salsa and the rhumba. He could hold his own alone. But he wasn't ready for partner dancing and they both knew it.

"Let's try again," said Skippy.

He took Eddie's left hand in his and placed his right on Eddie's back. They waited for a good starting place in the song, and both stepped forward with their left legs at the same time.

"Ow." Skippy was glad for his steel toed boots.

"I'm sorry." Eddie stepped back. "So sorry. Why can't I do this backwards? It's like I'm just—"

"Stop, stop, stop." Dave stood and removed his suit jacket. "This is painful to watch."

"What are you gonna do about it?" Skippy turned unhappily. If the man was going to sit there, making cracks...

"I'm going to take his place, Skippy," Dave said mildly.

"You what?" asked Eddie.

Gabe's mouth fell open.

"I can dance." Dave rolled up his sleeves. "I'm smaller than you. You guys seem to think this is a worthy cause, ergo—"

"I'm not dancing with you." Skippy's fists clenched.

"Afraid I'll cop a feel?"

He rolled his eyes. "I just don't want to hear about it for the rest of my life."

"Look, you want to learn or not?" asked Dave. "I can do this. Forward, backward, standing on my head. I'm a good dancer. Afraid to give it a shot?"

"Since when?" Gabe still had that stunned look on his face.

Dave sent a frosty look his way. "You don't know everything about me."

"All right." Skippy capitulated before he could change his mind. And then just to take the high road, he said, "Thanks for the offer."

"My pleasure." Dave glared as if it was anything but.

Instead of worrying why Huntley would offer if he didn't want to help, Skippy kept the image of Kelly Ann in his mind. Dinner by candlelight. Wine and fine food. An hour or two of dancing, where he could show off how hard he'd worked for this.

He took Dave's surprisingly soft hand in his left and put his right hand on Dave's back, just like he had Eddie's.

Dave took a half step forward. "I don't bite, Skippy."

"Just making room for the long arm of the law, Detective."

Dave's lips twitched. "You can begin any time now."

On the beat, Skippy stepped forward, then back, performing each step of his combination just like Eddie taught him.

One thing was clear right away: Dave was light on his feet. He followed well too. With very little coaxing, they were making turns. Dave spun when Skippy directed him. They got through one set of steps and Skippy stopped, breathless, anticipating some snide remark that didn't happen.

"Not bad." Dave tilted his head. "Go again?"

Without speaking, they went three more times. Skippy decided to change the order of the steps and turn when he wanted. He spun Dave while he executed a sideways move of his own, and Dave easily followed.

When they were done, Skippy's forehead ran with sweat. The problem wasn't the exertion, it was Huntley, who remained cool and unflappable—as if he salsa danced with guys like Skippy every day.

Skippy ignored the tingling sense of danger. He'd said he wanted to learn to dance, and if this was how he had to do it, so be it.

Eddie stood by, watching. "You're doing great, Skippy. How does it feel?"

Skippy glanced between him and Dave. On the one hand, he wanted to say it felt awesome. On the other, there was Huntley, and he didn't want to give him the satisfaction. "It's...good."

"Is that the only dance you're learning?" Dave asked. "Salsa?"

"He learned the rhumba, but—"

"Let's do that then." He met Skippy's gaze. "That's the dance of love."

Gabe said, "Jesus, Dave. What the fuck are you up to?"

"Nothing. For God's sake. Why can't I help without having ulterior motives?"

"Because you're normally an asshole?" Eddie offered.

"Me?" Dave had given Skippy shit since he came aboard Brothers Grime, but now he looked genuinely hurt. "I'm a nice guy."

"Not to me." Skippy said quietly. "And I get why, but—"

"Well, yeah. You tick all my boxes. You wear a story on your skin, Skippy."

"Well this is a new chapter."

"So you tell everybody." He let the words fall between them while holding Skippy's gaze. "*But.* You're important to my friends. That makes you important to me. Don't let us down."

As if he'd let them down. *As if* he'd do a single thing to hurt the men who'd given him a fresh start, who'd become almost as important to him as his family. Skippy's throat hurt.

Now he had to include *Dave Huntley* in that group. Shit.

Huntley was a smartass. From what Skippy saw, he could be kind of a dick with his lovers, since he didn't want to admit he was with them out loud.

Turned out, Skippy'd dance with the devil himself for Kelly Ann.

Hiding his own smile, he prepared to rhumba with Dave.

Eddie could teach him the steps, but it took Dave for him to finally learn to dance. Plus, putting Dave through all those dance moves almost satisfied Skippy's suppressed desire to shove his head through a wall.

They were good together, and he knew it. If he had ever liked dudes...

Hell no. He wasn't going there at all.

They stopped when he had gone through enough songs that he felt comfortable he could repeat his success with Kelly Ann.

"Thanks." He couldn't help it. He saw Dave with fresh eyes. Maybe he was one of the good guys, after all.

"Have a good weekend, Mr. Romance." Dave's sneer was back. "Try not to fuck it up."

"You got this." Eddie patted his back. "Make me proud."

"Good luck, Skippy," said Gabe.

"Thanks." With the music still going, he turned and half-walked, half-danced, to his car.

Late Friday night, the hostess led Skippy and Kelly Ann to a booth in the back of the steakhouse Ryan recommended. He'd done more than make a reservation, apparently, because she seated them at a tasting table covered in an immaculate white tablecloth with a candle lit floral centerpiece. A waiter brought them a silver ice bucket with a bottle of champagne nestled inside.

"Compliments of Mr. Halloran," he said as he opened it with only the slightest hiss. He poured them each a glass and left discreetly.

Skippy was almost afraid to find out what Kelly Ann thought of all this. Since they normally ate at home, neither one of them was used to the royal treatment. Would she think he was trying too hard?

"Your boss did this?" she asked now, eyes a little too wide.

"Jack's man. The nurse."

"That's very kind of him." Kelly Ann looked so pretty. Her blue cocktail dress made her brown skin glow and highlighted her figure.

She dazzled him, from her pretty high heels to the hair she pulled up to control, but not restrain, her natural curls. His breath caught when he looked at her.

"Ryan knows the owner." He picked up his glass. "To my gorgeous wife."

"To a wonderful husband. Thank you." She picked up her glass and took a small sip before wiping her lips with her napkin. For some mysterious chick reason, her lip color stayed, even though her gloss made a little kiss on the glass. She folded her pretty hands on the table and sighed. He glanced around, looking for something he could comment on.

"Your nails look nice," he said. "Pretty color. What would you call that?"

"Purple." Her eyes sparkled a little, and then her lashes fluttered down.

"Goes nicely with the dress."

She nodded. He knew her well enough to see she was anxious.

"Feels weird without Lalo, huh?" he said quietly.

"I miss him." She gnawed her lower lip. "Are you sure Jack and Ryan can handle him? All weekend? He's—"

"Baby. I trust them. Give it a chance."

Their waiter came back. "As I'm sure you've noticed, we didn't give you menus. That's because this is a tasting table, and that means chef will prepare a menu just for you from local, seasonal ingredients. May I ask if either of you has any food allergies?"

They both shook their heads.

"Any hard limits?" he asked mischievously, "do you balk at beets? Cringe at carrots? Mandate that mushrooms be left off the plate?"

They glanced at each other. Skippy answered, "No?"

"In that case, I suggest you enjoy your champagne, I'll be out in a flash with your starters, and bon appetite."

Did Ryan and Jack do this kind of thing often? Jack was blue collar as they came, and Ryan was a nurse, but from the looks of his house, he came from money. Skippy drank a little more champagne.

Kelly Ann whispered, "What if all I want is a salad?"

"I'm not sure we have a choice." He leaned toward her and lowered his voice. It's what Ryan called a tasting menu. Chef decides."

"But it must be expensive. We don't have to--"

"Nah, baby. This is a special night for us. I can take you out to a nice place once in a while, can't I? We're not gonna make a habit of it."

She quirked a little half-smile. "Okay. This once."

"Just okay?"

"It's very nice."

"And?"

"And..." She twisted her napkin. "What if I worry the whole time? What if I can't even taste it, because all I can think about is the baby?"

"Sweetheart, Ryan's a nurse. Lalo will be fine."

"Are you sure you have your phone?"

"I do." He placed it on the table between them. "If they need us they'll call or text."

"But—"

"Is this really gonna a problem for you?" He believed they were doing the right thing—keeping their marriage healthy would help them be better parents. And of course, he wanted time alone with her. He'd looked forward to their weekend so much. But if it made Kelly Ann this anxious, they could pick up the baby and go home. Nothing was worth making her unhappy.

"No," she said. "I just feel nervous. I should be watching the baby, shouldn't I? What if something happens?"

"Like what?"

"Like...they go off by themselves and forget about him."

"Lalo? He has a way of reminding you he's there. You gotta admit."

She chuckled, "Yeah."

"Look. My boss is a responsible guy. You know he used to be a firefighter. Ryan's a nurse. They're not reckless dudes."

"I just can't even imagine..." He heard her unspoken words: *life without Lalo.*

He couldn't imagine it either. "I can't believe spending two nights away as a couple will jeopardize what we have," he said carefully. "But isn't about just me. If you really want to go, we can. I want you to be happy."

"You wouldn't think I'm some control freak helicopter mom?"

"I wouldn't think that, but it doesn't matter. I care about how you feel. If it's too soon--"

"It's not though. I'm being ridiculous." She picked up her glass and took another sip. "All new moms go through this, right?"

"Dunno."

"It's probably a total cliché. And look at all this. No one will even believe it when I post about it. Our own menu?"

"Let's enjoy it, okay?"

"You think we should?"

"We can leave. Any time. Say the word. You have that option."

"No." She took a big, deep breath. "We need time together. Just us."

"That's what I hoped you'd say." He finished off his glass of champagne. After all, that was why they'd taken a rideshare. He didn't have to be Mr. responsible tonight. He just had to show Kelly Ann a good time.

They made small talk while in the background, soft, live music played.

"So what else is in your plans, mister?"

He winked at her. "Tonight? I figured we'd make it an early night."

"Did you now?"

"Yeah. Because dinner comes in stages, so we'll be here a while." He took her hand. "And when we leave, I figure we'll at least be a little tipsy."

"Oh, we are?" She gazed up from beneath her lashes.

"Then we can go back to the hotel," he teased, "take off our fancy clothes, and get an undisturbed, restful, night's sleep."

"Oh *wow*." She kissed him, and his heart caught fire. "That is the sexiest thing I've ever heard you say."

On Saturday morning, Skippy woke at the usual time. He checked his phone. There was no news from Jack. That was probably a good thing, right? He sent Jack a text, asking, "Everything okay?"

Jack sent back, "It's all good. Have fun!"

He sat in their little arm chair, undecided. He could wake Kelly Ann, and they could go down for breakfast, or he could go down and make her a plate. Breakfast in bed. *Boom.*

He didn't want to leave, though. Didn't want her to wake up alone.

She stirred. "What is it? Everything okay?"

"You want to go down and eat?"

"Mmph." She rolled over and pushed her head into the pillow. "Sleeeeepy."

He stood. "I'll bring breakfast. You sleep."

Muffled by the pillows, her words sounded like "Fank oo."

He checked the room was locked and headed for the elevator.

The restaurant the night before was sensational, even if Kelly Ann was a little bit nervous about leaving Lalo. But re-connecting turned out to be harder than he'd expected. Like strangers, they'd stumbled a bit coming up with things to say.

Of course, there was the baby. They could talk about him all night. But they'd made a sort of pact to talk about other things, and they'd shorted out pretty quickly. They'd acted like two uptight, exhausted people who didn't know what to talk about unless it was their kid.

At the buffet, he filled plates with fruit, bacon, potatoes. He added an omelet and a waffle from the hot bar. Carrying everything plus condiments and flatware wasn't so easy, even with a tray, but in no time he opened their door and placed their food on the table.

Kelly Ann joined him. She still looked half asleep.

"I texted Jack, he said everything's fine." He gave her the phone.

She studied the screen. "That's good to know."

"Today, I planned Downtown Disney. We can walk around a little, do some shopping, eat gumbo at Jazz kitchen, and see a movie."

"Really?" She didn't sound thrilled.

"You love that place, don't you?"

"Yeah." She took a bite of melon and chewed. "You really gave this some thought."

"Of course I did." He forked up a bite of waffle. "Gonna do all the things you love this weekend. Want this to be just about you."

"It will be so crowded." Her expression told him to slow down. They hadn't gelled instantly the night before, but he could still read her pretty well.

"Is that a problem?"

"Normally no." She flopped against her chair back. "I usually love going shopping."

He waited to see if she had more to say. There had to be more, right? If she loved it but she didn't want to, then why not?

"But not today?" he prompted. Was it him? Was it because of the baby, and the time they spent apart, and their lack of time together?

"Being a new mom is a whole different world. And for a while, I was so exhausted, I could barely get off the couch."

"I remember." He wished he'd realized she was depressed sooner. It had never occurred to him.

"Today, even thinking about Downtown Disney makes me tired. The crowds will make it extra stressful."

"I see."

"I'm such a mole." She covered her face. "I'm not fun, anymore."

"You are nothing like a mole." He pulled her hands away and kissed her. "But if you need to stay in and sleep, why not?"

"I don't want to sleep. I just." She spread her hands helplessly. "I can't deal with that many people right now."

"Okay." He could come up with a plan B. "What about the arboretum? You want to take a nature walk? It's probably pretty this time of year."

"That sounds wonderful. Yes. Please." She broke into a smile so happy he felt like he could slay dragons. Or tame them. Yeah, he'd tame them and then ride them.

Instead of planning for some fancy couple's adventure, his goal should have been to make Kelly Ann happy, whatever it took.

They might have lost the art of small talk, but he'd rather have silence if it came with Kelly Ann's smile.

Maybe he and Ryan had gone about this the wrong way.

After a long quiet walk and another amazing dinner, Skippy and Kelly Ann strolled past the bars and restaurants of Fullerton's SoCo district. He told her what he originally planned next.

"*You* want to go dancing?" Kelly Ann asked incredulously. "Did you lose a bet?"

"Dancing was my original plan, but you said you couldn't face crowds, so now, I don't know if you want to go."

She was intrigued enough to ask, "Where?"

"My friend Eddie told me about a place one street over. It's Latin night."

"A club?"

"Not exactly." Skippy had seen the sign a hundred times and given it no thought at all. "It's a ballroom, so it wouldn't be a crush like some bar."

"Well, I am dressed up." Tonight, she wore a red dress that fit her like a glove. It was his favorite. Maybe she knew that?

"Let's go look," he offered. "And then you can decide if you want to stay."

She hesitated. "If it's too crowded can we go back to the hotel?"

"Sounds great either way." He lifted an eyebrow.

"All right. Let's go," she agreed.

They paid a cover at the door and then walked up a flight of wooden stairs to an old disco, where a few dozen couples danced to a driving Latin beat.

Most were dressed up, but a few college-age kids wore shorts and T-shirts. They had the right idea, because the room was overly warm, even though industrial fans aided an overtaxed A/C.

There was even a spinning mirror ball, god help them, and flashing lights.

Skippy's anxiety ratcheted up. This was the moment of truth. Kelly Ann seemed to like the place. She began to sway to the intoxicating rhythms. Her heels tapped lightly on the wooden floor.

She turned to him. "Did you check on the baby?"

He nodded. "After dinner, when you went to the powder room. Jack said everything's fine."

"Do you believe him?"

"About Lalo? Sure. I don't know if Jack's fine. He sounded frazzled."

Her brow furrowed. "Frazzled how?"

"Frazzled like a guy who took care of a baby for twenty-four hours. But Ryan's home from work now. They're fine."

"If you're sure." She bit her lip. "Okay. Let's do it."

The time had come.

He started to sweat. Eddie said they mostly played salsa music. Skippy recognized the rhythm. The other dancers did the same moves Eddie taught him. He had this.

But what if he messed up?

What if he stepped on her feet, or bashed into someone on

the dance floor? He'd faced a lot of scary fucking shit in his life-time, but this? He shivered, despite the heat.

This is about Kelly Ann.

She deserves this. Anything. Everything.

"Would you care to dance?" He held out his hand.

Breathlessly, she took it. "I'd love to, mi vida."

He guided her among the dancers, looking for an open space to begin. Goddamn his mental image of Beauty and the Beast. Once he had it, he couldn't get rid of it. He caught her hand just like Eddie taught him and started with the basics. She followed his steps like a dream. Like she was liquid in his arms—no, *flames*.

"You really dance!" she exclaimed. "How come you didn't tell me before now?"

"I just learned."

"How?" He tried a turn and she moved with him.

"Eddie taught me." Unlike Dave, Kelly Ann's hips did a sexy little swivel with each step. Oh, man, that was hot. Skippy turned the next move into a spin.

"*Wow.*" She giggled as she went under his arm. "This is amazing. I'm picturing you and Eddie dancing together—"

"Eddie taught me the steps," he told her, "but Dave was the one I danced with."

Her eyes widened. "The cop?"

"Yup. Detective Dave."

"Oh my God."

"It wasn't that bad, actually." The music ended and they stepped apart. "Hope the next one's the same. I only know how to do two dances."

"Which ones?"

He waggled his eyebrows. "Wait and see."

Another salsa-tempo song started, and he took her in his arms again.

His confidence grew as they danced through four more songs.

Kelly Ann's cheeks bloomed with color. Her eyes sparkled. Skippy couldn't believe he was allowed to hold her like that in public. He inhaled her sweet fragrance and luxuriated in the feel of her body against his.

This dancing stuff was awesome after all.

They took a break for some pop, and then the music changed to a rhumba. He pulled her onto the dance floor and made one of Gabe's silly faces.

"Dave calls this 'the dance of love.'"

"It's wonderful. I never imagined a night like this."

"With me, you mean. I figured it might show you how much I love you." He wished he could offer her so much more than a few dances. "That even though I'm still only a thug—"

"Don't call yourself that," she said fiercely. "I've never once seen you that way."

"I see myself that way." His throat burned. "Remember how we met?"

"You were recovering from stab wounds. That's...unforgettable."

"So you know what I mean," he insisted. "They can laser off the ink, but the things I did—"

"You have to live with your past." She folded his hand in both of hers. "What matters to me is what you do now."

"I want to be a good man." His gaze fell to their joined hands. "*Your* good man."

"You've always been that."

"But—"

"I left everything behind, for you," she said. "I made a baby, with you. You're the guy who turned it all around for both of us. You want to be a good man? You're my fucking *hero*."

He closed his eyes. "I love you, Kelly Ann."

"Oh, God. Me too, honey." She pulled him in for a hug. "Try

to see yourself the way others see you. Look through my eyes, for a change."

"Thank you." He opened his eyes and found tears shimmering in Kelly Ann's.

This was her night. That would never do.

"Come on, gorgeous. Let me show you some more of my hot moves."

"One more dance." She nipped his lower lip. "And then we can go back to the hotel. You can show me some of those horizontal moves, papi."

"Oh yeah?"

"Oh, yeah. Bring it." Her eyes sparkled with happiness and love. "I'm a good enough dancer to follow you anywhere."

GRIME'S SURPRISE BABY

AN EXTRA BONUS SHORT!

Jack used his new key to unlock Ryan's front door. Their key exchange had only happened the weekend before, and he still felt strange entering Ryan's house on his own.

Memories of the room at the end hall on the first floor, where Nick had ended his life, still hung over the place. He hoped new memories with Ryan would obliterate them, with time.

Water ran somewhere upstairs, so Ryan must have been taking a shower. With a grin, Jack made his way up to join his lover. Stairs were slow going with his gimpy leg, but the hot water would do him a world of good. So would whatever Ryan was game for.

He shucked his clothes on the way and knocked on the bathroom door before entering.

"It's me." Probably sounded stupid, but he didn't want to startle Ryan.

"Hey you." The glass door opened, and Ryan peeked out. His

short blond hair stood up in wet spikes and his eyes shone like blue gemstones. His lips looked pink and delicious.

"Mind if I join you?"

That got him a sweet smile. "I'd be disappointed if you didn't."

Jack stepped behind him and caught the warm spray after it splashed over Ryan's body.

"Here"—Ryan pushed him to the front—"let's get you wet."

"Mm." Jack tilted his face up and let the hot water stream over him. "This is nice."

"Long day?"

"Little bit," Jack murmured. "We did a job where an elderly woman was dead for a while before anyone discovered her. Family in Washington wanted the place cleaned so they can sell it. I guess they need the cash."

"Always sad when someone dies alone."

"Yeah." He didn't want to be a downer so he changed the subject. "You save any lives today?"

Ryan rolled his eyes. "It's flu season. My god. The ER was packed. Did you get your flu shot?"

"I did." Jack was careful about things like that. Especially now that he had Ryan looking over his shoulder. He took vitamins, ate right, and everything.

"Good."

Jack let his head fall against Ryan's shoulder.

"Ooh, I like this." Ryan took a pump of body wash and spread it over Jack's chest. Jack's nipples peaked as Ryan scraped them lightly with his fingernail. Jack's chest tightened. His heart beat faster.

Ryan nibbled the skin below his ear, which got him squirming. He turned in Ryan's arms, and spread the soap between them in the best way possible. Ryan's cock rose.

"Somebody's happy to see me."

"Not just him. I am too," Ryan nudged him. "Just sayin'."

"Turn around," Jack urged. Ryan did as he asked. With a soapy hand, he caught hold of Ryan's cock and gave it an experimental pump. "This okay?"

"In what universe"—Ryan gasped—"do you imagine I'd say no?"

Jack laid a line of kisses on Ryan's shoulder, across his neck, and over the other side, all the while jacking his cock with firm pressure at an easy pace. Lazy and slow and sweet. Just how he liked it these days. This was all about Ryan.

"Oh. *Jack.*" Ryan moaned.

Jack nuzzled into the nape of Ryan's neck. He tongued the skin there, tasting salt and the soap. He nibbled Ryan's ear lobe gently.

Ryan responded so sweetly, every time. His breath came in huffs and his shoulders rose as if Jack was tickling him. Jack had this thing he did, stroking Ryan's dick hand over hand. Ryan's legs trembled when he did it. That was a rush. Ryan turned his head to meet Jack's lips in a desperate kiss. Ryan wanted more. Jack wanted to give it to him.

He picked up the tempo, gliding one hand over Jack's cock while he tugged lightly at Ryan's smooth balls with the other. From that angle, he couldn't stroke Ryan's taint so he pulled his hand back to skim his fingers down the sweet slash of Ryan's ass crack and lightly brushed his hole.

"Yes." Ryan head fell on Jack's shoulder as he spread his legs wider.

That was all the invitation Jack needed. He circled Ryan's hole, careful to be gentle, careful to keep soap away from that sensitive skin.

Ryan kept waterproof lube for that, and now Jack gathered some on his fingers and worked to soften him up for the ass play he loved.

"Mm." Ryan sank onto his finger so nicely. "More."

"*Shh.*" Jack ignored his pleas until he was sure two fingers would slip easily inside him.

This was meant to be sensual and relaxing. He didn't want to just plunge in, he wanted to drown Ryan with pleasure, not pinches of pain.

"Better?"

"Yes." Ryan quivered all over when Jack found his sweet spot.

He accelerated things, forcing Ryan to move between his hand and his fingers, picking up the tempo on both until Ryan whined with need.

"*Jack.* Please. Please. I want to come—"

"I've got you, honey." With only a few more strokes hot jizz streamed over Jack's hand. He braced his trembling lover and kept the sensations going as long Ryan let him.

"My God, Jack." Ryan sagged against him, spent. "That was..."

"Good?"

Ryan bit his lip. "Spectacular."

Jack teased, "Yeah, I know."

"You arrogant shit."

Jack held him beneath the spray and rocked him to rinse off.

Ryan reached for Jack's cock. "Here. Let me—"

"It can wait." Jack was hard. No doubt about it. But he had other things in mind then a hand job in the shower.

Ryan sought his lips again. "All right."

They shared kisses and finished washing each other, standing under the spray until the water turned cold.

Jack got out and wrapped a towel around his waist. Then he got one to towel Ryan off. "Here you go, baby."

Ryan kissed his nose. "What did I do to deserve you?"

Jack was equally bemused by the fact Ryan loved him. Like

Skippy was doing with Kelly Ann, Jack had planned an extra nice evening for Ryan. Jack wanted to show him how much he cared.

"I love you," he said simply.

Ryan nestled into his arms. "Me too, Jack."

The look he sent Jack's way was both tender and incendiary. Things were just heating up again when the doorbell rang.

Ryan stiffened. "Shoot. I have to get that."

"Really? No. It's probably missionaries or something."

"What if it's Karen?" Dave's mother often dropped baked goods off for him.

"Don't you think she'd come back if you didn't answer?"

"I don't want her to think I'm ignoring her." The bell rang again. "Your car's parked out front. The lights are on. Whoever it is knows someone's here."

"You really want to answer?" Jack asked. "*Now?*"

"Er..." Ryan shifted his gaze. "I was hoping you would go down."

"Are you serious?" At Ryan's pleading expression, Jack let out a loud sigh.

Now whoever was at the door started knocking. "Maybe it's an emergency?"

"All right." Jack turned to leave. "Hold dirty, dirty thoughts for me. Back in a second."

"Wait. You're not going to answer like that?" Ryan squeaked.

Jack glanced down at the towel wrapped around his waist. "Unless you have a better idea."

"Take my robe," Ryan offered. "And try to lose the boner, will you? You don't want to knock someone over."

Shaking his head, he grabbed Ryan's robe and headed for the stairs.

He tied the robe's sash on the way as he took the stairs one at a time. He wouldn't have thought Karen could knock like that—

like her son and his cop colleagues. The sound was insistent and authoritative.

"Hang on, I'm coming," he said more politely than he felt. He opened the door and found Skippy outside, holding his baby in a car seat.

"Hey Skippy." They eyed each other. "What's up?"

Skippy wore a suit and tie. Jack smelled cologne. The Mazda sat in Ryan's driveway, lights on, with Kelly Ann in the passenger seat.

"I don't know what to do, boss. I don't even know how to ask, but Kelly Ann's mom has a cold—"

"I don't understand," Jack stared at Skippy and the baby, whose little arms flailed.

"I'm trying to tell you. Kelly Ann's mom can't watch Lalo, and I made all those plans, and I was hoping you *couldwatchthebaby*." Skippy ran the sentence together so quickly Jack had a hard time understanding him. "You were hoping what?"

"Who is it, Jack?" Dressed in loose pants and a t-shirt, Ryan stepped close behind him. He saw Skippy, he offered a wide smile. "You look awesome. Ready for your big weekend?"

"That's the problem, see—" He looked toward the car and waved at Kelly Ann. "Kelly Ann's mom has a cold."

"Hope it's not flu. This season is"—Ryan gasped—"Skippy, is that the baby?"

"I don't think it's the flu, but obviously, she can't watch Lalo, and I was hoping you could."

"That's not a good idea, Skippy," said Jack. "I don't know very much about little kids."

"But Ryan does." Skippy turned to Ryan. "Don't you? You're a nurse, right?

Ryan's hand went to his throat. "Well, yes, but—"

"You guys are the only hope I've got. Gabe's out somewhere. Eddie's with his family—"

"But Skippy—"

"I'm working this weekend." Ryan spread his hands. "If we take Lalo, only Jack will be here during the day to watch him."

"Could you show him what Lalo needs?"

"I can give him a crash course in babies, but—"

"What are you saying?" Jack turned to Ryan. "Are you actually considering this?"

"Kelly Ann needs this time away, remember?" Ryan lifted his brows. "We helped Skippy plan the whole weekend. I don't see why we can't help him out with Lalo."

"Thanks, Ryan." Skippy handed the baby over, along with a sizable backpack. "I'll owe you a million favors. I'm good for it too. There's some more stuff in the car. Jack, can you help me get it?"

Bemused, Jack started down the lighted walkway with him. He waved to Kelly Ann. She waved back.

"You have no idea how much I appreciate this." Skippy opened the trunk of his car. "I brought everything you'll need: The travel crib, and the bouncy chair and formula and clean bottles. This is his favorite blanket and he likes this stuffed dinosaur best."

Jack let Skippy load him down with as much as he could carry. Skippy brought the rest, muttering advice that contained words like *fussy*, and *obstinate*, and *teething* while Jack's life slipped silently out of his control.

"You sure this is a good idea?" he asked again. "I really don't know anything about kids."

It wasn't the brash, almost feral Skippy who stared back at him, but an anxious young father who only wanted a night away with his wife.

"You've got a good heart." He poked Jack's chest. "And you've got Ryan. I think you'll do okay."

Ryan held Lalo's bucket seat while Skippy and Kelly Ann

waved goodbye. They watched as the small car backed out of the drive.

"I hope they have a great fucking time this weekend." Jack shut the door after the Mazda's red taillights turned the corner and vanished from sight. "Because somebody should."

Ryan undid the straps and scooped Lalo into his arms. "Hear that, Lalo? Uncle Jack is a Grinch, huh? We'd better hide Christmas, huh?"

Jack rolled his eyes. "I see how this is going to be. You get to be the nice uncle."

"Oh, I am the nice uncle." Ryan's smile went straight to Jack's cock. "And that makes you the enforcer."

"As if." A surge of fondness swelled Jack's heart. "Christ, you really think we can do this?"

Ryan nodded confidently. "We've got this."

Friday, 20:00 - "You know what? You look good doing that." Jack couldn't define the feeling he got when he watched Ryan feed the baby. Something dangerously soft and squishy inside him liked it. A lot. The image gave rise to others he wasn't ready to experience, much less admit.

"He's hungry." Ryan held the bottle while Lalo greedily ate. "Pace yourself, little man. You hold the bottle like this, see? So he doesn't get too much air in his tummy."

"Got it." Jack made a mental note. "I can't believe I'll be doing this alone tomorrow. You sure you can't take off work?"

"I'm sure. You can handle it. He can't exactly outrun you."

"That's one person, anyway."

Friday, 23:00 - "What does he want?" Jack's heart beat frantically. "I've ridden on firetrucks that aren't this loud."

"He needs a diaper change. Can't you smell that?"

"Well...I wasn't gonna say anything."

Ryan gaped at him. "You thought it was *me*?"

"Um..."

"Here are his things," Ryan said archly. "Have you ever changed a baby before?"

"You do it on the floor?" Jack's knee caught fire as he got on his hands and knees next to Ryan.

"I'm going to use a pad beneath him, but yes." Ryan glanced over. "You should probably do it on the bed."

"On our *sheets*?"

Ryan ripped the Velcro tabs and opened the diaper. "Save your leg."

Jack's stomach churned. "Christ. What do they feed him?"

"Poop stinks. What do you want from me? You've really never done this?"

"Hell no."

"Your firm cleans crime scenes for a living, and *this* is what bugs you? Suck it up, buttercup."

"All right, all right." Jack lifted his arm over his nose and mouth. "That's really bad, though."

"Uncle Jack's a big wuss, huh, Lalo." Ryan glanced over. "Don't forget to cover his penis with something while you do this or he'll pee in your face."

"He'll what?"

"It's not personal with babies. Just business. But yeah. Unless you want a mouthful of pee—"

"Got it."

Saturday, 01:00 - "I really thought babies his age were supposed to sleep through the night," Ryan admitted, after he'd walked Lalo around the living room for about twenty minutes. Lalo showed no signs of settling down.

Jack turned on the television and muted the sound. "You said they cry if they're hungry, wet, or tired. Obviously you're working on bogus intel."

"He could be teething I suppose. Does he seem to be drooling more?"

"More than what? It's not like I know the average drool volume of—"

"I'm just gonna... You know what?" Ryan felt the baby's forehead and cheeks. "He might be running a slight temp. Teething can do that. It's probably why he's fussy. I hope he's not coming down with something."

Jack sat up. "Should we call Skippy?"

"His temp isn't high enough to be alarming. He's about nine months old, isn't he?" Ryan felt along his gums with his pinky finger. "Oh, yeah. Feels like a bump here. *Ow*"—he pulled away sharply—"he's teething. Can you check the diaper bag and see if Skippy left any teething toys?"

Jack opened the voluminous backpack Skippy had given him and started searching its many pockets. "What would they look like?"

"Chew toys?"

"Like for a puppy? I found these." Jack held up a colorful set of fat plastic keys and a soft, water-filled ring.

"Perfect." Ryan took the keys. "Put the ring in the fridge for later."

"M'kay." Jack slogged into the kitchen. "You want anything while I'm in here?"

"Water would be awesome."

Jack brought two water bottles to the living room where they'd set up a camp, of sorts. Baby things covered nearly every surface now—travel crib, blankets, toys, a waste pail for diapers, a basket for laundry. They'd decided to sleep on the couches to be closer to Lalo's cot and the kitchen.

"How is it possible the place looks like this after only six hours?"

"Babies take over people's lives." Ryan took the water gratefully. "It's what they do. Hold him while I look for Tylenol drops, will you?"

Ryan handed Lalo to Jack, noting that strings of saliva stretched between them. "Elevated temp, check. Cranky, check. Drooling like a St. Bernard, check. Definitely teething."

Jack lay on the couch and settled Lalo on his chest. "Sh-sh-sh, baby. I got you."

"Hey, found it." Ryan called out. "This will help."

He pulled dosing instructions from his phone and carefully measured out the right number of drops. Lalo fought like a tiger when they tried to take the plastic keys away.

"I'll give it back." Ryan soothed. "It's just for a minute. Here you go, champ. You'll feel better in a bit."

Jack worried his lower lip. "I wouldn't have known about any of this stuff."

"He'll be fine. He's uncomfortable and he wants company for his misery."

"I've got you, little man." Jack leaned over and kissed Ryan's cheek. "You're a good guy, Ry."

Ryan leaned into him. "So are you, babe."

Saturday 05:00 - Jack picked up Lalo before he could really start wailing and walked him to the kitchen. He'd worried about carrying the baby in one arm while using his cane, but if he took it slow, things were fine. If worse came to worst, he knew how to fall and protect whatever he was holding. He'd only done it a million times.

He listed Lalo's feeding procedure in his mind as he checked off each step. *Warm the formula. Shake the bottle well. Test the temperature. Tilt the bottle just so.* "Here you go little man. Bon appetite."

He swayed side to side, leaning against the sink and staring out the window while Lalo ate his breakfast.

God, Ryan's yard was gorgeous. In the bluish light of dawn, late summer flowers bloomed in profusion beneath fruit trees, some heavy with nectarines and plums. He'd spent enough time with Ryan to know how hard he worked to keep things nice out there. When Ryan was wasn't at the hospital or with him, he spent his time in his grandmother's garden, tending vegetables, weeding, gathering fruit from trees she'd planted a generation ago.

Jack was so mesmerized by the view he didn't hear Ryan come up behind him before he felt a kiss drop lightly on the back of his neck. "You're up early. Did Lalo fuss?"

"Just enough to let me know he was hungry."

Ryan had dark circles under his eyes. "He'll probably want to play for a little bit after he eats. We should let him crawl around and explore his toys on a blanket for a while. I need a shower and then I've got to go."

Jack said nothing. Anything that came out of his mouth would sound like cowardice and begging. He glanced down at Lalo, silently beseeching the baby to be chill while Ryan wasn't home. As always, Ryan seemed to read his mind.

"Don't panic. You've got this." Ryan turned him to kiss his lips. "Say it."

"I've got this." Jack hoped it was true.

Saturday 11:00 - "He bit me on the nipple. Through my shirt. WTF?"

"Is he hungry?"

"Oh."

Saturday 11:30 - "He won't stop crying."

"Did you feed him?"

"Yes."

"Did you change him?"

"Affirmative."

"Did you put him down for his nap?"

"What nap? I'm supposed to initiate that?"

"Did you expect him to ask?"

"Saturday 14:00 - "I found cartoons. They're totally different than what we used to watch. There's barely any violence! Also I'm fucking tired. Feels like pulling a double shift in fire season. How do people do this all the time?"

"You're supposed to sleep when the baby sleeps."

"What? How? I had to clean and do his laundry while he was sleeping."

"Poor Jack. Next time he drops off, get a quick nap."

"When are you coming home again?"

"I'll bring dinner at 6:30."

"You're the best boyfriend ever."

Saturday 17:00 - "Seriously? How often do these things eat?"

Saturday 17:15 – "FML, I look like I walked under a flock of seagulls."

Saturday 17:30 - "I have new respect for Skippy and Kelly Ann."

Saturday 17:45 - "You would totally gag if you got a look at this diaper."

Saturday 18:00 - "Does it seem like time is standing still to you?"

Saturday 18:15 - "Oh, God. It's like you're never, ever, ever coming home again."

Saturday 18:30 - "Where aaaaaaare yooooooou?"

"I'm in the driveway. JFC! Gimme a minute. Which one of you is the baby?"

Saturday 20:00 - "Jack?" Ryan whispered. The snore he got was prolonged and loud. He stifled a laugh while he placed Lalo into his travel cot.

As a firefighter, Jack worked for days at a stretch, but it only took one little baby a few hours to destroy him. Lalo wore him as thin as those places in his slouchy old jeans that caught Ryan's eye whenever he shifted snoozing positions on the couch.

Jack was gorgeous. Fun. Interesting to be around. He had a code Ryan recognized and respected from being a fellow first responder.

Jack had been a little bitter when they met. They both had. But now, he filled Ryan's days with happiness and his heart with fantasies that they could maybe make things work, together.

Ryan didn't know what Jack wanted, but he'd always believed children were in his future. Time spent with Skippy's baby detonated an explosion of that desire in his heart, making it almost painful to breathe.

He had no idea how long he stood over Lalo's cot, making small circles on his sturdy back before Jack asked, "You okay?"

He breathed in the scent of a freshly washed baby before he stood. "Sure. Why?"

"You were so quiet." Jack sat up and patted the space next to him on the couch. "Sorry I fell asleep. Want to watch a movie?"

Ryan dropped into the cushions beside him. "Can we do it with the sound off? I don't want to wake you-know-who."

"Sure." Jack kept his voice low and keyed the remote. "See? Subtitles."

Saturday 23:00 - "Jason Bourne's not the same without gunfire and explosions, is it?" Jack whispered into Ryan's ear.

Ryan dropped his head on Jack's shoulder. "I'm not sure I was actually watching."

"You weren't, unless you can see out roof of your mouth."

Ryan laughed and turned to Jack. "You'll be amazed by the things I can do with my mouth."

"Oh, I already—"

"Shh." Ryan turned his whole body and straddled Jack's lap to kiss him deeply and with serious intent. Jack's slid his hands up Ryan's thighs to cup his ass cheeks.

Behind Ryan, Lalo rolled over and let out a pitiful howl.

Sunday 03:00 - "Didn't you say babies Lalo's age slept through the night?"

"Eh, your mileage may vary. Maybe they don't do as well when they're in a strange environment and teething and their parents aren't there."

"Come on." Jack picked the baby up and jiggled him. "It's gonna be okay, Lalito. You're okay. When did you last give him those drops?"

"Before bedtime. He's due for a re-up."

Jack picked up his cane. "I'll get his teething ring from the fridge. He digs that. Don't you, bubba?"

As tired as they were, he and Ryan worked pretty well together. After about half an hour, Lalo finally drifted off, and they were able to crawl onto the couch together.

Ryan pressed his nose into Jack's neck. "We did good. He's down for a bit."

"That tickles." Too tired to squirm away, Jack dozed off.

Sunday 05:00 - For the second day in a row, Jack woke at the slightest sound from Lalo. He found the baby lying awake in his cot, that curious gaze drifting around the room. He brightened obligingly when he saw Jack.

Some unexpected burst of happiness flooded Jack's veins.

Dawn had been Jack's favorite time of day when he worked as a firefighter. Rising early, cleaning and outfitting the rigs, breakfast with the others from his station—often, that was the most peaceful part of the day. Then rush hour would begin, and traffic accidents with it. They worked till they dropped, often enough.

His love for the stillness of early morning had never left him. Today, dawn carried new promises with it. A sleeping Ryan by his side, and happiness he'd never believed could be part of his life.

He slipped outside and down the path to the trees, letting Lalo wave his hand through the leaves, and pat the fruit. He didn't have enough hands to carry any back with him, but that was okay. He stood in the crisp clean air, eating a perfectly ripe nectarine, and imagined what it would be like if he could do this every day.

Might there ever be a boy or girl with Ryan's bright smile and strawberry blond hair in their lives? The sudden *want* crushed him under its unexpected weight.

From the baby in his arms to the earth he stood on, to the man who slept on the couch inside, he wanted everything. Wanted it now. Wanted it so badly the desire stung his eyes and burned like fire in his belly.

Just like with Tasha the cat, Skippy had inadvertently—or purposefully—given him another glimpse at something he didn't realize he needed until it was essential.

Jack wasn't ready to tell Ryan. He didn't have a clue when

he'd be ready. But now that he saw his future, he couldn't unsee it.

Grinch, Schminch. Jack's heart grew *ten* sizes.

"Lalo." He kissed the baby's fuzzy head. "I think your dad's positively Machiavellian."

Sunday 14:00 - Skippy didn't bring Kelly Ann with him when he picked up Lalo.

"How'd your big weekend go?" Jack had packed all Lalo's things and put them by the door—all but the blanket where they'd been playing with him.

"It was the best, boss." Skippy flushed deeply. "Kelly Ann was so happy. We made it an early night on Friday so she could sleep, and last night we danced. She loved my new moves."

"I'm really glad you had a good time."

"How was Lalo? Was he too much trouble?"

"Not at all. We gave him some Tylenol for teething. Otherwise he's been a champ. How's your mother-in-law?"

"She's still got a little cough. Nothing too bad." Skippy laid Lalo into his baby bucket and clicked the safety straps into place. "If it wasn't for you, we'd never have been able to go. Thanks, Jack."

"It was our pleasure. Really. He was no trouble at all." He might have sold the words better if he hadn't let out a gargantuan yawn.

Skippy snorted. "Don't lie. You look like hell."

Jack shrugged. "Yeah, well. We'd both do it again. He was fine. He's cute."

"I know, right?" Skippy sounded awed. "He's fucking awesome, isn't he?"

Skippy picked up the car seat, and Jack walked him to his car. His arms felt strangely empty.

"You know..." Skippy didn't look up while he buckled Lalo's

bucket into the back seat of his car. "I was wondering if you and Ryan would consider being Lalo's unofficial godparents. I mean, not like church godparents, but—"

"Sure. Yeah." Jack didn't even have to think about it. "I can't speak for Ryan, but I'd be honored. Your little monster grew on me."

"He kinda does that." Skippy gripped his kid's foot and gave it a little jiggle.

"I'll talk to Ryan about it."

"Thanks." Skippy met his gaze. "I appreciate everything you've done for me, Jack. I wasn't sure we could make a go of things out here when we moved—"

"It was a lucky day when we hired you. But I gotta ask. Why the nickname Skippy? Is that what your boys called you back home?"

Skippy's eyes lost focus, as if he saw something Jack couldn't. "No. They called me Chino...it was kind of a racist thing, 'cause someone said I look Asian once and it stuck."

Nicknames came from weird places. "You're Eduardo on all your paperwork. So why Skippy?"

"When I first came in, I had to wait for Gabe to end a call. There was a jar of peanut butter on his desk. You know how he eats it with apples?"

"No shit."

Skippy shrugged. "Figured Skippy sounded like the kind of guy who'd get hired, where Eduardo—"

Jack frowned. "I hope you don't think that now."

"Nah. But I let the nickname stand."

"You want me to call you Eduardo?"

"Nope. I kind of like being Skippy now." He grinned. "Dude named Skippy's gotta be harmless, right? Skippy built my new life. Eduardo only ever burned shit down."

Jack nodded. "Got it."

"*This* Eduardo"—Skippy indicated his boy—"is gonna be amazing."

Skippy waved as he drove away.

As Jack entered the house, he took in the too-neat living room, listened to the empty space, and wished he could bring Lalo back.

He took out his phone and texted Ryan. "Skippy came for Lalo."

"If the baby human was still alive? Our work is done."

Jack couldn't help a smile. "Going back to my place for a bit. I need to check on Tasha."

"Got plans for dinner?"

"I plan to eat, shower, and sleep for three days."

"Mind if I join you?"

They were still young. They had plenty of time.

But he might as well get the ball rolling.

Jack replied, "I'd be disappointed if you didn't."

AFTERS

I'm always aware that you have a ton of books to choose from, and I want to thank you for reading mine!

I'd really appreciate it if you'd leave a review wherever it makes sense to you, on Amazon or Goodreads or your favorite blog sites.

Reviews really do **make a big difference** to an author's visibility in bookstores and on the web. That means you can help me get noticed by new readers every day.

Thanks in advance for taking the time to help me out!

Best wishes and happy reading,

ZAM

WHAT TO READ NEXT...

As for what to read next?

If you enjoyed Jack's story, then be sure to read Eddie's! The Brother's grime are at it again, and there's plenty of work to go around.

This time, Eddie's got a bunch of secrets.

Eddie and his niece's teacher Andrew have dynamite chemistry. But Eddie is profoundly dyslexic, and Andrew lives to read. Andrew is pathologically disorganized, and Eddie likes things neat and clutter-free.

Andrew is desperately ashamed of his hoarder father, and Eddie is embarrassed by his lack of education.

When Andrew's father's condition deteriorates and he nearly dies because of his compulsion, Eddie and Andrew must learn compassion begins with loving oneself because *Grime Doesn't Pay*.

Here's a sneak peek to get you started:

Chapter One

Eddie checked his hair out in the rearview and gave a final pat to his tie before he got out of his car. His niece Lucy unbuckled herself, got her things, and climbed out of the two-seater, all the while complaining he was taking too long. *Of course* he was taking too long. They might see Lucy's teacher, Mr. B. Andrew Daley, and Eddie was determined to make one hell of a good impression.

What Eddie really wanted was to knock the breath from Mr. B. Andrew Daley's lungs in the same way the officially *awesome* Mr. B. Andrew Daley always knocked the breath from Eddie's lungs, but what could he do? Rome wasn't built and all. Eddie was holding to his course, making himself indispensable, helping with science projects and chick hatching, and chaperoning farm field trips. He'd become Daley's official event photographer.

In all, Eddie had probably spent more time with Daley than he had with any other guy, and he still called him Mr. Daley, for God's sake.

Finding a guy on a dance floor who wanted to suck him off was a piece of cake for Eddie "Cha-Cha" Vasquez, but asking a guy on an actual date? He couldn't remember ever doing that. Was he too old to learn new tricks?

Asking Daley out was fraught with more tension than he'd imagined.

"Come on already, Uncle Cha-Cha. How come you keep looking in the mirror?"

"I'm not." He turned in time to see one of Lucy's delicate eyebrows arch up, exactly like his sister-in-law's did when she was not impressed.

"You are too. I saw you just now." She frowned at him. "And how come you're dressed like you're taking Grandma to church?"

"I'm not," he said. He'd worn his slickest black suit, burgundy shirt, and black silk tie. These were the clothes he looked his best in. He looked *GQ* good.

"Are too." Like all the women in his family, Lucy could see right through him.

"I just like to look nice."

"But I'm going to be late for early bird library." She tapped her foot on the sidewalk in front of the car.

"Still like your lunch box?"

"Yeah," she said. "No one's got a lunch box like it, except my spoon and fruit cup clank when I walk." She held herself back to slip her little hand into his as they walked along.

"Metal lunch boxes are classic." He loved seeing her carry a tin lunch box, even if it was leopard-print smiley cat. "So the way you see it, is being unique a good thing or a bad thing?"

"What do you mean?"

"Are you the kind of girl who likes to have the same things other people have, or are you the kind who likes to be different?" He was quick to add, "There's nothing wrong with either one."

Her brows drew into a thoughtful furrow. "I like some things other people have. My girlfriend Ariana has a plastic polka-dot lunch box that keeps her food cold. Her mom puts in tuna salad."

"Tell your mom to freeze your juice box if she's going to put perishable food in your lunch, and have her wrap everything in a cloth napkin. That will keep it fresh and quiet. Best of both worlds. I almost got you another lunch box the other day with Charlie's Angels on it. The television show, not the movie."

"Mami says you were born at the wrong time."

"She did, did she?"

"Yeah, she says you should have been born fifty years ago, 'cause you like old things."

"Hey, now. I like classic things." Before Eddie could explain the difference, one of the upper-grade teachers walked up.

"Hello, Mr. Vasquez. Lucy. How are you this morning?"

"Just fine, thank you, Mrs. Calvin."

Mrs. Calvin nodded to Lucy. "Early library day?"

"Yes!" Lucy jumped and landed on her tiptoes. "I'm in reading level 6.2!"

"The kids sure work hard for this," said Eddie. The top three students in each grade got to spend an extra hour in the library in the morning. The privilege of extra time and extra books was turning Lucy into a first-rate student.

"It's been a pretty successful program." She smiled at him and leaned toward him to whisper, "It doesn't hurt that there's contests and prizes."

"I won last month, did I tell you?" Lucy asked. "I won *Teacher's Pet* pencils."

"I think you mentioned that, honey. Once or twice."

Or a thousand times.

"I read the whole first Harry Potter book and took a test on it. I got a perfect score."

"Good for you, Lucy. That's upper-grade stuff." Mrs. Calvin checked her watch. "Better run along, or you'll be late."

Lucy picked up speed, and Eddie gave a helpless shrug before chasing after her.

"Cool your jets, Lu-lu. We've got plenty of time." She dashed past the last of the classrooms and headed for the main library doors. By the time he caught up, she was already opening one to go in without a backward glance. "Hey, what do I get?"

She dimpled prettily. "Thank you for driving me, Uncle Cha-Cha."

"Put it right there." He pointed to a spot on his jaw as he leaned down. She gave him a kiss before turning to run away. "Anything for you, *pepita*. Have a good day."

"Bye," she said. She must have had her head in the books already, or she would have groused at him. *I'm not a pumpkin seed, Uncle Cha-Cha.*

Eddie didn't suppose he blamed her. Library was her favorite thing, and he was only her ride. He turned to leave, mildly disappointed without a real reason for it.

Lucy was one hell of a kid. He'd like a couple of kids of his own someday, but a lot of guys thought kids—like carrying metal lunch boxes and wearing a jacket and tie to look nice in the hope of seeing that special someone—were a little old-fashioned. "Hetero-normative brainwashing" was what the last guy he'd dated called it.

As if the desire for a family and a child was beneath Eddie's dignity.

He knew plenty of guys who didn't want kids, and that was fine for them. But Eddie liked family. He came from a big one. Growing up, he'd had six different houses to call home and a ton of family at school to keep the bullies away. That was how he liked it.

"Mr. Vasquez." A rich tenor voice stopped his train of thought—derailed it, actually—and made his mouth go dry. He turned to find Mr. B. Andrew Daley leaning against his classroom door with his hands in his pockets.

How Eddie wanted to be those hands. Since they'd met in September, Eddie'd had the feeling his heart was already inside one of those pockets, clenched tight in Mr. B. Andrew Daley's lovely, capable hand.

Is there such a thing as love at first sight?

Or had the feeling come on as he'd watched Mr. Daley work?

Daley was always fair. Always patient.

He listened.

He liked kids for who they were, not what society expected them to be.

Daley genuinely cared. He was like a magnet and Eddie wanted to melt all over him like a hot metal blanket.

Eddie cleared his throat and managed a dumbstruck smile as he ambled over to say hello. "Mr. Daley."

Daley appeared freshly shaved, and his light brown hair was trimmed close over the ears and collar but fuller—a mass of haphazard curls—on the top. He'd dressed in a mouthwatering combination of low-rise jeans, a blue button-down, and a slim V-neck sweater under a navy sport coat. He had a goddamned scarf wrapped negligently around his throat.

In southern California.

It had probably dipped to a chilly sixty-five that morning. Eddie dared a look at Daley's feet. *Oh God. Combat boots. Kill me now. I'm done.*

Daley is the hottest man ever.

"How's teachery things?" Eddie asked stupidly. He breathed in deeply when he approached Daley, who smelled like glove leather and laurel-leaf crowns and Madagascar vanilla.

"Going along fine. Did Lucy tell you she won the prize in Early Library last week?"

"Yeah." Eddie had the fleeting thought there was nothing he wouldn't do for a *Teacher's Pet* pencil. "She's so happy. This year has been great for her."

"She's my most voracious kid when it comes to books. I'd say she was the best reader in the whole first grade."

"That's good to know." Eddie couldn't take his eyes off Lucy's teacher.

"Do you like to read, Mr. Vasquez? I find a child's love of reading usually starts with family. I only ask because I've been rereading *Maurice* for about the hundredth time and—"

"I don't, actually." Eddie felt his face heat. Whatever *Morris* was, he'd never read it. He never would unless listening counted as reading. "I'd like to, I mean. But reading is for people who have more time on their hands than I do. I have to go to work now."

Eddie turned to run, but Daley's voice stopped him. "Wait. I don't—"

"It's okay." Eddie figured his face must match his burgundy

shirt. Why had he worn that? It made him look like a thug. "Um... have a good day."

Daley tilted his head like a cat with a question. "It was good to see you again, Eddie."

Eddie shivered when Mr. Daley spoke his name. He couldn't help it. He tried out a jaunty salute that probably looked like a tic, and headed back toward the parking lot.

One of these days, he thought.

One of these days, I'm going to figure Mr. Daley out.

ANDREW WATCHED LUCY'S uncle walk away yet again. On the one hand, Eddie "Cha-Cha" Vasquez seemed interested. On the other, every time Andrew hit on him, he ran off like a possum with a can tied to its tail.

One of these days Andrew was going to throw caution to the wind and just ask the man out.

What's the worst that can happen?

Andrew genuinely liked Eddie. He treated his niece, Lucy, like gold. Like she was the most important thing in his life. But aside from that, Eddie was pretty forbidding. Big and built and a little bit rough around the edges.

He could break Andrew in half if he didn't like Andrew's attention.

Andrew was no fool. Gay pride parades and the eradication of Don't Ask, Don't Tell and PROP 8 aside, this could still be a dangerous world for a guy who hit on the wrong man. It was only that Eddie stared at him sometimes when he thought no one was looking, and it made Andrew feel *licked* all over. *Kissed.* Worshipped even, by dark brown eyes that gave away nothing but a certain hot intensity that made Andrew's knees weak.

A curious noise caught Andrew's attention, an odd humming that seemed to be coming from behind him.

Andrew turned in time to see a woman wearing a filthy pink

tracksuit amble up to the door of the next classroom over. She was thin to the point of emaciated, and her silvery hair was matted and oily. She'd gripped the door handle and pulled it hard, but the room must have been locked. She fumbled some keys out of her pocket and tried each one unsuccessfully.

Andrew made his way toward her as he asked, "Can I help you?"

She turned her blank gaze on him. "I can't seem to open my classroom."

Andrew recognized the woman as a teacher who used to substitute back when he'd first started teaching at Taft. "Mrs. Henderson?"

"My key doesn't work," she muttered, frustrated.

Parents dropping off early bird kindergarteners had started staring. Andrew felt an unreasonable irritation with them. Obviously there was something really wrong with the woman. She didn't need people gawking at her.

Andrew stepped closer so he could talk to her without letting his voice carry to the parents and other teachers whose curiosity was aroused. That was when he noticed the smell coming off Mrs. Henderson's clothing.

The scent was faint, but it was rank.

The closer he got, the less bearable the odor was—like something between unwashed human and rancid meat. Even as Andrew's gut twisted, he tried to keep his face neutral.

"Mrs. Henderson, are you all right?"

She frowned. "Why, of course. I—"

"Do you think maybe you could wait in my room with me while I make a quick call?"

"I need to get ready." Mrs. Henderson tried another key. "The children will be arriving any minute."

A murmur went through the crowd of gawkers. The older kids hid laughter behind their hands. Andrew understood the impulse. Sometimes uncomfortable things made him laugh too, but he couldn't stand seeing anyone laugh at someone in Mrs. Henderson's condition.

"Maybe you could come inside while I call the office," he offered. Thank God she let him lead her into his room where he could close the door on the outside world. He dialed the number for the school secretary.

To Mrs. Henderson, he said, "Have a seat for a minute while I see if the office can get things sorted." He left her there and stepped back out while he talked to the office staff about getting a police officer and maybe paramedics because something obviously wasn't right. At the very least, the poor woman looked like she needed a decent meal.

When Andrew reentered his room, he discreetly started opening windows. Had Mrs. Henderson been living on the street? What was that smell?

"Someone's on the way to unlock the door right now. In the meantime, can I get you a bottle of water?"

She accepted water and some graham crackers, accepted that he was telling the truth.

God, he hated lying to her.

Andrew sat down and waited with her, hoping the police would get there before he had to open his classroom for the children. Andrew and Mrs. Henderson gazed at one another in awkward silence while he tried to figure out something to say besides, *Mrs. Henderson, what the hell happened to you?*

Stay tuned, for **Eddie: Grime Doesn't Pay**, with even more bonus material, coming August 20, 2019!

ABOUT THE AUTHOR

Z. A. Maxfield started writing in 2007 on a dare from her children and never looked back. Pathologically disorganized, and perennially optimistic, she writes as much as she can, reads as much as she dares, and enjoys her time with family and friends. Three things reverberate throughout all her stories: Unconditional love, redemption, and the belief that miracles happen when we least expect them.

If anyone asks her how a wife and mother of four can find time for a writing career, she'll answer, "It's amazing what you can accomplish if you give up housework."

ZAM loves to hear from readers!
www.zamaxfield.com
zamaxfield@zamaxfield.com

ALSO BY Z.A. MAXFIELD

Novels

Crossing Borders

Drawn Together

Family Unit

ePistols At Dawn

Gasp!

The Pharaoh's Concubine

Rhapsody For Piano and Ghost

The Long Way Home

Home the Hard Way

The Bluewater Bay Novels

Hell on Wheels

All Wheel Drive

The Plummet Series

Plummet to Soar

Hawai'i Five Uh-oh

Three Vlog Night

The My Cowboy Series

My Cowboy Heart

My Heartache Cowboy

My Cowboy Homecoming

My Cowboy Promises

My Cowboy Freedom

Honky Tonk Hellion

The Stirring Series

Stirring Up Trouble

All Stirred Up

The Brothers Grime

Grime and Punishment

Grime Doesn't Pay

The Deep Series

Deep Desire

Deep Deception

Deep Deliverance

The St. Nacho's Series

St. Nacho's

Physical Therapy

Jacob's Ladder

The Book Of Daniel

Novellas

Lights! Camera! Cupid!

Blue Fire

Fugitive Color

Through the Years

Holiday Stories

A Picture Perfect Christmas

I Heard Him Exclaim

Lost And Found

Secret Light

What Child Is This?

COPYRIGHT

Made in the USA
Coppell, TX
14 February 2020